Too Far in THE DARK

by

ANTHONY HUGER

ZALINO PUBLISHING, LLC

Published by:
Zalino Publishing, LLC
96 Linwood Plaza #267, Fort Lee, New Jersey 07024

www.zalinopublishing.com
Zalinopublishing01@yahoo.com

Zalino Publishing is the cornerstone in publishing world class novels, ebooks, and educational articles in all genres.

ISBN: 9781732717848
LCCN: 2018911585

Book Layout: Ravi Ramgati

Dedication

In loving memory of my father, Anthony, and grandmothers, Helen and Pearl.

Also by Anthony Huger

"Sly Fox"

Table of Contents

CHAPTER 1

Harlem, NYC "1966"

Charles wiggled in a sweaty sandwich on the twin-size mattress. His two younger sisters, Tracey, and Joyce enveloped him like sesame seed buns on a hamburger. He pushed off Tracey and managed to stand up. She didn't feel anything, but Joyce did. Her tiny arm clawed at Charles' leg, a crab pulling another back inside the barrel. Charles stepped off the mattress barefooted. The cold floor tiles sent chills up his seven-year-old frame. He gazed back at the bed. Joyce's claw now pacified her, she slipped a thumb in her mouth and soundly went back to sleep. Tracey, a deep sleeper, snored louder. A meteor could strike their tenement building, and Tracey would sleep through it. Charles snuck out the room on the balls of his feet. The hallways to the apartment were cluttered in junk. The ripped-up floor tiles deemed hazardous for visitors; Charles mastered long ago. He could maneuver on the floor tiles blindfolded and barefooted without catching a single splinter. Charles twisted a crystal doorknob smeared in white paint, identical to the paint on the walls, and slipped inside a closet. On Charles' left was a collection of vinyl records stacked up in milk crates, sprouting an inch below the ceiling. It was the finest collection of music on Harlem's Westside, and it belonged to Charles' Uncle Steve.

On the right side of the closet sat Momma's fine China wrapped in old newspaper. Charles gently moved a couple of dishes aside and grabbed a bundle of newspaper tied tightly with brown shoestring. He tiptoed across the hall to the bathroom. On the bathroom's door hung a long-cracked mirror, Charles stirred at the seven-year-old boy looking back. He wore green pajamas that evaporated around the knees. Charles was the average height for a seven-year-old boy. He didn't have cantaloupes for shoulders like Teflin, the six-year-old who lived a floor above Charles, but nobody did. Charles saw something special in his chocolate reflection. His light brown eyes and button nose were compliments of Momma. His peanut-shaped head was an early inheritance from Poppa, but Charles' favorite attribute came from Uncle Steve. He smiled at the small part on the left side, of a small crop of black hair. The part wasn't a hairdo. It represented being cool in his Harlem neighborhood. Whenever a small hair growth threatened to replenish Charles' coolness, he took to the part with Daddy's razor. The clock above the hamster read 11:45 p.m. Charles hurried, not wanting to keep Uncle Steve waiting. He stood on the toilet seat and squinted over the rolls of toilet tissue in the bathroom window. On the corner of 117th St. glowing under a streetlamp was Uncle Steve's white Oldsmobile 88, the car Ike Turner made famous in "Rocket 88," arguably the first ever rock & roll song. Charles leaped off the toilet, and tore open the bundle of old newspaper, inside was a dark blue suit, white dress shirt, and a pair of shiny black penny loafers. After Charles dressed, he peeked into the living room; Momma was asleep on the foldout sofa. The Freeman family's newest edition, baby Belinda, slept beside her in a small crib. Poppa worked the overnight shift every Friday. If not, this secret rendezvous wouldn't be possible. The last three Fridays, Charles snuck to the Dessie club to watch Uncle Steve's band perform. The Dessie Club was located on the corner of 117th and Seventh Avenue. It was Charles' and Uncle Steve's little secret, and Charles intended for it to stay that way. He quietly unlocked the door and eased out of the apartment, eager to join the night.

On the streets of Harlem after dawn, there wasn't a vice that couldn't be provided for a fee. Junkies, thieves, peddlers, and prostitutes shared the bloodstained sidewalks. The corrupt police force feed off the community's illegal economy, protecting and serving the number banks instead of the people. Dignified Caucasians left their civilities below 110th street, when venturing uptown to Harlem to satisfy their animalistic needs. The whorehouses, gambling dens, nightclubs, and abundance of narcotics made Harlem, NYC's largest adult playground. Charles lived on Harlem's main vein, Seventh Avenue. It wasn't unusual to see children wandering the streets of Harlem late at night. Children could sale thousands of dollar capsules of heroin without garnering police attention or slip through the smallest crack to jumpstart the burglary. The children did the dirty work for the neighborhood player's trying to keep their cat paws out of the fire.

The crowd outside the Club stretched to the center of the block. Charles walked between a maze of blacks speaking a language only the coolest of cats could comprehend. The bouncer at the Dessie Club saw Charles and unhooked the velvet rope.

"Clear the way for a little man!" he said. The crowd ignored him. "Clear the motherfucking way, before I knock me a motherfucker out!" the bouncer screamed, and nobody doubted him. He punched at least one customer out every night.

"You shouldn't be cursing around no child, Stanley," a brown-skinned woman sulked in a purple dress said.

"This ain't no child, your uncle's by the bar." Stanley said. Charles passed the velvet rope, the purple dress stepped up. "Where the fuck you going?" the bouncer asked.

"I've waited out here for half an hour, and you letting this kid in? Nigga, you gonna let me inside this club," she said, jamming a finger in Stanley's chest.

"I ain't doing a motherfucking thing, you motherfucking barracuda. Nobody wants to rub up against the motherfucking wolf pussy, anyway."

The crowd outside the Dessie laughed and the woman slapped Stanley clean across the part in his head.

Charles heard Stanley's scream before the club's music faded him out. A large cloud of smoke dimmed the lighting inside the Dessie. People surrounded the stage, dancing to the tunes of some homegrown talent. Charles choked on the second-hand smoke while walking across the thick burgundy carpet. The Dessie's L shaped bar had stainless steel stools with red cushions running the length of it. Charles pulled on the sleeve of a dark blue suit.

"Hi Chuckie, did anybody see you sneak out?" asked Uncle Steve. "Nope, I did the trick on the locks, the way you taught me." Charles said.

A light-skin, attractive woman wearing a red dress and bright red lipstick hooked her arm in Steve's.

"Rachel, I want you to meet my nephew Chuckie."

Charles stared at the dead fox wrapped around her shoulder.

"Hello Chuckie, aren't you a little too young to be partying in nightclubs?" Rachel asked.

"Chuckie's a little big man, he's one of the Stones, ain't that right?"

Uncle Steve extended an open hand. Charles smacked him the hardest five.

"That's right, I'm a stone," Charles said proudly.

"The Stones are on in five minutes!" Irv Conway called out. "Rachel, you, and Chuckie stay right where you are.

The Stones are going to give a performance you won't ever forget!"

Luis Freeman walked the bus depot parking lot with a group of transit workers, after finishing a twelve-hour shift. Luis cherished the camaraderie the bus drivers shared. He always enjoyed being a part of something bigger than himself. The roads to New York City were bumpy, and potholed. The same words described Luis's career as a transit worker. He was among the first African Americans hired by the Transit Authority. A city job was an admired one. The corner grocer increased Luis' tab, and the barber kicked customers out the barber chair to cater to him. To Luis, the burden of being a pioneer outweighed the neighborhood perks. The white transit workers didn't mask their displeasure of having to coexist with blacks. The hostilities they dealt Luis and other black workers sometimes seemed unbearable. A few blacks submitted to the constant degradation and resigned. The thought of quitting never crossed Luis's mind, not with a growing number of mouths to feed at the dinner table. Luis ignored the pranks, the name- calling, and focused on doing the job, day-in and day-out. He earned the respect of his peers and superiors. Five years later, the white drivers invited Luis to their cookouts, and everybody referred to him as Mr. Freeman.

Luis wasn't a born city slicker; he migrated to New York City by way of Louisiana. Luis Charles Freeman, born May 4th, 1939, the first born to a clan of ten children, spent most of his childhood working on the Freeman family farm. He rose early in the morning and trooped the five miles to a wooden shack; the town of Pineville called it an elementary school. The long hours in the cornfields cooked his skin tar black. It also instilled in Luis an appreciation for hard work.

In June 1957, Luis became the first member of the Freeman tribe to graduate high school. In the Deep South during the 1950s, not many opportunities existed for ambitious young black men, even those who earned high school diplomas. To accommodate, many African American Southerners relocated North in pursuit of the American Dream. The ones that found them a slice of the pie returned to the South, flaunting their success. Luis had a first cousin, Miles Freeman, who went north to Chicago and became a journalist for the Chicago Defender, at the time, the country's most influential black newspaper. Miles dazzled Luis with tall tales of the Windy City. Luis was sold on Chicago. He planned to room with Miles the following spring, but Miles reneged and eventually their correspondence ceased. That summer, Luis's younger brother Steve graduated high school, and set his sights on New York City.

"I 'ma be the biggest blues singer ever, bigger than Muddy Watters," Steve bragged to whoever listened.

The younger Freeman grew up singing lead in the church's choir, and captivated audiences. Steve was dark-skinned like Luis, but much taller and more handsome.

One hot summer day, Steve burst into Luis' room counting a fistful of greenbacks.

"Where'd you get that money, Steve?"

"I won it playing poker in Denny's barn, four hundred dollars." Steve peeled back the greenbacks.

"That's a lotta money, you sure there won't be no trouble over it?" Luis asked.

"No way, I won this money fair and square, and guess what I 'ma do?" Luis shrugged.

"I 'ma buy us two bus tickets to the big apple, big bubba."

Luis and Steve arrived in New York City's Grand Central Station in July of 1958. Their farm boy overalls singled the brothers out amongst the trendy dressed New Yorkers. They hailed a taxicab uptown to Harlem. The yellow cab stopped at the curb of 125th and Lenox Avenue, Steve paid the fare, and Luis lugged their belongings in a woven straw suitcase. "We in Harlem, Lou!!" Steve said, nudging Luis as the taxi sped away. They, like many other African Americans, yearned to be in Harlem, the capital of Black America. They walked the streets in utter amazement. Never before did they see blacks living so extravagant. There were black-owned businesses, blacks driving fancy automobiles, and blacks dressed in the most expensive fabrics.

"Luis, you scared?" Steve asked as they climbed a steep hill on 145th St. "I ain't scared of nothing."

"Well, I am. The pastor said every man gets a little nervous at the gates of paradise."

Luis and Steve rented a basement apartment in a three-story brownstone on 149th street between Convent and St. Nicholas Avenue, in Harlem's Sugar Hill section. The bourgeoisie of Harlem resided in Sugar Hill's prime real estate. Steve put a large portion of the four-hundred-dollar jackpot on the apartment's down payment.

The luxury amounted to a heavier burden, a handsome monthly rent bill. Luis woke up at seven o'clock in the morning to search the city for employment. Steve did his job-hunting at seven at night. Steve picked up quicker on the city's fast pace and started running numbers on behalf of Harlem's notorious policy king, Leon "King" Atkins.

The Harlem numbers king bankrolled the Atlantic-Uptown policy wheel, the biggest policy wheel in New York. Leon's hands touched everything-guns, narcotics, union organizing. Atkins shaded his illegal income with his management company. The business front fooled nobody; everybody knew Leon Atkins preferred breaking legs over artist. Leon signed Steve to a shady management contract and let him juggle policy numbers to help pay the sky-high Sugar Hill rent. Harlem's party life accepted the handsome, witty Southerner. On the rare occasions when

Leon did book Steve a singing gig, it would be in grimy lounges full of reefer smoke and goons. At one of these gigs, Luis eyed a red bone barmaid named Beatrice. He mustered the courage to ask her on a date, and Beatrice willingly accepted. A Harlem pastor's only child, Beatrice attended nursing school and bartended part-time at the Star Bright Lounge. The sassiest employee at the Star bright, Beatrice had high cheekbones and curves like a Coke bottle. She spoke in a demeanor woman from the South wouldn't dare, that's what attracted Luis to her. Their courtship wasn't long, the couple married in January 1959. Luis and Beatrice relocated to their own apartment on 117th St and welcomed their firstborn, Charles Luis Freeman. A trio of girls, Tracey, Joyce, and Belinda came later. Luis had a good job and a loving family. He achieved everything he dreamed about on that long bus ride from Louisiana to New York.

Years on the hustle finally wore Steve down. A foot-long criminal rap sheet and intense paranoia was all he owned. Steve parted ways with Leon Atkin's management hoping to salvage a stalled music career. The blues genre was out, and the new sound of Rock & Roll dominated pop culture. Steve jumped on the bandwagon forming a Rock & Roll band along with four musicians he met traveling the old blues circuit. They named the band "The Stones" and performed anywhere they could fit. The last twelve months proved plentiful for the Stones. The band found a great manager, an Irishman named Irv Conway. Irv booked the Stones for shows up and down the Eastern seaboard. The steady income from touring enabled Steve to bid farewell to the Harlem hustle. That coming Monday, the Stones had a meeting at Capitol Records.

"Remember this weekend, fellas. It'll be your last living in poverty. Come Monday, we'll be rich," Irv Conway told the Stones that night at the Dessie.

A tin lunch box clanged on top of a rusty "58" Plymouth Fury. Luis fumbled in deep pockets for a set of car keys.

"See you tomorrow, Freeman," a co-worker said honking the horn. "Alright, buddy."

Luis folded in the Plymouth's driver seat. He rubbed the dashboard smoothly.

"Listen, Betty, I don't want no problems out you this morning, you hear. I want you to get me out of Brooklyn and back to Harlem, safely" he said, then succumbed to Betty's mercy.

"Please." Luis turned the key in the ignition. Betty choked, shot out a black cloud, rattled, and then completely cut off.

"Stubborn bitch!" Luis muttered.

On a bar stool, inhaling Rachel's perfume, Charles fell in love. The Dessie's crowd let the rhythm of the music shuttle them to ecstasy. They danced in a groove. Music ruled their emotions and overpowered the problems of today and worries of tomorrow. The love of music pierced Charles' heart. That night Steve's showmanship hit a new orbit, showcasing a new collection of dance moves. One instance after rising from a spinning split, pink lace panties parachuted down on Steve's pompadour. The Dessie customers got their money's worth. After the show, Steve, Rachel, and Charles piled into the Oldsmobile 88 and headed west to Broadway's famed ice-cream parlor.

"Once Irv gets my advance money, we're going on a vacation. Maybe Las Vegas," Steve said.

Rachel wiped lipstick stains off Steve's cheek.

"Where's Las Vegas?" Chuckie asked seated next to Steve in the small booth inside the parlor.

"In Nevada, Chuckie. It's a long strip of bright lights and casinos." Steve scraped the last remnants of hot fudge out the sundae's glass. "When school's out we'll fly out there, Chuckie," he said.

"It's bad enough he's club hopping, you want to fly the boy to Sin City?" Rachel said then her expression changed.

Two men entered the parlor, their muscles ripping the seams of their polyester suits.

"Give me a second." Steve slid out the booth.

"What the fuck do you want?" He asked the men through gritted teeth.

"Leon wants a minute of your time." Steve glanced back at Rachel and said.

"Now is not the time, I'm with my gal, and my nephew." One bodyguard opened his polyester jacket, showing the butt of a black handgun.

"Leon wants a minute of your time, and what Leon wants, he gets." Steve saw the black Cadillac limousine double-parked outside. "Since I don't have a choice," Steve let himself out the door. A bodyguard jogged ahead to open the Cadillac's door.

"Care for a drink?" Leon Atkins asked pouring some scotch into a crystal glass.

"No" Steve said sitting in a seat opposite the gangster. One bodyguard squeezed beside Steve, the other took the wheel. Leon twirled a 21-karat platinum and diamond ring on his stubby pinky finger.

"This is how you treat old friends, Steve? I gave you the first hundred- dollar bill you ever seen, remember? You still smelled like the cotton fields of Louisiana," Atkin reminded him.

"I earned every dollar, my rap sheet will prove it," Steve said, unintimidated.

"I see you singing in a band of washed-up musicians, that little mick you call a manager somehow got the attention of Capitol Records. It's time for me to collect on your outstanding debt."

Steve was astonished at how fast news travelled on the Harlem wire, but then again, Leon Atkins was the King of Harlem.

"I don't owe you shit. I'm under new management. You got any problems, talk to Irv Conway. Excuse me."

The bodyguard didn't budge until Leon nodded.

"I always thought you were smart, Steve. I guess that's how it is when big money comes around, you kick your old friends to the curb."

Steve crawled out the Cadillac. The sun started its ascension. He'd have to rush to get Chuckie home before Luis.

"I'm doing my own thing Leon, nothing personal. Just business," Steve said.

"It's personal to me." Leon said closing the Cadillac's door.

"Is everything ok?" Rachel asked Steve as he neared the booth.

"We have to get Chuckie home before my brother gets uptown, let's go." Steve cruised in the white Oldsmobile across 125th St, chatting with Rachel above the sounds of the FM radio. He turned right on Seventh Avenue and drove down to the Dessie Club. Frank Sinatra's new hit "Strangers in the Night" spun on the radio.

"Every time you're about to get out the car, the radio plays the good songs," Steve said. Rachel put her hands in his.

"So stay here till the songs over." A black Ford rode alongside them. Suddenly the Ford accelerated, then *Boom! Boom! Boom!* The first bullet smashed the Oldsmobile's windshield, the others landed in Steve's scalp. Tires screeched loudly, but not louder than Rachel's screams.

Luis had to park the Plymouth on St. Nick avenue, the blue "DO NOT CROSS" police barricades blocked off 117th St. the extra walk tipped his balance.

"Damn Muslims," Luis cursed shuffling to Seventh Avenue. The aftermath of Malcolm X's assassination the year prior sparked a bloody war. The Nation of Islam led by Elijah Muhammad, feuded with Malcolm X supporters,

Muslim Mosque Incorporated. The MMI firebombed the nation of Islam headquarters days after Malcolm's murder. The two factions warred on Harlem soil. Luis wasn't a Muslim, therefore he had nothing to worry about, but the Muslims were becoming a nuisance to all of Harlem.

The police gathered around the Dessie Club, Stanley, the club's bouncer sat on Luis' stoop.

"Hi there, Stanley." Luis tapped two cigarettes out a pack of Lucky Strikes and offered one to Stanley.

"No thanks," Luis heard Stanley's voice crack and saw the tracks of his tears.

"Someone shot Steve this morning, Lou," Stanley cried. "They shot up the Oldsmobile 88 with little Chuckie in the backseat. The ambulance rushed them to Harlem Hospital."

Luis' feet switched to autopilot and he jetted uptown to the Hospital.

The receptionist at the hospital's front desk didn't raise her head out the newspaper, when an out of breath Luis asked for Steve and Charles Freeman. She pointed to a clipboard and said.

"Sign in."

"Ms., you're not listening, my son and my brother got shot! For Christ's sake, look at me!" Luis smacked the desk in frustration. The receptionist wasn't amused by the tantrum.

"You have to sign in and wait your turn," she said.

"Is there a problem?" The on-duty cop at the hospital asked the receptionist.

"Yes!" Luis answered. "I want to see my son, Charles Freeman."

Luis began spelling his last name at the receptionist. The cop's face turned red, he clubbed Luis in the back of the head. Luis went limp on the hospital floor.

"God damn junkie," the cop spat.

A Week Later

Charles hadn't uttered more than ten words since Steve's murder. He stayed to himself and declined any offers to leave the house as he sank deeper into his shell. Losing Steve crushed Luis, but to see Charles in this condition was too much to cope. A desperate Luis sent Charles to a psychiatrist. The doctor explained Charles' symptoms were normal behavior for a child who witnessed a homicide, he was traumatized. The doctor recommended a new environment to help erase the horrors of Steve's death. Luis declined, Harlem meant the world to him. As time went by, somehow word travelled that Luis Freeman's boy could identify one of Steve's killers. Leon Atkins' thugs started hanging at the Dessie Club, and asking questions. Luis and Steve considered

Harlem their thing, a place they discovered together, a life they created together, but now Steve was gone. Luis' family depended on him to make the decisions that brought them security. Luis decided to leave Harlem.

Hell's Kitchen, NYC. 1 Month Later

Mickey threaded through soggy cornflakes, floating in a bowl of milk. The metal spoon submarined over and under the milk's surface. He leaned his head on a closed fist, elbows propped on the kitchen table, obviously lacking enthusiasm.

"Are you going to eat or mope over your breakfast?"

The first words spoken at the table, since Mickey stumbled to it half awake. Mickey's stepfather Henry lowered the daily newspaper beneath lifeless eyes. Mickey surfed up a flake in the center of the spoon and swallowed it. Henry hissed in disgust, and went back to reading the morning paper. Mickey waited until the morning's headlines shielded the tyrant before he mumbled, "Motherfucker."

Mickey dreaded the days his mother's hectic job schedule wouldn't permit her to beat the sun home, because he'd have to share a silent, awkward breakfast with Henry. The doorbell rang. Nobody offered a "Who is it?"

They both knew exactly who it was. Henry folded the newspaper; the doorbell rang again. Henry tilted a pint of

Irish whiskey into a plastic cup, drinking down the whiskey smoother than tap water. He burped a stench of alcohol, and said, "Go." Henry's word was a gunshot at a world- class track meet. Mickey grabbed his school books, and dashed to the third ring of the doorbell.

"Bring your ass straight home afterschool you hear! Don't make me come up on that damn roof!" Henry yelled in a thick Irish accent.

Mickey said, "Yes."

Matty stood over the green clovers on the welcome mat, eating a meatball sub.

"Where's your mom?" Matty asked with tomato sauce stains around his lips.

"She's working, the bar must've been busy," Mickey said skipping down the staircase.

"Shit, I dreamt about her banana pancakes." Another reason Mickey hated waking up to Henry, cereal was the only meal on the menu. Matty stalled on the stairs to savor the meatball sub.

"Matty hurry up, you're eating a sandwich and complaining about missing out on pancakes."

"You can never have enough food." Matty's obesity vouched for his statement.

Matthew Hart lived on the fifth floor in building 458 West 36th, two floors above Mickey. They'd been friends since diapers along with Matty's twin, Eddie. Their fathers grew up on the same plot in Londonderry (Northern Ireland). The Tansy and Hart family connection went back centuries. The families followed each other to New York's Ellis Island, and eventually to Hell's Kitchen. Matty's twin, Eddie Hart, waited in the lobby of the building against the dusty mailboxes, clutching a plastic lunch box. Matty's lunch never made it out the building. Although Matty and Eddie were twins, the brothers shared nothing in common. Matty was fat with black hair and brown eyes. Eddie was slim with sandy blonde hair and green eyes. Matty cracked jokes, Eddie hated horseplay.

"I'll give you half my allowance money for half your meatball sub," Matty propositioned Eddie.

"I'll give you one half of a half, for half your allowance money," Eddie said. Matty agreed and devoured the quarter sub right in the lobby.

"You're a pig," Mickey said before they all walked out the tenement building.

Hell's Kitchen is a neighborhood on the island of Manhattan's Westside. It runs from 34th Street to 57th Street, from Ninth Avenue to Twelfth Avenue. The name Hell's Kitchen first debuted in print in the 1890's to describe the rough section of Manhattan, where a New York Times reporter used the term to describe a triple homicide in a housing block in the area. As the years passed, the neighborhood continued to live up to its infamous reputation. In the 1920's, street gangs liked The Gophers carried on the tradition and plagued the

Westside. The Gophers not only terrorized residents, they scared the NYPD shitless. The gang liked to fire handguns at the cops for fun. To an outsider, Hell's Kitchen was a place to visit when you lacked the guts to commit suicide. To the people of the Westside, it was a sanctuary of limestone and linoleum. The old timers gossiped on the building stoops and wouldn't hesitate to discipline a neighbour's kid. If a kid got caught doing wrong, they'd get four beatings before getting dragged to their stoop. The majority of Hell's Kitchen's population was Irish and Italian. A seasoned Westsider could tell the difference from an Italian block or an Irish block. The Italians treasured their restaurants, the Irish, their pubs. The pubs and the Hell's Kitchen piers provided employment for most Westside residents, so did the factories. Hell's Kitchen was a cesspool for organized crime. It flourished in all aspects on the Westside; every bar and pier had its own gangster representative ready to squeeze the eagle off your quarter. A mob of organized crime figures grew up in the neighborhood but none rose higher on the criminal pedestal than Irish racketeer, Oweny Madden. The gangland boss hijacked, extorted, and murdered his way to the millionaire tax bracket. Madden's holdings included the world famous Cotton Club in Harlem. Besides the nightclub interest, he controlled the taxicab business. The modern day Irish mob on the Westside operated under the leadership of Timothy "Matches" Volpe. A gangster from the Oweny Madden lineage, the police called" Matches" mob the "Lucky Charm Crew" because of their headquarters, the Lucky Charm pub, on 48th street and Tenth Avenue.

The clouds ganged up on the sun, a wind blew south, scattering the lightweight trash down the street. Mickey, Matty, and Eddie walked in silence, preparing themselves mentally for another day of the third grade. A cop directed traffic on 37th Street, the smell of freshly baked muffins drifted out the Italian bakery welcoming them to 38th, an Italian block. The last member of the gang lived on 38th Street in the heart of enemy territory. The Ravens, an Italian street gang marked 38th Street as their stomping grounds. The president of The Ravens, an up and coming thug named Johnny Sticks, declared war on all Irish gangs in Hell's Kitchen. That declaration included the boys on 36th Street, who at the time weren't really a gang, but The Ravens, labeled them one to justify their attacks. Johnny Sticks called Mickey and the Hart twins, The 458s because it was the number on their tenement building. The 458s' fourth member was an Irish kid named Jackie who had the misfortune of living on 38th Street. The Ravens used Jackie as their personal punching bag. To minimize his beatings, Jackie joined the nearest Irish gang, the 458s. The three of them stopped at Jackie's tenement building. Jackie Ward prided himself on being Hell's Kitchen's richest kid. He saved twenty-six hundred dollars in a bank account; the money belonged to Jackie and nobody else. He earned the dough running a newspaper route and chopping meat part- time in his father's butcher shop.

"What are you going to do with the dough?" Mickey asked Jackie.

"Calculated investments," he responded. Jackie was eons ahead of the other kids in terms of money management. Finally, Jackie walked out in a brown corduroy jacket, eyes half sealed by the cold.

"The Ravens outnumber us. We can't be waiting down here forever," Mickey complained.

"I forgot my book on the radiator. I had to run back to get it. Any of you see the Jimmy Dean show last night?" Jackie asked, switching subjects as they marched in the school's direction.

"No, I fell asleep," Eddie answered. Mickey's family didn't own a television set.

"What about the nigger family in your building. Did you see them?" Jackie asked.

The black family moving into the empty apartment on Matty's floor was the talk of 36th Street. Mickey brushed a blonde lock out the center of his face and imagined sitting in front of a television set.

"Yeah, I saw them out my window. A lady and three little girls," Eddie said.

"These niggas better stay the hell out of Hell's Kitchen, and go back to the zoo, where they belong."

Hatred filled Jackie's little heart.

"It's one family, Jackie. Cool out." Mickey's baby blue eyes darted the block for a Raven.

"My dad says that's how it starts. We let one stay and in comes a thousand more."

"Jackie is right, we should do something," Eddie suggested.

Mickey jumped and snatched a small branch off a lifeless tree. Jackie skipped in front of the gang turned and backpedalled, he always did this when he wanted center stage. The smallest 458 member had to be crafty to get everyone's attention.

"And there's a boy our age in the family. I saw him at the deli on 35th street."

"Jackie, it's a bunch of girls," Mickey swung the branch like a magic wand.

"I'm serious, there's a boy."

"There is a boy," Fat Matty finally intervened. Jackie continued back peddling. "I told you so."

"Why didn't you say something Matty?" Mickey snapped the branch in half. This changed everything. He and the Hart brothers ruled 458 West 36th street, now a black boy threatened to overthrow their regime.

"I forgot about it but who cares," Matty said.

"I do," Jackie said. Everyone awaited Mickey's response as president of the 458s, he had the last word.

"The showdown with the Ravens is on Friday night. We'll get ready for battle and after the rumble, we'll send the black boy packing," Mickey said.

"Class, can I have your attention," Mrs. Thompson addressed her third graders in a sweet but authoritative tone. Her pleasant face didn't have a trace of makeup, blue sapphire earrings dangled on the shoulders of her blue turtleneck.

"I want to introduce you to our newest class member, Charles Freeman." She said Charles stared at a pair of black Chuck Taylors All-Stars.

"I want everybody to give Charles a warm welcome." Mrs. Thompson smiled. Thirty students behind wooden desks studied Charles harder than any class assignment.

"Let's not repeat the tragedy that happened to the last black," Mrs. Thompson restrained herself. Charles looked up. *Repeat the tragedy that happened to the last black,* he thought. Mrs. Thompson's smile flinched a bit, but she quickly recovered. "Charles, your desk is in the back of the classroom, next to Mickey."

Charles looked to the two secluded desks in the back. He knew the desks weren't' for the privileged students, more for the outcasts.

"Mickey, raise your hand so Charles can see you. You're lucky for the company. If this class wasn't overcrowded, you'd still be alone," Mrs. Thompson scolded Mickey. Charles went to the desk next to the half-raised hand.

A reddish brown haired boy spun around and whispered, "That's him, Mickey."

Charles remembered seeing the boy yesterday at the daily on 35th street. Charles dug out a black and white composition notebook and a number 2 pencil. Mrs. Thompson turned to the blackboard and a paper ball bounced off Charles' cheekbone, giggles broke out in the classroom. The last bell signaled the end of the school day.

Charles waited outside the school, exhausted from bobbing and weaving paper balls for the first four class periods. Someone stuck gum on his chair after lunch. Mrs. Thompson called Charles up to the blackboard to solve a math problem. The class went hysterical at the sight of pink gum stuck to the ass of his black pants. He spent the next period in the boys' bathroom, scrubbing away gum. That's where he got formally introduced to The Ravens and Johnny Sticks. Charles' left side still throbbed from the breath-taking body blows.

"Welcome to Hell's Kitchen, nigger boy!" a Raven blurted, while Charles winced in pain. It wasn't the warm welcome Mrs. Thompson preferred. The rusty Plymouth rattled on the side of the pavement. It took Charles three hard tugs to open the passenger door. He repaid the door with a hard slam once inside.

"Be careful boy. You almost broke my damn door!" Luis yelled. Charles wanted to yell back, "It's already broken!"

"How was your first day?" Luis asked. He left the girls at home.

Luis thought these manly sessions would help Chuckie get over the hurt of losing Steve.

"Another school day." Charles chose to edit out the racism and bullying. The move to Hell's Kitchen meant a lot to Dad, so he'd have to persevere.

"Did you meet any new friends?" Luis asked. "No but it's the first day, I got time."

Luis snapped to James Brown's "Night Train" playing on his mental radio. "That's right, Chuckie, once those kids realize how cool and smart you are, you'll be the most popular kid in school."

Chuckie was certain the Ravens would kill him long before that ever happened, but Chuckie laughed and said.

"Yeah, Dad, I'll be the most popular kid," because it made the old man happy.

CHAPTER 2

Hell's Kitchen, NYC. "1966"

Rita McMillian was a naïve teenager when she fell for a hotheaded Irish thug named Mickey Tansy. The phrase *swept off her feet* was an understatement. Mickey's blonde locks hung shoulder length, his blue pupils sliced through her soul. Tansy was twenty-five years old, high on the beliefs of the Irish Republican Army. Rita was seventeen and even higher on him. She'd see specks of Mickey in his son. Big Mickey was charismatic, kind- hearted, but when in rage, deadly. He never went anywhere without his younger brother, Thomas. The two extorted storeowners on the Westside. The money provided stability for Rita and her newborn son. Rita's friends envied her for not having to work to acquire life's necessities. Big Mickey's involvement in the IRA increased. He began smuggling guns across state lines. The day arrived when Mickey's beliefs were put to the test. A state trooper stopped Mickey's pickup truck, stockpiled with rifles and ammunition. Mickey shot and killed the state trooper and wounded two bystanders. A federal judge sentenced him to life plus one hundred years in prison.

Rita faced two options: survive or perish. She swallowed her pride and worked two jobs in order to feed little Mickey. The neighborhood took pity on Rita but no one offered any help except Mrs. Hart, who babysat Mickey while Rita worked double, sometimes, triple shifts. Mrs. Hart encouraged Rita to start dating while she still had the looks. Rita doubted any man would want to be burdened with another man's child.

A prizefighter named Henry McMillian visited the Lucky Charm Pub where Rita bartended. Henry was the pride of Hell's Kitchen, and many predicted the next light heavyweight champion of the world.

Henry adored Rita and his growing fight purses helped her financial situation. Rita moved Henry into her two-bedroom apartment on 36th Street. Henry McMillian debuted on Ring Magazine's Top Ten Light Heavyweight Contenders list in 1961. He celebrated by marrying Rita at St. Patrick's Cathedral. Rita accepted Henry's proposal but deep down, never truly loved him. In the spring of '62, Henry fought Harold Johnson for the light heavyweight crown. He suffered a second round technical knockout. Henry never regained his earlier prominence. He lost his next five prizefights. The last one, so one-sided that after the fight, Henry's boxing promoter voided their contract. The former prospect soaked his sorrows in whiskey and only KO'd one opponent, Rita.

Mickey mastered the chain of events, a simple conversation escalated into an argument. The argument catapulted to smacks, punches, and kicks. Mickey willed his mind out the room, out the apartment. His thoughts sailed uptown to 48th Street, to Uncle Tom's apartment. The T.V. displayed Mets rookie pitcher, Tom Seaver. Uncle Tom loved the New York Mets, and Mickey loved Uncle Tom's girl, Gwendolyn.

The gorgeous black woman taught Mickey the new dance crazes she learned up in Harlem. The Temptations played on the record player. Mickey held Gwendolyn by those wide hips. Uncle Tom smoked those tightly rolled white papers. Tom's Irish friends never approved of Gwendolyn, but Mickey overheard Tom telling a friend.

"If I cared about what you think, I might as well hand you my balls and cannonball into the Hudson River." Nobody else butted in Tom's personal life. The pots falling off the stove brought Mickey back to reality. He heard the drunk rage, Rita's cries. Mickey mastered the chain of events, he'd end the night with a busted lip or worse, a broken nose, because he'd intervene. Mickey would rather endure the beating together than cower to her screams alone. A slap, a scream, another slap. It neared the time Henry balled the smacks to fist. Mickey grabbed a miniature baseball bat and walked out the bedroom, hoping Hell's Kitchen wouldn't serve him another cold plate.

Charles roamed the apartment looking for an excuse to get out. It was Friday and the ritual continued whether uptown, downtown, or around town. Momma's best friend, Mrs. May came over every Friday afternoon to fry fish and play bingo. She'd bring her three daughters, the most aggravating little girls Charles ever met. Daddy went back to working the overnight shift, so the house would be full of females. Yup, he had to go, go, go!

Charles entered the kitchen and there it was, a way out. He twisted the ends to the stuffed garbage bag.

"What in the world are you doing?" Momma asked, using metal thongs to flip fish in the frying pan.

"I'm getting rid of this smelly trash," Charles said. Beatrice never kept a man from work, especially when it made her job easier.

"That's great, Chuckie. Pick me up some potatoes at the 35th Street deli." The garbage was a decoy to leave the apartment. Momma's store request just boomeranged him right back.

"I'll come back for the potato money," he said.

"Why can't you get everything out the way in one trip?" Momma asked. Hot grease leapt out the frying pan. Charles hated to do it, but she left him no choice. "Ever since the night Uncle Steve died, my mind doesn't work so well" Charles hung his head and shook it. Beatrice cuffed Charles' head under her left breast. "Poor baby," she said, fighting back tears. "You take the trash and I'll send Mrs. May down for the potatoes."

Charles slung the garbage bag inside the dumpster on 36th Street. He thought of places to hide until nighttime. He'd hike uptown in the slow drizzle to 117th to visit Teflin, to see the old crew, and the old neighborhood. Charles walked uptown to 38th Street and saw Jackie Ward speeding downtown, Jackie didn't see him. Charles crossed the street, he learned the gangs and their territories quick. It was a matter of survival. Jackie kept looking back, holding tightly to his bag. He looked like prey himself on the Westside streets. Charles continued up another block contemplating whether he possessed the stamina for the journey uptown. Ten feet away, Johnny Sticks strolled out a penny candy store. A group of Ravens backed him. They wore purple cardigans with black Ravens stitch on the right breast. They all were holding brown paper bags filled to the brim with one-cent candies. The candy storeowner's voice rung out the store.

"Someone call the cops, please!"

The few Ravens still looting inside punished the owner for squealing. A door buzzed off to the building on Charles' right, an act of God! Charles dipped inside the building and ran up to the roof.

The 458s shot the breeze in their clubhouse on the roof of 458 West 36th street. They transformed a deceased neighbor's birdcage into the gang's hangout. A slight drizzle of rain drummed on the tin roof of the birdcage. Eddie skimmed through a Superman comic book sitting on a ripped cloth sofa. Mickey and Matty sipped Coca Cola's and discussed battle tactics. Matty, the 458s warlord and second in command earned the position beating up rival gang members but lost the fight for the 458's presidency to Mickey. Henry's boxing lessons gave Mickey an advantage against other kids. Jackie walked on the roof's tarmac, perspiration streaming under a New York Yankees baseball cap.

Mickey opened the latch on the birdcage. Jackie slammed the bag on a coffee table. Mickey eagerly rubbed both palms together. "Show me."

Jackie ripped the paper bag open and emptied it on the table. A spray can of mace, brass knuckles and a blackjack fell out. Matty reached for the blackjack but Eddie beat him to it, so Matty settled for the brass knuckles.

"That's all, for twenty bucks?" Mickey asked.

Jackie went inside his corduroy jacket for a black and silver switchblade. He pushed the silver button, and watched the 5-inch blade flip out. Mickey relieved Jackie of the knife.

"The blade's mine," he said.

The throw down was at nightfall on 40th Street, no man's land. The rumble marked a dawn of a new era in gang fighting. In the past the two gangs fought with strictly fists but The Ravens violated the no weapon treaty when they smashed Jackie over the head with a beer bottle. The two gangs' appetite for destruction was fueled by James "Snapps" Mitchell. A member of the Lucky Charm Crew, Snapps supplied both factions in their race for arms. Snapps' morale didn't suffer the slightest indignation from selling eight-year-olds weapons.

"There's a lot more of them than us. We can win if we fight back to back," Matty said.

"If they pile on you, get one of them and hurt'em."

The 458s sported black knitted sweaters, with green clovers stitched down the front. Rita sewed the sweaters on her lunch breaks at the sewing factory. She thought the boys started a social club to help clean up the neighborhood, not a gang to help tear it down.

"When can we beat the crap out that nigger?" The black kid weighed on Jackie's mind more than the Ravens.

"After the throw down," Mickey said.

"I want to bring something to the gang's attention." Eddie's face went somber.

"The president warned us to stay away from the nigger in the building. I witnessed our warlord and my own brother leaving the nigger's apartment yesterday afternoon." "What?" Jackie gasped and grilled Matty, the ultimate betrayer. "Is this true?" Jackie demanded.

Eddie grinned at Matty. He found pleasure watching Matty try to crawl out of this one. Eddie waited to disclose this information at the perfect time. Matty's demotion meant Eddie's promotion.

"Yeah, I went in the house," Matty confessed. "I carried the lady's groceries upstairs and she fixed me a plate of food."

Matty's mouth watered in reminiscence of the tender pork chops. "Some of the best food I ever ate, so what?" Matty said unapologetically. "And another thing, the kid Chuckie, we did our math homework together." Matty figured if he told it, he had to tell it all.

"Chuckie! He's calling the monkey by his name!" Jackie screamed.

"I motion for Matty to be stripped of warlord status and put on probation," Eddie said.

"I second that motion," said Jackie.

Once again, they all looked to the president. "What's your decision, Mick?" Eddie asked.

They didn't stand a chance at winning the rumble without Matty.

Mickey knew this.

"I'm giving Matty a warning. He's still our warlord." Eddie's grin hitchhiked to Matty.

"This is bullshit!" screamed Jackie.

"Shut the hell up, I call the shots," Mickey said.

Charles played a game of cat and mouse with the Ravens. The ability to spy on his enemies without them knowing gave him a feeling of empowerment. The adjourned rooftops allowed him to move freely a block north and an avenue across. Charles followed the Ravens from up in the sky to their clubhouse between the avenues. A group of ten Ravens smoked cigarettes and drank beer outside an abandoned storefront. As the day aged, the traffic on the block got scarce. The Ravens went inside the storefront and returned holding bats, chains, and pipes. The gang rallied around Johnny, who gave instructions with a wooden baseball bat. The Ravens marched to the avenue. Charles crossed the roofs keeping up with them. They turned the corner on 39th Street and went up to 40th. Charles crossed four more roofs. Johnny Sticks slammed the fat end of the baseball bat into the palm of his hand. The Ravens launched rocks at the bulbs on the streetlamps; three of the five poles went black. Charles looked to the two still shining and saw four figures approaching the middle of the street.

He recognized Matty, the day before they did homework together. Matty offered to be Charles' secret friend for a plate of food every Sunday. Charles agreed to the shakedown, what the hell? He was lonely. A light bulb shined over Charles, the 458s, and the Ravens were about to throw down. The gangs in Harlem did the same but whenever Charles' crew threw down; he'd fake a flu. Charles laughed to himself. The two gangs who tormented him were set to kick the shit out of each other, and he had tickets to the cheap seats.

Car horns honked behind them, Mickey led the pack, the wind sending the hair on his head behind him. Ravens spread out, blocking off the street, yelling their war chant, "Ravens! Ravens!" Ten birds' brandished weapons, fear clogged Mickey's throat.

"Half of them are chumps," Matty said.

He must've heard Mickey's heart beating. Matty and fear were never acquainted. It didn't live in him and he could detect whenever it came around him.

"They ain't no real brawlers," Mickey said, amping himself. "They're scared whops," Eddie said. Jackie seemed hypnotized by Johnny Sticks' bat.

"Jackie, put your game face on and don't shit your pants," Matty said.

"We should have bought a gun," Jackie said under the Raven's rants.

"Stay by my side," Matty whispered.

"I thought you Micks weren't showing up!" Johnny Sticks screamed. They stood footsteps apart.

"Your mother kept us waiting, you dumb Whop!" Johnny's temper sizzled his cool. Mickey jumped back, out of reach of Johnny's swing with the bat. A car door swallowed the Louisville slugger. The two gangs swarmed in, and mayhem broke out. Johnny dug the bat out the car dent, but Mickey's right, left combo connected first. Johnny stumbled back, shook the punches off, then began swinging the bat wildly.

Mickey back pedalled and weaved the slugger, until he tripped over Eddie's leg. Johnny held the bat in both hands and lifted it high above his head, then brought it down like a sledgehammer. Mickey rolled over in the nick of time, and managed to get two hands on the bat, him and Johnny struggled for control. Johnny and another Raven collided, knocking him down. Mickey held the bat; He stood up and swung at the Raven who bumped out Johnny. The Louisville slugger made contact. The crack was louder than a Mickey Mantle homer. A fist stung the back of Mickey's head, Johnny's right hook.

Another Raven bear hugged him to the concrete. Mickey fell on the bat and curled up to protect himself, Eddie curled up beside him. A flash of white light spotted Mickey's vision; drivers left their cars in the street, trying to escape the medley. A hand lifted Mickey up.

"Stay the fuck on your feet," Matty said before tackling a Raven.

The two Ravens who pounded Mickey, were laid out cold by Matty's brass knuckles. Police sirens blared in the night.

"Coppers!!" a Raven screamed.

Mickey's blood boiled, he let the craze consume him. He flicked out the switchblade and saw red. A Raven climbed Matty's back choking him with a thick metal chain. Mickey stuck the blade into the Raven's back and twisted it. The Raven immediately released the chain and fell off Matty. Mickey stabbed another gang member, the Raven howled out in pain. Johnny Sticks pulled himself up on a parked station wagon and spit out a tooth.

"Johnny, help, I'm bleeding. Someone stabbed me!" cried Mickey's first victim, paralyzed on the pavement. The police sirens were closing in. Johnny pulled a .22 caliber two shot Dillinger out his cardigan. Scared and confused, Johnny sent two shots at Mickey and fled.

The police sirens snatched Charles out of the intensity of the ongoing brawl. The apartments lit up on the top floors. Charles thought a tenant might see him on the roof and mistake him for a burglar. The thought of going to jail scared Charles senseless. He ran down the stairs to the building's first floor. The flashing lights reflected in the glass of the building's front door. Charles used a stack of telephone books as a stepping stool, to see out the glass. He watched in disbelief, as the police officers began to beat the young gang members with nightsticks. Charles went to run back to the roof, but something called him back. He cracked open the door.

"Mickey!" Mickey circled the brawl in a deranged state, blood flowing down his face.

"Mickey, over here!"

Mickey skipped up the stoop to the building.

"This way." Chuckie leaped up the stairs, three steps at a time, until he hit the roof. "Come on," Chuckie said, crossing over the rooftops. Mickey followed.

"We can climb this wall and run down the fire escapes to the backyard." Mickey touched the brick wall.

"Wipe the blood off your face," Chuckie said. Mickey stared at the clover sweater soaked in blood.

"I'm bleeding." Mickey realized he was still holding the bloody switchblade. He raised the knife, Chuckie jolted back.

"What you plan on doing with that, man? I'm trying to help." Mickey threw the switchblade over the wall, down to the gutters of the backyard.

He pulled off the sweater and wiped at the blood.

"Holy shit, you're shot," Chuckie touched the graze on Mickey's forehead.

"Seriously?" Mickey asked, more excited than frightened.

"It ain't bad. In Harlem, I seen people get shot all the time." Chuckie did just witness a murder five weeks earlier.

"I heard a lot of stories about Harlem. That's where you from?" Mickey asked.

"Yeah, you're bleeding again," Chuckie pointed at the wound. "If you want, you can come to my house. My mom's a nurse."

"Cool, I'll go," Mickey said.

"Ouch!" Mickey tensed on the toilet bowl seat.

"I'm almost finished. Two more stiches," Momma said, biting on needle and thread.

"This scar ain't come from no damn stick ball," she mumbled. Belinda leaned on Mickey's leg sucking on a chicken bone.

"Chuckie, find Mickey some clean clothes to change into. "Belinda popped the chicken out her cheek and offered it and some drool to Mickey.

Later That Night

"But what if the boy you stabbed dies, did you think of that?" Chuckie asked.

"Then he dies," Mickey shrugged wearing Chuckie green pajamas.

"You'll be in jail forever," Chuckie said, legs folded Indian-style on the twin-size bed.

"In Hell's Kitchen, it's about who's the toughest. The toughest gang gets respect and respect gets you everything." Mickey picked up Chuckie's Hess truck.

"I'm not scared of jail. Maybe I'll see my dad, get him to kill my stepfather."

"Why do you hate your stepfather?" Chuckie asked.

"He doesn't care about me or my mom. I'm staying the night at your house and he won't even know I'm missing." Mickey drove the Hess truck up the dresser.

"You're lucky, I wish I had your family."

"Lucky? I'm public enemy number one in Hell's Kitchen," Chuckie said.

"We were supposed to kick your ass tonight," Chuckie lunged the pillow at Mickey.

"Be careful, I'm shot!" Mickey touched the stiches on his forehead. "Join the 458s, you already live in the building, use the gang for protection. Jackie does"

"You think the gang will let me join?" Chuckie asked.

"You're alright with me and I'm the president. Matty's the warlord and you know what floats his boat."

They both said, "Food" simultaneously.

"Want to listen to some music, Mickey?" Chuckie walked to the closet and brought out the record player. Mickey peeked in the closet at the large record collection.

"These all your records?" Chuckie blew dust off a 33 ⅓ RPM 12-inch vinyl.

"Yeah, they belonged to my Uncle Steve but he's dead now." Chuckie placed the vinyl on the record player and dropped the needle.

"My uncle is the closest thing I got to a father. If he died, I'd go crazy.

How did your uncle die?" Mickey asked.

"They shot him. I was there, I saw everything" The scene reeled in Chuckie's head.

"Damn Chuckie, you're strong. Way stronger than I am," Mickey said.

Chuckie nodded and Little Richard shouted, "Good golly Miss Molly!"

CHAPTER 3

Queens, NYC "1975" 9 Years Later

Pallbearers lowered a black coffin lined in eggshell velvet into the ground. There were more mourners in the Queens cemetery than expected. The deceased wasn't a person of enormous popularity.

Her death wouldn't affect a nation or cripple a movement. There would be no schools closing or flags flown half-mast, the world wouldn't skip a beat. Her death didn't belong to the world; it belonged to the few in attendance, making it sentimental. The smaller the circle, the greater the loss, the chain of events proved detrimental.

Mickey thought he mastered the chain of events, but the chain on the bicycle broke, no longer able to spin the grooves into motion. Mickey tried saving it. He flipped the bike over on its handlebars and seat. He wheeled the pedal but the chain didn't slip off, it popped! No more riding, no more Rita.

The thongs to the rose pinched blood out Mickey's fingertip. He held it tight stirring at his mother's casket. The lone rose, he'd lay on the coffin after the priest chopped up the Holy Trinity and said, "Ashes to ashes and dust to dust."

Mickey would lay the first rose and everybody else would follow. Ashes to ashes, dust to dust, no hesitating, no more. Mickey chastised himself. If he hadn't hesitated, Rita probably be alive, but he did. Mickey hesitated standing over the unconscious drunk on the couch, holding Uncle Tom's army-issued .45 caliber pistol. When it counted, he froze, clammed up, and hesitated. Henry accomplished the goal he set out on long ago, beating Rita to death. Mickey wasn't in the apartment when it happened, nobody was, when Mickey found her head positioned in a way that wasn't humanly possible. Well, a living human, one without a broken neck. Mickey tried fixing the chain but it broke. It popped!

The police caught Henry days later at a motel in the Catskills of upstate New York. The former contender forever an offender. The red rose landed on the casket, tucked in its eternal resting place.

"No hesitating, no more," Mickey whispered.

"She's with God, Mickey." Chuckie patted him on the back.

"Where was God when Henry broke her fucking neck," Mickey said, loud enough for the mourners to hear. A pair of dark sunglasses covered half his face but you didn't have to see the face to know that it was cold, colder than the ground Rita rested in.

"Over your mother's grave, you use that filthy language. Get lost," Tom said.

Mickey sized him up. Mickey grew to six feet, two inches. Tom stunted at five foot seven. The blonde hair and blue eyes ran in the Tansy genes. Tom wore his hair short and combed it to the back, his short stocky frame resembled a bull. Uncle Tom was Mickey's new guardian. Mrs. Hart wanted to adopt Mickey but her strict ways didn't appeal to the youngster. At Tom's place there were no rules, Tom lifted a wooden cane at Mickey.

"You hard of hearing, numb nuts? Get out of here."

Mickey turned hard and walked harder to the caravan of cars parked on the cemetery's dirt road.

"I didn't mean to lash out, Chuckie. This shit is driving me fucking crazy." Mickey paced near Matty's Pontiac, patting his jacket pockets for a lighter. He clenched the butt of a cigarette with his teeth, no lighter. Mickey kicked the Pontiac's tire with a platform shoe.

"You left the lighter in the car," Chuckie said. He and Mickey were the same height, but Chuckie's wide afro gave him a few extra inches. They were seventeen and seniors in the same high school, though Mickey seldom went. Mickey opened the Pontiac, unlocked the glove compartment, and found the lighter. He sparked a Marlboro and blew a cloud at the clouds. A gold Cadillac Eldorado shimmered in the sun's light, cruising on the dusty road. Mickey and Chuckie knew the car, everybody on the Westside did. It belonged to JB Volpe, Matches' younger brother and co-leader of the Lucky Charm crew.

The Cadillac stopped beside Matty's brown Bonneville; Matches Volpe sat in the passenger, boss of the Irish Mob.

"Ha, Little Mickey," Matches called the teenager over to the Eldorado. "I'm sorry about Rita, she was a saint. She worked the Lucky Charm for sixteen years, never stole a dime." The godliest thing a woman could do was not steal Matches' money. Mickey was surprised Matches even knew his name.

"Thanks, Matches, she really loved working at the bar."

Matches had a strong and distinctive face, compacted with stress lines and freckles. His hairline receded to the crown, perfectly trimmed gray hair on the sides. A black eyepatch covered his left eye. The right eye was green and doubled up on awareness. Matches assessed everything in their surroundings.

"If you need anything, Little Mickey, come to the bar. Don't be shy. You're a part of the family." Matches dropped a fifty dollarbill on Mickey and JB drove out the cemetery.

"That's Matches Volpe," Chuckie said. "Yup, the boss himself." Mickey said.

"He knows your name?" Chuckie asked.

"Of course, I'm the leader of the 458s. I'm somebody on the Westside." Mickey said. Matty joined them wearing a blue varsity football jacket, at seventeen he'd already grown a full beard.

"I saw JB's Cadillac," Matty said.

"Yeah, Matches funded our pot party." Mickey held both ends to the fifty and popped the bill.

"Half a yard, that's enough to get us stoned for the week."

Matty had grown the tallest, He sat two hundred plus pounds on the Pontiac's hood. Mourners approached the dirt road, funeral over.

"Matty, drive us uptown, I need to get high," Mickey said.

East Harlem, an Hour Later

"If the police roll up drive to 110th Street and Lexington, we'll meet there." Mickey exited the Bonneville for the slums of Spanish Harlem to score some pot. The block of 107th Street between Lexington and Third Avenue was an open-air drug market and the destination for good marijuana.

Chuckie shrunk in the backseat afraid they'd get busted. He'd rather wait in Hell's Kitchen and let Matty and Mickey cop the drugs. Matty turned back laying his arm along the top of the seats.

"Fifty-seven sacks, that's my career total," he said. Matty boasted about a stellar high school football career before parking by the "Do Not Park" sign.

"Football is too dangerous. Every play someone's trying to rip your spine out."

Chuckie wasn't a fan of sports, especially those involving extreme contact.

"That's why I love it! When I'm on the football field, I'm in my zone. I thirst for the action," said the all-state linebacker.

"I can knock a guy out and not get in trouble." That's the same line the coach said to convince Matty to come to tryouts.

"I get a natural high listening to music and I don't wake up to sprains and aches," Chuckie said.

"Yeah, but music isn't paying your college tuition, football's paying mine. I'll deal with the pain, plus I give more than I take," Matty smirked.

"You really love hurting people, you're sick Matty." Chuckie said, "At least I'm handsome," Matty chuckled.

"You decided which college you want to play for?" Chuckie asked. "I've got recruitment letters from Nebraska, Oklahoma, and Notre Dame. I'm going to Notre Dame. It's the gold helmets that gets me, gives you a sense of royalty, grid-iron royalty."

Chuckie was a bit jealous. Matty knew exactly what he wanted in life and he still hadn't made any plans for the future.

"What's the hold up?" Chuckie asked turning to stare out the window again.

"Two ounces of grass, and don't short me either," Mickey said.

"I'd never do such a thing, white boy. I 'ma businessman," said the skinny Puerto Rican in a red derby hat. His place of business, a neglected tenement building hallway decorated in graffiti.

"Cop a cutie pie, I'll give you a good price." Tito pitched his sale. "What's a cutie pie?" Mickey asked.

"A quarter pound, cat daddy." Tito dug in a mailbox for his stash of drugs.

"Next time, Tito. Two ounces of weed will do for now" Tito refused to break the fifty-dollar bill for change.

"I've got a fresh package of the best girl on the Eastside. I'll break you off proper if you're down for it." Five thin gold chains choked Tito's neck, laying on a silk black shirt opened wide enough to show nappy chest hair.

"Cocaine isn't my cup of tea."

"Everybody snorts a little girl. I do it, helps numb the pain of living in this fucked up world." Tito gave Mickey the two ounces and a neatly wrapped piece of aluminium foil.

"Numb the pain," Mickey said.

"Numb the pain, white boy." "Alright, I'll try it." Said Mickey.

Tito's baby face glittered. Fifty bucks for less than two minutes' work. "White boy, you can't come copping suited up. It's bad enough you're white. You're gonna lead the police right to me." Tito lifted a pants leg. "Go up to AJ Lester's and get you a pair of these," Tito twirled a red snakeskin shoe.

"Some dress slacks. You want a foxy woman to notice you, you got to look like money," Tito said, ushering Mickey out his office.

Mickey rolled two joints for the voyage back to Hell's Kitchen, the potent weed fogged up the car.

"It's better than last time," Matty said. The Flame red-eyed as Matty stemmed on the joint. Chuckie sat up in the backseat.

"I'm high and hungry."

"Chuckie, you're stoned off two joints. I've got two ounces of this shit and a surprise," Mickey said.

"What's the surprise?" Matty asked, straightening out the steering wheel.

A red cherry lit up on a gray Chevrolet.

"Fuck! The police!" The three instantaneously started fanning the weed aroma out the Pontiac. Matty pulled to the corner of 56th Street. Mickey tucked the aluminium foil in a sock, the weed between the seats. The cops stalled. The three waited nervously in the Bonneville.

"Un-fucking believable," said Matty to the rearview mirror. "What?" Chuckie asked.

"It's Sam Mitchell. He has a hard on for me because I embarrassed him at the annual Westside football game," Matty said, still in the rearview mirror.

"Who? Snapps' brother? I thought he went Federal," Mickey said. "The prick stopped me five times this month," Matty whispered. "His brother's the biggest crook in the neighborhood and he's top cop." Matty said.

"What a family." Mickey laughed.

"Hi Sam, haven't seen you since Tuesday," Matty said.

"Funny, prick. License and registration." Sam's flashlight searched the Pontiac.

"I see you got your pal riding shotgun. Hey, Mickey. Still stealing swag?" Sam asked.

"I'm on vacation, your brother is a fair employer," Mickey said.

Sam tilted six-feet-six-inches into the Bonneville. He was in his late twenties with an angular face and sharp features. His light blue eyes were deep set and engaging.

"Who's the new fella," he asked.

"I thought you were FBI, why are you doing traffic stops?" Mickey asked.

"Mr. All-State here is my recreation. The next professional football player out the Westside." Sam winked.

"He's mad I hit the pigskin right from under him in the Westside championship."

Sam winced at the memory of the bone crushing sack.

"An illegal hit. I don't care what the referee said." Sam removed his black Fedora from his black hair.

"I'ma teach you to respect your elders." He shined the flashlight on Chuckie. "Word of advice, kid, lose these two. They won't be in Hell's Kitchen for long." Sam tossed Matty's wallet into the Bonneville and walked to the Chevy.

Uncle Tom's Apartment. 48th Street and Tenth Avenue-Later That Night

Matty rolled up marijuana in whitepapers on a Harold Melvin and the Blue Notes album cover. He sold joints for one dollar. Chuckie was in charge of the music. He knew the right songs to play to get the parties going. They moved Uncle Tom's furniture into the back bedrooms and screwed red light bulbs on the lamps. At least a dozen neighborhood girls and twenty 458s kept the weed in rotation. Mickey charged a 50-cent admission fee, these parties usually made the gang good money, which they used to finance future parties. Over the last several years, the 458s gained strength in Hell's Kitchen by absorbing smaller gangs and building alliances. The Iron Clovers, an Irish gang forty clovers strong, was completely absorbed by the 458s. The merger boosted Mickey's gang membership to one hundred members.

"Jackie, you coming out to dance?" asked an eager brunette. Jackie went from Hell's Kitchen's richest kid to its richest teenager. He drove a brand new silver Corvette Stingray. Jackie Sr.'s chain of butcher shops operated in all five boroughs. At seventeen years old Jackie earned more money than ninety percent of the adults in the neighborhood, managing his father's butcher shops.

"Not now, save a dance for me later," Jackie said.

"Jackie pass that brunette off. She's twice your size,' Mickey said. "We're the same size in the stingray." Jackie smiled.

"You're hogging the pussy. You can't love them all, Jackie," Eddie said. "Oh but I do. I swear I do." Matty and Chuckie walked into the kitchen. "I need more weed, I finished the first ounce."

Matty passed Jackie the roll of dollar bills. Mickey got more weed out the cabinet under the sink.

"I almost forgot." Mickey carefully unraveled the aluminium foil. "Tito gave us some coke."

"Why did he give you that? We don't do coke," Jackie said. "Yeah, Mickey, what made you buy that shit?" Chuckie asked, agreeing with Jackie, which never happened.

"My mother is dead. I need something to numb the pain," Mickey said.

"I'll do some," said Matty. "Me too" Eddie said.

"I ain't putting that junk up my nose," said Jackie.

"We'll all try it for this one night. If the shit's a bummer, we'll flush the rest down the toilet."

Mickey scooped up some coke in a dingy dollar and snorted it up a nostril. He blinked like he'd walked into a wall. It was several seconds before Mickey could speak again. "That felt good." he said.

"I'm next!" said Matty.

The sunlight streaming in the bathroom's shades gave Chuckie the vampire affect, sending a sharp piercing pain through his brain. Chuckie laid on the floor tiles, saturated in vomit and urine, unable to get up.

"Dear God, if you give me the strength to stand up, I'll never drink again, I'll never smoke again, and definitely no cocaine, please God."

Chuckie prayed and pleaded. He waited a few seconds expecting to miraculously come back to life. Nothing happened. Chuckie got home at four a.m. high on weed and coke, piss drunk on Mickey's special rum punch. The night was a memorable one, the gang, the girls, the superior consciousness cocaine awards you, but the crash felt violent and treacherous. The crash left Chuckie on the bathroom floor.

"Chuckie, are you in there?"

Chuckie wanted to respond but he couldn't.

"Chuckie, get out the bathroom. I gots to get ready for work." Luis pounded harder on the door. Chuckie went back to battling the sun. A butter knife slipped between the door lock.

"Beatrice! Call an ambulance!" Luis scooped Chuckie up.

The smell of a hospital reminded him of death. That's why Chuckie tended to stay away. A thousand flowers, air fresheners or perfumes couldn't replace that smell. The hospital gown reeked of mothballs. A tray of awful food, yellow daises in a glass vase, and a wooden chair furnished the hospital room. The daisies happened to be Chuckie's favorite flower. Only Momma and Tracey knew that. Chuckie exercised his memory and embarrassment flushed him. The vomit, the cold floor tiles, the spouts of incoherent mumbling during the ambulance ride. Chuckie'd rather die than face Momma and Poppa about his drug abuse. Chuckie didn't abuse drugs. He experimented every other weekend at 458 parties. To Chuckie's parents, it wouldn't' matter. He'd be considered a drug addict, no different than the one's sleeping on street corners.

"I tried rushing back before these things got cold." Luis held two Styrofoam cups. "It's hot cocoa, drink some." He put a cup to Chuckie's chapped lips. Chuckie actually felt the steaming chocolate slowly sliding down his chest.

"Your little sisters sent you these flowers. They're disappointed but not more than I am. You're supposed to be oldest, setting an example for them."

"I went to a party."

Luis silenced Chuckie with another sip of hot chocolate. "I'm not driving these buses for my first born to be a junkie." "I'm no junkie," Chuckie said defiantly.

"Oh yeah, well the doctor said you had a bunch of junk in your system. Reefers, cocaine, alcohol." Luis counted the narcotics off on his fingers.

"The party got a little out of control, Pops." Luis put down the Styrofoam cups.

"I want you to have the best, Chuckie. The things I couldn't have in my life. Eventually you'll have to decide which road you're going to travel and I trust you'll make the right decision, son." Luis kissed Chuckie's forehead. "And another thing, those friends of yours, leave them alone."

"They're my friends, Pops," Chuckie said.

"I talk with Mickey all the time. He doesn't want anything that isn't in Hell's Kitchen. They're your friends but if you want to succeed, distance yourself, because they're going down the wrong path."

4 Months Later

The china bubbled in a bent spoon swaying over a lit wax candle. The white substance sizzled on the caked up silverware. A hypodermic needle dove into the spoon and sucked up the china. The needle squirted a pinch in the air, the anticipation quivered Tom's lips. He tied a leather belt around an arm tattooed in needle marks, holding the belt buckle between his clenched teeth. A small vein pressed up against his skin tissue. Blood clouded the heroin in the syringe when the needle entered Tom's vein. A dirty burgundy mixture vacuumed into Tom's arm. The rush slacked his jaw, releasing the belt buckle, the arm fell lifeless, the hypodermic needle still attached to the vein. The fix was strong, not the china white you'd find in Southeast Asia, but the closest thing New York had to offer.

In late '68, the U.S. Army drafted Thomas Tansy to fight in the jungles of Vietnam. The Army trained him to kill and Tom followed instructions very well. In the two tours he served in Vietnam, Tom's body count totaled twenty-seven, women and children included. The U.S. Army awarded him the Silver Star for gallantry in action and promoted Tom to Sergeant first class. The Vietcong Army's guerrilla tactics kept the frontline soldiers on edge. They sought something to calm the jitters, heroin, preferably china white, filled the void. The majority of minority soldiers returned to the inner cities heroin addicts. They fought bravely for a country who disowned them once back on American soil. There weren't any programs created to help veterans cope with the horrors of war. The shell shock, bloody nightmares, waking up in cold sweats. Many Vietnam veterans surrendered to heroin, others to crime. The slammed door ruined Tom's nod.

"Every time you two come in the house, you let the whole building know it." He snatched the hypodermic needle out his vein. Matty crashed on the couch, Mickey on a rocking chair next to a black and white Zenith television.

"You're usually in the bedroom, Tom. When's the last time you hung out in the living room?" Mickey asked, lining cocaine along the coffee table with a playing card.

"I used to hang out in the living room all the time before you assholes moved in." Tom packed up his works inside a leather satchel. Mickey snorted some coke and passed Matty the playing card.

"Where's your clothes?" Mickey asked Tom, who was sitting in white Fruit of the Loom underwear, and nothing else.

"This is my house, you're lucky I got these on." Tom ran a thumb along the elastic of the underwear and sniffed the last bit of cocaine off the playing card. A dot of white powder stayed on the tip of Tom's nose.

"The school is going on a class trip tomorrow. It costs ten bucks," Mickey said, turning the knobs on the Zenith television set.

"Class trip my ass; you want ten bucks to shove up your damn nose. This isn't going to work Mickey. You're a drug addict, I'm a drug addict. I'm living on a fixed income and my veterans check isn't worth shit," Tom said.

Mickey rocked in the rocking chair.

"I'm broke. What do you want me to do, get a job?" he asked.

Tom rubbed the tip of his thumb on the tips of his index and middle finger.

"You're not the nine to five type, Mickey."

"So how am I supposed to help out if I can't work?"

Tom left the couch for the bedroom. Mickey and Matty turned their heads to avoid Tom's hairy thighs.

"Put some pants on while you're in there!" Matty yelled. Tom returned without pants and a green attaché case.

"This is for you." He gave Matty the black army-issued .45 caliber handgun.

"And this is for you, numb nuts." Mickey took the chrome .32 caliber five-shot revolver.

"What's this for?" he asked.

"So you guys can get some nuggets, money, peso, whatever the fuck else they call it," Tom said.

"It's beautiful." Matty aimed the .45 at Ed Sullivan on the television screen.

"Careful Matty, it's loaded."

"I can't believe this, Chuckie's father is telling me to do something positive with my life and my uncle is giving me guns to pay the rent. Some role model you are, Tom," Mickey said.

"Call it what you want but I tell you this, that gun is the last gift you'll ever get from me. So enjoy," Tom said.

The near fatal drug-induced coma scared Chuckie straight. In the months following the overdose, Chuckie dedicated himself to hitting the books and avoiding the 458s at all cost. The resentment he received from the 458s was nothing in comparison to the disappointment he dealt his parents. One 458 didn't take offense to being cast aside.

"Everybody's doing their own thing, Chuckie, I'm not mad," Mickey said, bumping into Chuckie on a Westside street.

There wasn't a jealous bone in Mickey's body, and it made Chuckie feel guilty about giving him the cold shoulder. Mickey and the 458s wanted to be kings of the Westside. To them, nothing else mattered.

Chuckie rode his father's bus on the weekends, and the bus ride exposed him to another New York. He lived in New York every day for seventeen years and never left it, but was oblivious to the other New York coexisting in the same city. Chuckie's New York consisted of gangs, drugs, and abandoned buildings. The trenches, ghetto life, where everyone tries to get over and the strong prays on the weak. The other New York dined at the finest restaurants. Their chauffeurs conversed with their doormen, waiting for them to descend from their glass penthouses on Central Park East. The other New York read the New Yorker. Most of Chuckie's New York couldn't read. They rode to luxury midtown offices in Lincoln limousines and were CEOs and presidents of corporations essential to everyday living. The other New York was important, powerful, and respected. Chuckie saw this other New York on Pop's bus routes and none of the other New York shared his complexion.

The success stories in Chuckie's New York were the drug kingpins. The black dealers that lorded over criminal empires that rivaled any Standard & Poor Fortune 500 company in organizational structure and profit margins. The black drug barons gave out turkeys on Thanksgiving and sponsored neighborhood-sporting events. The ghetto's children immortalized the kingpins. Chuckie envisioned himself becoming a new version of the black kingpin, a legit version. A positive role model for African Americans, to ensure them their hopeless New York wasn't the only New York. Chuckie chased this dream of being an executive of a major corporation relentlessly. The acceptance letter he received to attend Howard University next fall, a mere baby step to achieving his dream.

The lint balls in Mickey's pockets outnumbered the U.S. currency. He fidgeted off one foot onto the other, waiting for Matty's Pontiac on 48th Street. The collar to his denim jacket flipped upwards. The October's cold huffed out Mickey's nostrils. He puffed on a lit Marlboro between two dirty fingers with a bug eye expression. He'd been up three days sniffing cocaine and smoking pot. A small boy in a police uniform approached him.

"Trick or treat."

It was Halloween. Mickey put two quarters in the kid's candy bag. "Where's the Sugar Daddies and Tootsie Rolls?" the boy asked.

"You don't want the fifty cents? Give it back," Mickey said, looking over the kid clocking the street's traffic. He looked back down on an orange cap gun and plastic handcuffs. "You're under arrest." The boy busted a cap. Mickey opened his denim jacket.

"Get lost or I 'ma shoot this."

The kid cop gasped at the chrome revolver and flew down Eighth Avenue. The Bonneville waited at the next red light, Mickey met the car in the street.

"Where's the drop off?" he asked once inside. Eddie drove, Matty sat in the back, the .45 caliber handgun sat on Matty's lap.

"It's on 104th Street," Eddie said, spinning the car into a U-turn. The flashy drug dealer stood out in a purple suit and matching snakeskin shoes. Tito swaggered down the avenue, a right hand paddling his stride. The 458s followed him slowly in the Pontiac to a newly renovated apartment building. A dark skinned woman in a fire red wig strutted to Tito in a form fitting miniskirt and knee-high boots. She handed Tito a package and they both entered the apartment building.

"Same as last week, same day, same time. That's the weekly supply.

She brings it every Wednesday," Eddie said.

"You sure? I'm not risking this for petty cash. For that we can rob the pizza delivery boy," Mickey said.

"I've hawked this motherfucker a week straight. That's the stash and that's the package. I'll guarantee it." Eddie said.

"If we ain't out in fifteen minutes, we ain't coming out." Said Mickey. "Then I'm coming in," Eddie said.

"With what?" Matty asked.

"My baseball bat." Matty unlocked the door.

"Eddie, stay in the car. Who's going to care for Ma if we're both dead?" Matty said.

The apartment number read 1E. Mickey pressed an ear against the freshly painted door.

"I treat you good. You're not sick, so why you stealing?" Mickey heard Tito say. The redhead conjured up some lame excuse.

"Cut this package up. Don't be tapping the shit." Tito opened the door. "I'll see you later."

When Tito turned, his long nose touched the long nose of Mickey's .32 revolver.

"You scream and you're dead." Mickey pushed Tito back inside the apartment.

"White boy, what's wrong, baby? We friends," Tito stuttered, getting pinned to a wall. Matty went to sweep the house, holding the .45 caliber as he went. In a nearby room, Tito's girlfriend weighed cocaine on a scale. She saw

Matty and instinctively began firing a .22 caliber pistol as Matty came through the door.

"Shoot him, baby!" Tito yelled, but she was so nervous; she emptied a six-round magazine into the wall instead of Matty. A hard slap knocked her across the room, the wig flew off, and the pistol fell.

"Stupid bitch!" Matty screamed. A brown stocking cap covered her natural black hair. She was in her early twenties and clearly strung out on heroin.

"Stay down!" shouted Matty as he waved the .45 caliber. Mickey threw a bleeding Tito into the room, cheerleading won Tito a gun slap. On Tito's dresser was a half-pound of cocaine, a triple beam scale, and measuring spoons. Matty bagged it all in a black garbage bag along with the .22 caliber pistol.

"Where's the rest?" Mickey asked.

"That's everything," Tito cried. Mickey clocked the gold watch. Matty pulled the gold watch off Tito's wrist and snatched the chains off Tito's neck.

"Why you doing this, white boy?"

Mickey looked around the plush apartment. A color T.V., a glass bar, fluffy white carpet. The skinny Puerto Rican lived like Julius Caesar. Mickey wasn't satisfied.

"Where's the money?" He asked, kicking Tito's girlfriend in the stomach. He put the revolver's barrel to her temple and spoke directly to Tito.

"If you don't give me everything, I 'ma put every bullet in this gun in her fucking head." Mickey warned. "Alright, in the living room!!!" Tito screamed.

Tito led Mickey to a hidden compartment in the wall unit, jackpot! A baseball size chunk of china white heroin, $24,500 cash in twenty-dollar bills and a .38 special pistol.

"That's it. I'm wiped out," Tito said. "You're in over your head white boy, my boss Fast Ricky is going to hunt you down and kill you."

Mickey slapped Tito again with the chrome handgun. "Now, he's got even more reason to come looking."

CHAPTER 4

Hell's Kitchen, NYC "1975"

The 458s sliced up the loot three ways, pitching 200 hundred dollars apiece to Uncle Tom. They hid the guns behind the boiler inside the building's basement on 36th Street. After they consumed every white crystal of the half a pound of cocaine. Tom unloaded the china white on a few war buddies; minus the bundles he slammed himself. The dope brought them another twenty thousand dollars. Mickey tricked on a color television, polyester suits and a dozen pairs of snakeskin shoes like Tito suggested. Matty traded in the Bonneville for a black '74 Oldsmobile 98. They paraded around the Westside in the new Oldsmobile dealing out the robbery money faster than they stole it. The old-timers began paying the young thugs close attention. When the robbery loot vanished, they robbed again and again. They robbed so many drug dealers uptown that Matty's black Oldsmobile became a symbol of terror. Whenever dealers spotted it, they took off running. The "White Boys," the name the uptown wire christened the 458s, pistol-whipped their victims in broad daylight, not wearing masks, not caring if they got caught. The notoriety uptown forced them to hunt drug dealers in Brooklyn and Queens. When that well ran dry, they prowled on grocery stores and discotheques in Greenwich Village. On major scores, Uncle Tom filled in as the driver and Eddie became the third gunman. Jackie made too much money to be stealing but he helped them blow the cash at expensive boutiques on Fifth Avenue and inside the hippest nightspots. As winter approached, the 458 wrecking crew had no idea 1976 would be their biggest year and Jackie would orchestrate their biggest heist.

It all started when Jackie Sr. introduced Jackie to a Jewish girl at a regional butcher's convention. The Jewish girl's family distributed meat products to small butcher shops and major supermarket chains across the tri state. Jackie Sr. and the Jews did business together, and Jackie thought hooking Jackie Jr. up with the daughter of New York's top meat distributor would merge the two families and secure Jackie's foothold on the business. Jackie resented the plum, Jewish girl but Jackie Sr. rallied for their union. In a desperate attempt to win affection, Jackie's plum lover spilled the beans on a family secret. The Jews stored away the freshest meat products for the Jewish butchers and sold meat spoiled or near expiration to the other customers, Jackie Sr. included. The revelation enraged Jackie. Hard work was being counterbalanced by a biased distributor. Jackie Sr. chalked it up as the price of doing business. The younger Jackie wasn't fond of rowing water under the bridge. He schemed on an act of retaliation and employed the services of the 458s.

Williamsburg, Brooklyn. February 1976

On the last Thursday of every month, the Jewish meat distributors delivered the bulk of its monthly inventory in 18-wheel trailer trucks. The diesel engines revved up, waiting for the warehouse security to clear them out the barbed wire security gate. In this section of Williamsburg, Brooklyn, factories and warehouses dominated the landscape. At 6:30 in the morning, the streets were empty except for the grumpy factory workers at the food cart, craving a wakeup shot of coffee. The security gates opened, four 18-wheel trucks filed out the warehouse. The first two in route to the Brooklyn Bridge, crossing over to Lower Manhattan. The other two 18-wheelers verged on the Brooklyn back blocks ready to deliver the borough's meat. The lead truck driver tapped on the brakes, a black four-door sedan clogged the intersection. The truck driver decreased speed, suspecting the car had broken down or run out of gas. It happened often on the road, young kids these days thought cars operated on solar energy instead of gasoline. The truck came to a complete stop and the two front doors opened on the stranded automobile. Two men wearing women's pantyhose over their faces, brandished guns, and descended on the truck's cab.

"Out! Get out! The fucking truck!" The driver checked the side- mirror, hoping to flee in reverse, but the truck behind him was being hijacked too. The truck driver complied, exiting the cab. The hijackers hogtied him in duct tape and left him in the middle of the street, next to the other truck driver.

Manhattan, Upper East Side. Eighty Days Later

Mickey borrowed Matty's 98 for the sit-down. The windshield wipers couldn't push the rainfall off the windshield fast enough. Mickey squinted out the glass trying miserably not to strike down a pedestrian. Anybody roaming Manhattan's Upper East Side in this rainfall had to be down on their luck or wishing for a lawsuit, and Mickey was a prime candidate, driving without a license or permit. Mickey drove to Madison Ave; there he saw Snapp's Silver Mark IV Lincoln Continental parked outside the Mayflower restaurant. The "new" Lincoln Continental, every year Snapps upgraded to the latest model. Last year's Continental was burgundy, the year before that it was black. Snapps Mitchell's reputation had risen to the clouds on the Westside. The Irish gangster's criminal endeavors earned him a bunch of money and younger brother Sam turning FBI strengthened his allure. A quarrel with Snapps Mitchell guaranteed the wrath of the Lucky Charm Crew and the FBI. No criminal could withstand those repercussions. The Volpe brothers depended on Snapps to keep order in Hell's Kitchen. He was Matches' main lieutenant in third in line to the Westside throne. Mickey parked between Snapps' Lincoln and a Cadillac Seville. He did a line of coke off the dashboard and read Tito's gold watch. Five minutes early, he treated himself to more cocaine, and skimmed through a billfold full of twenties and fifty dollar bills. Mickey developed a habit of carrying thousands in cash on his person. The Brooklyn hijacking netted them $120,000. Mickey, Tom, Eddie, and Matty split it four ways. Jackie didn't want a dime, vengeance paid him in full. Mickey stuffed the cash inside his pocket and Tito's .38 special in the small of his back. He grabbed an umbrella off the backseat and bypassed the expired parking meter.

Snapps ate a plate of spaghetti and veal at a roundtable in the non- smokers section of the 4-Star Italian restaurant. A white cloth napkin hung out the neck of his white open collar shirt. Snapps waved Mickey over, the gold ring on Snapps' pinky guarded a diamond the size of a mini ice cube. Mickey pulled a chair up to the baby-faced mobster.

"It's raining cats and dogs outside. I almost couldn't find this place.

Why couldn't we meet on the Westside?" Mickey asked.

"Expand your horizons, Mickey. New York is bigger than the Westside. This is a great restaurant owned by a good friend of mine, Vincent Salerno."

"An Italian?" "Yes," said Snapps.

"I got this nasty scar on my forehead from an Italian. I haven't liked any since."

"You don't have to like a person to make money with them" Snapps said.

"Does this joint sell burgers and fries?" Mickey whispered, unable to comprehend the lengthy menu.

"I already placed the order for you and a glass of coke." "You remembered."

"How many trips we took up to Yankee Stadium together. Now you're eighteen and I got to call the Pentagon to a get a hold of your ass." Snapps said.

"I tried returning your call sooner, but you know how Tom is." "How is Tom?" Snapps asked.

"High on heroin and war stories," Mickey said.

"Me, Tom, and your father were the Three Stooges of the Westside, Larry, Curly, and Moe. Then your old man went to prison, Tom went to war, and I stayed in Hell's Kitchen. The rest is history," Snapps continued down memory lane. "Your father got us out a lot of trouble. Tom's a tough bastard but compared to Big Mickey, he's a punk."

Mickey loved hearing stories about the old days.

"The war screwed Tom up, got him hooked on that junk, then that nigger girl."

"Gwendolyn," Mickey corrected Snapps.

"Yeah, Gwendolyn overdosed on horse and Tom never got it back on track. He blamed himself. Tom really loved that black girl."

I did too, Mickey thought.

"I've got to bring back Matty's car in an hour." The waiter put Mickey's food on the table.

"The wire says you rug rats capped a $200,000 caper pulling of some hijacking in Brooklyn."

"Who told you that?" Snapps laughed.

"When you're robbing drug dealers in alleyways, I turn a cheek. You start hijacking six figure loads; you're entering the major leagues, Mickey. It's a whole different ball game." Snapps coiled red wine in a wine glass. "Anything major in Hell's Kitchen has to have Matches' stamp on it." Mickey dunked a French fry in a mound of ketchup.

"Your source exaggerated. We scored $80,000 and if Matches wants a cut, I have no problem paying tribute." Snapps nodded in approval.

"That's good Mickey, shows respect. Matches doesn't want your money. He's swimming in money. He wants your robbing crew to come under the Lucky Charm crew. No more sticking up liquor stores. I got a list of banks in the Tristate area that are begging to be held up. Big risk, big money, are you in?"

"I'm offended you even had to ask," Mickey said.

"It's a slot open in the crew. Do a good job on these bank jobs and I'ma talk to Matches for you." Growing up, most kids wanted to be a New York Yankee or a Dallas Cowboy. Mickey wanted to be a Lucky Charmer.

Hell's Kitchen, NYC. "1976"

At ten in the morning, the Lucky Charm pub was free of its patrons. The bar stools were aligned upside down on the wooden countertop. A half dozen pyramids of shot glasses stood next to the antique cash register. Matches counted yesterday's handwritten receipts, signed the receipts and stuck them on an office ice pick. The light bulb hanging over the bar's counter shined dim, overpowered by the sunlight reflecting on the storefront glass, exposing the dust particles floating in the air. A white pit bull terrier decorated in brown spots curled up on a worn rug at Matches' feet. He won the dog at a poker game and named it Lucky. Then he won five grand fighting the dog against Snapps' pit-bull and changed Lucky's name to Hercules. Then Hercules killed five dogs in orderly fashion, but lost an eye in the last dog battle. In honor of their similarities, Matches renamed Hercules, "Matches" and treated the dog like a son. Matches jerked a wide head up at Matches. The only two eyeballs in the pub locked. Matches barked.

"Go get them," Matches barked back. The grand champion reached the pub's door in four strides, waiting on the trespasser. Matches continued barking. He knew the trespasser. If not, there would be no noise, just anticipation of chunks of flesh being torn off an erect doggy snack. It wasn't JB or Snapps. When they came around, Matches hid under the tables. He liked to let them get comfortable then charged at them full speed. The two ruined too many suits, fumbling whiskey in fear.

"Who the fuck is there? The bar doesn't open till noon."

"It's Vinnie." Matches opened the bolt lock and sent Matches to his bed, the rug.

"Come in buddy."

Vinnie came inside in a gray track suit and white Puma sneakers.

"I finished my morning jog in Central Park and said to myself, 'What the hell, Matches is right down the way.'" Vincent Salerno was a fast-rising Mafioso in the Traumanti crime family. The Traumanti Family was the Ivy League of organized crime compared to the other four Italian crime families in NYC. The family's boss and namesake, Tony Traumanti kept the organization's powerhouse in his hometown of Brooklyn. The East Harlem faction of the Traumanti family was based on Pleasant Avenue and were the moneymakers of the mob. At the young age of thirty-two, Vincent Salerno was the capo of the East Harlem crew. Vincent ran a huge numbers operation in Harlem and owned the Mayflower restaurant on Madison Avenue. Vincent's Harlem numbers racket earned the Traumanti family twenty million dollars annually. Vincent's second most lucrative racket was supplying heroin to black drug kingpins. Matches pulled two stools off the counter.

"I run four miles every morning, that's how I stay fit." Vincent's tall body and sloped shoulders eased on the stool. He looked around the pub.

"Buy a house, Matches. You could be living anywhere,"

"I don't want to live anywhere else. I got my bedroom in the back, my dog, and a fully stocked bar in my living room. You have to be a lunatic to not be jealous of me," Matches said.

Salerno laughed.

"What's your business on the Westside?" Matches asked. Vincent stared at the one-eyed Irishman contemplating whether to collaborate or manipulate.

"I want someone killed," Vincent said, moving a hand through thick, sweaty black hair. Salerno had olive skin and beady brown eyes.

"I buy slot machines and jukeboxes from you, Vinnie, and they're beautiful." Matches glanced at the slot machines by the unisex bathroom. "I also know your boss Mr. Traumanti has a stable of killers. Why come to the Westside for something your in-house shooters can handle?"

Vincent respected Matches' brain. He came to the right man. "Here's the whole scoop." Matches' grin said play at your own risk. "I got a rock in my shoe named Fast Ricky Williams, the biggest black heroin dealer on the East Coast. This nigger flies to Las Vegas every month to lose a quarter million dollars at the blackjack tables," Vincent said.

"Blacks are getting rich selling heroin to their own people, It's nothing new. You guys don't sell dope, what's the problem?"

Vincent frowned. "The commission rule is you deal, you die. Do you really think wise guys are going to let the spics and niggers take over a billion-dollar industry?"

"That's why you can't go to your own people to whack out the doper. Mr. Traumanti will suspect you're in the heroin business," Matches said. "Tony T is a hypocrite; all the bosses are hypocrites. They don't say shit as long as they get their cut. Then the shit hits the fan and everybody's surprised how they got the money to finance their new cigarette boat." Matches set up two shot glasses on the bar's counter.

"I know your circumstances. Why do you want to kill the dealer?" Matches asked.

"I supplied Ricky's crew, now he's making so much money, the punk cut me out of the picture."

"You lost a good customer, maybe you're taking it a bit too personal," Matches said.

"Ricky held a business convention in Atlanta, twenty of the biggest black dope dealers in the United States."

Matches poured two shots of bourbon; a black convention gave him dry throat.

"One of my spies at the meeting said the main topic was breaking the Italian mob's monopoly on the heroin trade. The black dealers are pooling their money together to purchase hundreds of kilos of pure heroin directly from the Corsicans. They'll control the entire market. We can't allow that."

"I'm going to help you but I want a piece of the heroin pie. This Fast Ricky business is our secret and the cornerstone to our new alliance." The boss of Hell's Kitchen and the capo of East Harlem shook on it.

Mickey blew out the candles on a cake dripping in vanilla icing and diced strawberries. "Happy Birthday, numb nuts," said Tom, grinning proudly in his house clothes, white Fruit of the Loom underwear. The Hart brothers and Jackie, offended by Tom's nakedness, endured it. The man wasn't putting on pants, they surrendered. Matty cut into the cake, everyone thought for Mickey's slice, until he bit down on the piece.

"What the fuck, Mickey's supposed to get the first slice," Eddie said. "Says who?" Matty asked, munching away.

"It's a ritual, this fat fuck just ruined the party." Tom limped away from the cake he spent the day baking, Eddie and Jackie behind him.

"It's a cake, Mickey can have the next slice." Matty carved out a new piece. "Look, Mickey's eating the cake. Come back he's eating the cake."

"Fuck off!" Tom yelled, barricading himself in the bedroom. "Mickey's not even mad and it's his birthday!" Matty screamed.

Eddie and Jackie ignored him. Julius Erving slammed dunked a red, white, and blue basketball on the color T.V.

"I didn't mean to ruin your birthday, Mick. I saw the cake and I wanted it," Matty said. No self-control, no excuses.

"I'm not mad, long as everybody eats. I don't care who eats first," Mickey said, licking frosting off a finger. Someone grunted in the living room, a Matty despiser.

"I'm out of smokes. Walk with me to the deli," Mickey said. Matty held open a beautiful powder blue coat that cost Mickey $200 at Leighton's. Mickey slipped on the jacket. "Butler duties, you must really be sorry," Mickey teased.

On the other side of the street was Snapps' silver Lincoln Continental.

"There's Snapps," Matty said, cuffing a carton of Marlboros. Snapps and JB argued on the sidewalk. When the argument ended, JB went inside the Lucky Charm, Snapps inside the Lincoln. "Hi Snapps!" Matty yelled.

"What you calling him for?" Mickey whispered. "Being nosy." "Mickey!!" Snapps screamed.

"See, Matty, I'm the one who has to talk to this old nut."

"Maybe he has another bank job. I'm leaving for Notre Dame. I could use the dough," Matty said, eyes scaling up the building to the third floor fire escape, Tom's menacing face was framed in the bedroom window.

"Tom's pissed off about that cake," he said. Mickey looked up.

"Yeah, don't go upstairs without me. Tom might shoot you." "If I stay here, he's liable to throw a sink down."

Tom mouthed a slew of obscenities at Matty.

"Least you can dodge a sink. You can't dodge a bullet, definitely not with Tom behind the trigger.

"I'll be right here. Hurry up," Matty said.

Snapps flipped down the sun visor and two C-notes fluttered out. He gathered the hundreds.

"Happy Birthday, Mickey."

"Thanks." Snapps unscrewed the cap on a gold flask and swigged. He offered Mickey some troubles.

"Any bank jobs come up?" Mickey sipped slowly.

"Next week, a little Federal Union bank upstate in Sullivan County.

Why? You broke already? I thought I told you to save your money."

"It's not me, Matty's going to college soon. He wants some extra cash." Mickey hissed from the liquor.

"What you and JB arguing over?"

"He's upset because Matches chose me over him," Snapps said. "Chose you for what?" Mickey had enough, he nearly threw the flask back at Snapps.

"We narrowed down the candidates for the open spot to you and JB's boy, Georgie. Matches has a special contract he wants handled. Whoever does it gets made a Lucky Charmer."

Snapps waited.

"Matches gave us the contract." Mickey grinned. Like him, Georgie was a young Irish thug raised on the Westside and destined to be a leader of the new school.

"Smile, but it isn't official until you fulfill the contract. This is murder, Mickey. One mistake and its Attica until the sun burns out."

"I'm ready, Snapps. I waited my whole life for this."

"Here's your chance. The mark is a black dealer goes by the name of Fast Ricky," Snapps said.

"You're in over your head, white boy, My boss Fast Ricky is going to hunt you down and kill you." Tito's words echoed in Mickeys' memory.

"I heard of this guy. He's pushing dope in Harlem., Mickey said.

"Fast Ricky is pushing dope in twenty-two states, no small fry. That's why the hit has to be done right. I went to Matches and vouched for you. My reputation is on the line. I want this smack dealer dead, yesterday."

Harlem, NY. June 1976

The black Oldsmobile drove slowly up to 155th street. A black Thunderbird with a white top sat in a reserved parking spot outside an overcrowded playground.

"What's this a cookout?" Tom asked watching kids hold their balance atop the park's gate to get a glimpse at the activities going on inside.

"It's a basketball game," Matty said from the back. "It's at least a thousand people in that playground"

"It's the championship game for the Rucker Park basketball tournament. The black guy who led the Nets to the World Championship the other night plays up here."

"The Doctor?" Tom asked, amazed. "Yeah, the Doctor" said Matty.

"Why didn't you say so?" The doctor cured everything for Tom. "Whoever the Doctor's playing against, good luck."

"He's playing against Fast Ricky," Mickey said, swinging into a broken U-turn for an empty parking space.

"The guy we came to kill?"

"Snapps says Ricky's some playground basketball legend. Says he turned down a big contract to play professional ball." Matty loaded bullets into the magazine of the army-issued .45 caliber.

"It doesn't matter why he's mark for death, let's just make him dead," Matty said.

"You're both babies when it comes to this. I've got more killings under my belt than both of you have years on this earth. The name of this game is patience. We'll wait until the game's over and follow Ricky," Tom said. "Can I be the trigger man?" Matty asked, draped across the back of the front seat between Mickey and Tom.

"I'm the professional. Go to Notre Dame and play football, Matty. My nephew wants to be a half ass gangster, so I'm doing his dirty work." Tom's attention drifted to the playground. "Fucking Snapps gives an eighteen-year-old a murder contract. The boy's still a baby."

"I wanted this contract. Once I become a Lucky Charmer, I'm untouchable," Mickey said.

Tom spun the loaded cylinder to a .357 Magnum, then closed it with a quick jerk of the wrist.

"Stupid prick. Long as I'm alive, you're untouchable," he said.

Fast Ricky's Thunderbird sped down Harlem's Eighth Avenue, bodyguards chased the boss man in a gray Cadillac Seville. Ricky was used to being followed by undercover cops, he chopped up the city's traffic laws, knowing only the police would follow him and reveal themselves. Ricky ran four red lights, dashed the wrong way up a one-way street and threw in illegal U-turns. He shook them all off him including the carload of protection. Mickey drove around Harlem looking for Ricky. He finally found Ricky outside a record shop on St. Nicholas Avenue.

"The bodyguards found Ricky before we did. I'ma find another parking spot and we'll wait it out," Mickey said.

"What if he gets in that damn T-Bird and plays speed racer again." Tom counted three bodyguards.

"You said the name of the game is patience, Tom."

Mickey was coasting towards the stoplight when Tom yelled, "Fuck this!" and jumped out the moving car. The four-man entourage on the corner froze up, thinking the short white man hopping out on them was police. Tom raised the .357 Magnum and sent a slug travelling 800 mph through Ricky's cheekbone. Fast Ricky went limp in the arms of one of his bodyguards. The right side of Ricky's face chopped off like the top of a coconut. Tom ran to the still-rolling Oldsmobile, the brake lights flashed. Tom limped the last few feet, ignorant of the armed bodyguard chasing him.

Matty's gun hand appeared out the back window; four bullets pushed the pursuing bodyguard between two parked cars.

"Drive!" Tom screamed finally in the passenger seat.

The third bodyguard ran to the yellow divider in the middle of the street, .38 caliber slugs shattered the fleeing car's back window.

6 Hours Later

"Matches is ecstatic. The blacks don't know where the hit came from; they think the NYPD set Ricky up. You really did good Mickey," Snapps said. "So why do I feel like any second the police are going to pull this Lincoln over and haul my ass to jail."

"The first one is always the hardest. Mickey, you might see Ricky in some nightmares but as time passes, he'll go away." Snapps hooked a left on 52nd Street; water from the hydrant splashed the side of the Mark IV.

'It's a beautiful night." Snapps inhaled deeply. "Relax, Mickey. The hit went perfect. Bask in your moment. It's official, you're a Lucky Charmer."

Mickey wiped away beads of sweat.

"I remember when I joined the crew in '64, I spent two weeks in a whorehouse." Snapps laughed. "Go get laid, Mickey. You'll feel brand new."

"Matty, set up a double date for us tonight. Some chicks off Eighth Avenue," Mickey said.

"Good, go on the date. Here." Five crisp hundred dollar bills. "Buy the broads something nice on me," Snapps said.

"Don't spoil me, old man."

"This is the tip of the iceberg. You inherited Richie's share of Matches' bookmarking operation. That's an extra two grand every week for your pockets," Snapps said. The money lightened Mickey's mood.

"Take the Lincoln. You roll up in the Mark IV. Sends the right impression," Snapps said.

"You don't let nobody drive your car, you sure?" Mickey asked. "It's not my car anymore, Mickey. It's yours."

"I can't believe Snapps gave you this car," Matty said, caressing the burgundy leather.

"Matches gave me a piece of the book too. Soon I'll be flooded in cash." Mickey's hands caressed the wide steering wheel.

"A piece of Matches' book, too?" Matty asked.

"Yeah, it's too bad you're going to Notre Dame." Matty estimated the pussy he'd miss out on in the new Mark IV.

"Pretty soon I'll have my own section of the Westside. That's even more cash and my partner won't be around."

"Yes, I will. I can come back every semester. Then it's Spring Break, Christmas vacation," Matty said.

"Right, Matty, I'll have so much cash, I'll fly you to the city every weekend. You can stay at the apartment I'm going to buy on West End, great views of the Hudson River."

They waited on their dates outside a tenement building on Eighth Avenue. "Fly me in every weekend, apartment on the West End," Matty said.

"It'll be the least I can do, for the man who helped me get to where I'm at. It's a shame half of this is supposed to be yours." The allure of the fast life pulled Matty in.

"But you rather be in cleats and shoulder pads. While I'll be in diamonds and Lincolns," Mickey said.

"I can't believe Snapps gave you this car." Matty repeated. "Where's these broads?"

"They're worth the wait; two sisters. A slim brunette and a redhead heavy in the right places. The red heads yours because I met the sister first," Matty said.

"I pray they don't look like those two Amazons you snuck out the Staten Island Zoo," Mickey said.

"Stop holding that against me." "I'll stop when…"

The redhead walking out the tenement building squandered Mickey's thoughts. "Any complaints?" Matty asked.

"What's her name?" She had on a navy blue skirt that came to life at every switch of her hips. A white short-sleeved blouse that tried its best to contain two bursting breasts.

"Pamela," Matty said as they exited the Lincoln. Pamela's red hair fell down to her lower back, tiny diamonds pinned to her ears, maroon on her lips. She was something to see and Mickey wasn't the only man in the city with eyes for the job. Matty made the formal introductions. Mary snugged under him.

"Isn't he so cute?" Mary asked Pamela, proud of her catch.

"Where are you taking us?" Pamela asked, with a slight trace of an attitude, striding in blue spiked heels.

"To the Copa," Mickey said.

"Is that your father's car?" Mickey helped Pamela off the sidewalk. "My father's been in prison for the last seventeen years. It's my car, I got it today."

"What's a young guy like you doing driving a Lincoln?" Pamela asked.

"What's a beautiful girl like you doing not riding in a Lincoln?" Pamela stammered.

"Don't worry, I'll correct it," Mickey said.

Federal Union Bank, Sullivan County, One Week Later

"Everybody on the floor! You move, I shoot. Do we understand?!" Mickey foot printed deposit slips on the bank's counter. A sawed-off double barrel shotgun calmly watched over the bank's customers and tellers ducking down. Mickey adjusted his ski mask.

"No surprises!" Eddie yelled, guarding the bank's entrance disguised in a blue ski mask, himself holding an M14 rifle with a pistol grip. Matty swept the cash bundles off the bank teller's registers into a black garbage bag and hurried to the next cubicle.

"You're doing great people. A couple more seconds and we'll forever be out of your lives. No heroes, no casualties." The bank's security guard buried his face into the blue carpet.

"Twenty-five seconds!" Matty hustled harder, the garbage bag wasn't heavy enough.

"How am I looking in the parking lot!" Eddie looked at Tom in the stolen Impala, no cops in sight.

"All's well," Eddie screamed. Mickey counted down from ten and ran out the bank, swinging the shotgun, clearing Matty's path. Eddie issued a few more threats at the petrified bank customers and ran for the Impala. The Impala tires screeched the parking lot and onto a nearby freeway, easy money.

Tom wrapped a blue rubber band around a wad of bills and jotted a figure down on a yellow writing pad. The Federal Union's money was spread eagle on the motel's bed. Eddie shuffled through a stack of bills calling out the amount, Tom wrote down another figure. On the other bed, Matty coached Reggie Jackson through a 3-2 count; bases loaded, ninth inning, Baltimore Orioles, American League east supremacy on the line.

Mickey watched the game half interested, wanting to make up an excuse to get to the payphone and call Pamela. They went on two more dates and caught a karate flick on Times Square. The night before, they were together at Tom's apartment. Their steamy sexcapades projected in Mickey's mind.

"What's the take?" Mickey asked.

"I'm not a machine. It's a bunch of fives, tens, and twenties. Fat boy over there is allergic to fifties and hundreds," Tom said talking about Matty.

"I 'ma call Snapps and give him an estimate on the loot. I need a quarter for the phone."

"It's a phone over there. Charge it to the room," said Tom.

"You crazy? Not on the motel's line. It'll leave a trail," Mickey said. "We're four towns away." Tom said.

"It doesn't matter. You're counting thousands, crying over quarters." Tom gave up the change.

"I'm not paying the toll back to the city," he said. Mickey took the change and Tom's .38 special.

"Tell Pam I said 'Hi.'" Matty smirked.

"Fuck you." Mickey walked from the adjourned motel suites down to the front desk. There, he bought two packs of smokes out the cigarette vending machine and dialed Pamela's number on the payphone.

"Hello." It wasn't Pamela.

"Hi, Mary. Where's your sister?" he asked. The question went over her head.

"Where's Matty? He hasn't called in two days. Who the hell does he think he is?"

Mickey switched the receiver to the other ear. "Matty told me to tell you he'll 'see you later.'"

"Matty's there? Put him on the phone."

Mickey unwrapped the wrapping off a pack of Marlboros. "Actually he's not exactly here?" he said.

"Don't lie for him," Mickey puffed on the cigarette he just lit up. "I'm not, I'll bring him by later, I promise."

"Ok, I'll get Pamela," said a content Mary.

"Hello, Pamela, your sister's a piece of work," Mickey said.

"She's been to 36th Street twice already looking for Matty's car," Pamela laughed. "Where are you?"

A black pickup truck parked in a vacant spot outside a suite. "I'm upstate."

"Will you be back in time for the show, George Benson is performing at the Copacabana. You paid all that money for the tickets." She worried more about Mickey's money than he did. The driver stayed in the pickup, Mickey shivered.

"I'll be back in time, but I can't talk for long."

"Ok. I'll see you later, I love you." The second time she said it. The first time Mickey said it back.

"Love you too." He hung up quick. Mickey held the .38 in his jacket pocket. In these hick towns, the police were hard to detect. As he began the walk back to the suite, the door to the pickup truck opened. A short stubby white man cocked a shotgun.

"You measly fucking home wrecker," he drawled out. "What?" Mickey asked, moving backwards.

"You're fucking my wife, you young punk." Mickey raised the hand that wasn't on the pistol.

"You're making a mistake. I don't know your wife. I'm from the city," he said.

"You city boys coming up here stealing away our women." The deranged husband's face looked a pinkish red, cheeks fat from a lump of tobacco chew.

"I swear, it's not me. Think before you do something stupid." The motel suite opened between them.

"John, what are you doing?" the wife asked, wearing a white terry cloth towel.

The husband turned back to Mickey with the devil in his eyes. Mickey already freed the .38, he bust off three rounds. The husband slid down the black pickup truck.

"Freeze, sheriff 's department!" screamed the wife's lover, aiming a police revolver, half-dressed in a sheriff 's uniform.

"Drop your weapon!"

Behind the sheriff in the doorway of their motel suite, Tom held the M14 rifle. Mickey shook out a "no" and dropped the discharged .38 revolver on the asphalt.

CHAPTER 5

Sullivan County Jail "1976"

Mickey Tansy Jr!" screamed a lawyer at weary detainees locked in a bullpen. Mickey slept uncomfortably on a steel bench in the rear of the holding cell. A suit jacket wrapped around him, a pair of shoes his pillow.

"Mickey Tansy" the lawyer shouted, aggravation setting in.

"Over here," Mickey answered in a groggy voice, using a thumb to slide the shoes on his feet. The lawyer went to the small steel conference area on the right of the pen, designated for attorney clients' privileges. Mickey stepped around a junkie clinging to the concrete floor, fighting the early stages of withdrawal. The toilet inside the cell didn't flush and had more urine around it than in it. A family of shit flies hovered over a foot- long log of feces in the bowl. Mickey pinched his nostrils together and relieved himself in the toilet, no sense washing his hands. The sink was stopped up with tissue somebody used to wipe their ass with. In the closet sized conference area, awaited a short balding man in a blue rumpled suit and gold wire-rimmed glasses.

"Mickey Tansy, I'm Patrick Hinton, your attorney. Snapps Mitchell hired me to represent you."

A metal wired gate separated them.

"Where's Snapps, Is he in the courtroom?" Mickey asked, sitting down.

"Snapps is in Manhattan. He called me when he heard the news." Hinton dabbed a fingertip in saliva and rummaged a folder labeled "Mr. Tansy."

"The prosecutor's charging you with murder in the second degree." "He's dead?!" Mickey screamed.

"Unfortunately, the victim succumbed to gunshot wounds in the county hospital." The sincerity in Hinton's words didn't match his emotionless expression.

"You have a lengthy arrest sheet dating back to juvenile, including a felony arrest for a midtown burglary. The prosecutor is going to ask for a mandatory twenty-to-life sentence." Mickey looked at Hinton like he had seven heads.

"Twenty to what? You lose your fucking mind? This whole case is a big misunderstanding."

Hinton's arrogance cut into Mickey's rant.

"I heard the story, Mr. Tansy. The sheriff 's screwing the victim's wife. The victim thought you were the wife's lover, came to the motel, touting a shotgun. An awful case of mistaken identity, that doesn't change the fact that there's a stolen handgun with your fingerprints that killed Mr. John Blackman in a police evidence box."

Mickey put two palms to a mind grain.

"It's not the end of the world, Mr. Tansy. There may be a loophole for you to squeeze out," Hinton said.

"What's that counselor?" Hinton held out a carnelian and white Cornell University bumper sticker.

"That's my loophole?" Mickey asked, questioning Hinton's sanity.

"Me and the prosecutor went to Cornell. We received our law degrees together. This isn't the first time the sheriff 's been caught red-handed committing adultery. The D.A. is willing to offer you a good deal. Plead guilty to manslaughter and cop to a five- to fifteen-year prison sentence."

"Where the fuck did Snapps find you, the circus! How is five to fifteen years a good deal?"

"This is the time to put your thinking cap on. We go to trial, we'll lose and your life belongs to the state forever. We wait, the D.A. snatches the deal back and ups the ante." Hinton spread out the pages to Mickey's rap sheet.

"This is a good deal for murder, Mr. Tansy. You're young. Do your time, stay out of trouble, you'll be home in five years."

"You want me to plead guilty at arraignment?"

"The first offer is sometimes your best offer," Hinton said.

Five-to-fifteen or twenty-to-life, Mickey weighed the options on his mental scale.

"I'll plead guilty to manslaughter."

Hinton packed Mickey's file in a brown briefcase and rushed to the judge's chambers.

Washington, D.C. "1980" 4 Years Later

The couple exchanged "I do's" in a crowded courtroom at City Hall. An old priest wearing a Georgetown Hoyas sweatshirt instructed Chuckie to kiss the bride and pronounced them man and wife. Chuckie met the chocolate city beauty on campus in his sophomore year.

Claire Robinson, at the time also a sophomore attending Howard University, came from a highly respected African-American family. Her mother taught a business course at Georgetown University. Claire's father was a Surgeon at George Washington University Hospital. Claire aspired to join her father in the medical field. Chuckie and Claire first crossed paths at a sorority party, butterflies fluttered in Chuckie's belly every time and any place they encountered each other after. Claire wasn't a shapely woman. Slim and petite, hundreds of females at Howard University had her beat in the looks department. Claire's plainness suited her tailor-made personality. She didn't wear makeup on her dark skin. Her black hair was always pulled back into a loose ponytail, baggy university t-shirts, and windbreakers, her daily attire. Claire's smile highlighted her facial features. Her smile was inviting. Inviting whomever in her presence to share in her happiness. Chuckie wanted her happiness and she shared his butterflies. They fell hard, so hard Chuckie asked Claire to marry him after six weeks of dating. She accepted but wanted to postpone the wedding at least until they received their degrees. In two weeks, they were graduating. Claire and Chuckie, true to their promise, tied the knot in a quiet ceremony at City Hall.

Hell's Kitchen, 3 Weeks Later

After graduation, Chuckie dragged Claire up to Hell's Kitchen to meet the Freemans. When he introduced her as his wife, you could hear a pin drop in the apartment.

"That's wonderful! I can't wait to introduce my new daughter-in-law at tonight's Bingo game," Momma said, breaking the silence. They ate a feast Momma cooked. Chuckie's sisters pranced on Claire during the dinner, fearless cats, jealous of the girl who stole their brother's heart. Claire had a protector in Momma Freeman, who battled the cats away. After dinner, Claire and Momma went to the church to play Bingo. Joyce, Tracey, and Belinda did the cleaning.

"Who has a wedding and doesn't invite their sisters?" Tracy asked.

"That's what I'm saying," Belinda said.

"We wanted a small ceremony, nothing big. We're trying to save up for our own apartment," Chuckie said.

"I bet you she made you cut your afro," Joyce said, sweeping the floor. "I cut my afro because the low-cut is the new style. Claire's a great person. How can you hate somebody you don't even know?"

Pop Freeman came to the kitchen to refill an ice jug with faucet water. "Chuckie, I want to talk to you in my room." Pops filled the jug and left without another word.

"That's what you get for getting married and not telling nobody," Tracey mumbled as Chuckie trailed Pops to the bedroom.

"Chuckie, what's wrong?" Pops asked, reclining on the loveseat, putting the jug up to gray whiskers.

"Nothing's wrong. I'm doing what men do, get married, start a family," Chuckie said.

"We were in Washington D.C. last weekend for your graduation and you didn't mention nothing about marriage, son."

"Pops, I'm married, don't matter if I told you today or a week ago." "You're too young to be getting married. You don't have a job, school's over. Where are you going to stay?" Pops asked. "I was thinking of staying here." "Exactly," Pops grunted.

"If we're not welcome…"

Pops sat up. "Of course you're welcome here. I have nothing against Claire. She's smart, beautiful, but marriage is serious."

"Claire's the one, Pops. Trust me the way I trust you." Chuckie said.

Harlem, N.Y. "1980"

"246" called the white women behind the fiberglass on the office intercom. Chuckie's number read 276, thirty hopefuls ahead of him at the unemployment office. At the rate the woman called numbers, he'd get interviewed at midnight. He was becoming a firm believer of the saying, "It's not what you know but who you know." Claire's father helped her get a residency at St. Luke's Hospital. Chuckie's bachelor's degree overqualified him for minimal jobs and under qualified him for jobs he was certain he qualified for. To be precise, Chuckie's business degree didn't under qualify him, his race did. This was Chuckie's third time at the unemployment office. It didn't differ from the first visit, a wasted afternoon. He decided to skip the train ride home, the sunny day gave him an excuse to stroll and save a token. On 142nd Street and Broadway he saw a "Now Hiring" sign painted on a furniture department store. "Watt's Furniture, affordable for all, layaway available," read an orange neon sign on the two-story brick building. The store's stock workers lifted furniture samples off the sidewalk. Chuckie followed the stock boys carrying a cabinet into the store. A black man, average height with black pork chop sideburns punched buttons on the cash register. Chuckie bent down to place his suitcase between his leather shoes.

"This sign says you're looking for a new manager. I'd like to interview for the job."

Mr. Watts' sign mentioned nothing about a manager, but he closed the register and invited the ambitious youngster to the back office. The job interview ended up a detailed recantation of Mr. Well's troubled biography.

Chuckie smiled and occasionally added a "get out of here." That's all the fuel Mr. Watts' motor mouth ran on. He wanted to move to Florida and buy a few of those new condominiums people his age gossiped about. Mrs. Wells wanted him to get rid of the furniture store altogether, but Mr. Wells wasn't ready to relinquish a business he devoted a lifetime building.

"If only I can find a smart, trustworthy person to run the business," Mr. Wells confided in Mrs. Wells. On that sunny afternoon, Mr. Wells was certain that he hired that smart, trustworthy person.

On Chuckie's first day as manager of Well's Furniture, he fired an incompetent employee. The firing set an example for all employees. Watt's Furniture department store had a new sheriff in town. Teflin, Chuckie's childhood friend, filled the vacancy on the employee roster. The old friends reacquainted downtown on Columbus Circle, both on the hunt for employment. They made a pact, whoever landed a job first would put the other down on the gig. Chuckie hired Telfin as a salesman and Mr. and Mrs. Wells booked a flight to Florida. Two weeks later, Chuckie cashed a paycheck for $336.42, first month's rent and security deposit on the one-bedroom Claire circled in the *Amsterdam News*. The move to the apartment on Harlem's

Bradhurst Avenue brought Chuckie full circle back to his birthplace. It took two trips in Claire's Volkswagen Beetle to bring their belongings uptown. A fresh coat of wood polish glittered on the wooden floors. The walls were painted off-white, the windows faced Jackie Robinson Park. Chuckie popped the cork on a bottle of chardonnay in the apartment's only furnished room, the living area. The furniture was a wedding gift from Mr. and Mrs. Wells. The chardonnay bubbled in Claire's jelly jar glass.

"I can't believe this is our apartment, Charles. Our life is a blank canvas; we can paint any portrait we please." Claire cuddled against a shirtless Chuckie, wearing his flannel shirt, him, blue jeans and bare feet.

"The best portraits are the ones that aren't rushed. Patience paints the perfect portrait" Chuckie said.

Claire cupped his chin.

"I'm going to be the perfect wife," she gently kissed Chuckie's lips. A knock at the door parted them. Chuckie put on a white t-shirt that had seen better days, over a growing erection.

"This better be those sweepstakes people carrying a million-dollar check," he said.

"It's Tof," the guest answered without being asked. In Chuckie's absence from Harlem, Telfin shortened "Telfin" to "Tof."

"This is nice. Good paint job, shiny floors." Tof 's big bald head moved side to side, forearms pushing past the barrier Chuckie planted with the door. "You're drinking champagne, living the good life, huh." Tof picked up the chardonnay and drank out the bottle.

"Hi Claire," Tof said wiping his mouth with the back of his hand. "Hello, Tof. " Claire waved. Chuckie snatched back the bottle. "Who wants to drink this after your mouth been on it."

"Me," Tof said, reclaiming the chardonnay.

"What do you want, Tof? And how'd you get my address?"

"I stole it off Mr. Wells' desk. Be careful where you leave information," Tof warned.

"Yeah, be careful of people like you."

"You ready to go?" Tof asked in a brown suede bomber jacket. Chuckie stood dumbfounded.

"The party in the boogie down," Tof said. "What's the boogie down?" Claire asked.

"The Bronx. I told Chuckie about it last week. It's payday and my best friend is in Harlem. We gots to party!" Tof said.

"I'm helping Claire unpack. I can't party tonight."

"Yes, you can. Go enjoy yourself," Claire said, looking at the packed cardboard boxes. "I'll be alright."

Chuckie parked up Claire's Beetle on Prospect Avenue. Tof led him deep into a Bronx housing project. At the center of the projects, a speaker quaked giving birth to a bass driven beat. An extension cord ran out a first floor apartment window, juicing the party's sound system. A congregation of thrill-seeking youths seized control of the housing grounds. Tof pushed Chuckie to the nucleus of the commotion. Teenage boys danced on cardboard taped to the concrete. One dancer flipped around on his back and began spinning on the crown of his head, then he froze head on the cardboard feet in the sky. Everyone who witnessed the gravity-defying move went crazy.

"What is that called?" Chuckie asked. "Breakdancing," Tof said.

"The dancers are called break-dancers, break boys or B-boys for short."

Chuckie nodded to the loud music as Tof guided him through the crowds.

"The black cat manning the turntables. That's the D.J. The king of the scene, without him none of this is possible," Tof schooled. Everyone around them was having pure, unadulterated fun. "There's DJ's in every borough but my favorite is Flash the Grandmaster. See how Flash scratches and mixes the record? He's the first to do it, that's why we call Flash, the Grandmaster."

"Check out those girls."

"We call them B-Girls. Peep how they standing, arms folded over their breasts on a sideways lean. That's the B-

Boy stance, but girls can do it too." Tof slapped someone in the crowd a high five.

"Who's the guy surrounding Flash?" Chuckie asked.

"Those are the MCs or Master of Ceremonies. I call them ghetto poets, soon Flash will hand them the microphone and they'll rap over the breaks of the beat." Chuckie's diaphragm vibrated.

"Ain't nothing this hip in Washington D.C," he said.

"It's hip-hop Chuckie, birthed here in the South Bronx. It's our culture. It's how we express ourselves." Tof face tightened." Look at that chump with the dried up Jeri Curl. That's what you call a sucker MC. He banked me for one of my girls back in high school, but wasn't nothing to a true player," Tof said, ego still healing.

"What's your thing DJing, MCing?" Chuckie asked, shaking Tof out of a high school heartbreak. Tof 's face relaxed, it was shaved clean, hairless, except for two thick black eyebrows.

"I'm a graffiti artist. That's my tag spray-painted on the brick wall." Chuckie listened while the group of MCs rapped on Flash's break. The wordsmiths told vivid tales about fly girls, ghetto superiority and all despised the sucker MC.

Chuckie drove the Volkswagen back to Harlem solo, after the NYPD shut down the festivities. Tof went bombing, night raids graffiti artists did on subway tunnels to tag up on locked down trains. That night Chuckie couldn't sleep. He bounced around the new apartment trying to release the abundance of energy hip-hop surged in him. Hip-hop, a culture Chuckie related to with all his being. He was the seven-year-old in the Dessie Club, again. Chuckie needed someone to share it with, this epic moment. Claire fell asleep. Chuckie smiled to himself after deciding the perfect person to tell about his night. He rummaged the cardboard boxes for a pencil, writing pad, and wrote a letter.

Elmira Correctional Facility, Elmira, NY. 4 Days Later

Dear Mickey,

I tracked Tom down to get your new address. I know it took me a couple months to respond to your last letter. My life's hectic! I graduated from Howard University finally! I can't believe it, myself. Where did four years go so fast? My next line is going to set your mind ablaze. I'm married. Claire, the girl I've written to you constantly about is my new bride. I'm happy, Mickey. Claire's truly special. I can't wait for you to meet her. We leased an apartment in Harlem, on 150th Street and Bradhurst. It's small but perfect for the two of us. I'm the new manager at Wells' Furniture department store. It isn't the big-time corporate gig I expected, but it's a start. The neighborhood is not the same without you. Pops and Momma recently purchased a little house in Yonkers. They're leaving Hell's Kitchen once the summer's up. Matty's living on 8th

Avenue with that girl Mary. He quit school to help Mary out with the baby. Rumor has it Jackie is flat broke, Jackie Sr. went bankrupt, I'm not 100% sure. It can be just a rumor. Eddie's selling drugs on 36th Street, but I think he uses more than he sells. Mary's sister Pamela flew to the west coast, Hollywood, hot on becoming a movie star. There's this new culture swarming contagiously in the city called hip-hop. It's incredible Mickey, the music, dancing, graffiti, most of all, the attitude. It's unapologetic! Hip-hop is just a baby but it's going to grow and I'm going to grow with it. Remember we'd break night in my bedroom listening to The Four Tops, the Coasters and the Cadillac's on my record player. Music glued us together, closer than Siamese twins. I pray you stay out of trouble so you can make that first board. We need you home

Mickey!

Love always,

Your brother Chuckie.

Mickey folded the letter up after reading it out loud.

"That Chuckie is a very interesting character," said Rabbit, Mickey's cellmate. Rabbit had thirty years in the prison system and hadn't received a letter from the streets in a decade. He listened to Mickey's letters, eyes shut imagining the words crisp off the paper.

"Yeah, Chuckie's been that way since we were kids," Mickey said. Rabbit slapped a bookmark on Miyamoto Musashi's *The Book of Five Rings*. He shifted up on the cell's bottom bunk bed, two pale frail legs outlined in swollen blue veins down to the bunions, brushed the dusty floor. Rabbit scooted to the edge of the bed, bones poked out his skin, and skin dangled where bones didn't poke. At eighty-three years old, Rabbit was the oldest inmate in Elmira Correctional Facility.

"Where are you rushing off to?" he asked, blowing snot into a ball of tissue tougher than sandpaper.

"The yard to get stoned," Mickey said.

Rabbit, an avid reader, kept volumes of Ernest Hemingway and Niccolo Machiavelli. Rabbit's book collection claimed the most space in their cramped cell. The few bookless tiles on the floor were scratched from the friction of sharpened shanks. A cracked sink was on the left, crowned by a fluorescent light. Another small fort of books blocked the toilet bowl, where the floor sloped two inches. The double bunk cells were too puny for scuffles but cellmates still broke elbows on the solid walls trying to swing punches.

"You can't smoke this jail sentence away. It'll sneak up on you," Rabbit said.

"When it sneaks up, I'll up the dosage and put that mother fucker back down." Guys did time pumping iron, reading books; Mickey did his time chasing drugs in the yard. Mickey wrestled a white V-neck T-shirt on a chiseled upper body. A million sets on the pull-up bar filled out his physique. He'd grown a thick mustache in an attempt to look older and cut his blonde locks to a buzz cut. The new hairdo wasn't by choice. The prison's barber only had two hairstyles in his repertoire-buzz and bald.

"Want me to stop at the general library and pick you up some books?" Mickey asked, buttoning a green state shirt.

"It's enough in this sweatbox to keep me occupied," Rabbit said. The cell bars rolled open. Mickey walked a tight rope down the tier to the police bubble. On their tier there wasn't many minorities. In the free world, blacks and Hispanics were the minority, but in jail, everything flipped. The outnumbered white inmates were the minorities in the prison population. Racism flourished behind bars more than anywhere else.

The white inmates stayed amongst their own. The black and Hispanic prisoners did too. The unity within the race groups was a false front. The Italians hated the Irish, the Dominicans hated the Puerto Ricans, and the Cubans hated everybody. blacks out of Harlem didn't get along with blacks from Brooklyn, but if a race riot occurred, they'd bury their differences and unite. The multiple races sectioned off the prison yard by race. The blacks had the weight shack, the whites politicked on the bleachers, and the Hispanic inmates hung on the baseball field.

Mickey sat on the bleachers waiting for the lit marijuana joints to rotate, listening to the larger than life stories that prisoners told. There wasn't a con in Elmira who didn't drive a Lincoln, shop on Fifth Avenue, or sit front row at Muhammad Ali prizefights. A convict Mickey knew on the Westside to be a degenerate drunk who seldom had two brown pennies to rub together, changed altogether in Elmira, away from booze and bookies, bulky from tossing 125 lb. dumbbells. The con conned everyone into believing he owned the Westside. He'd beg Mickey not to expose him. On the streets or behind concrete walls, money governed all. The big money convicts were the connected Italians and bigtime drug dealers. Mickey, being a bank robber, swam at the bottom of the totem pole. What's a stick up kid without a gun? A jailhouse enforcer in an oversaturated market of toughs willing to cut, butt, slice, stab, bite and kill for cartons of smokes and sprinkles of dope. Mickey had blown the bank dough and Tom sold off the Mark IV the previous summer. Mickey hadn't heard from Snapps or the Lucky Charm crew since they fronted the bill for the lawyer. The money he'd stolen, the blood he spilled, forgotten. The Lucky Charm train steamed on without Mickey. JB's boy, Georgie, got Mickey's share of Matches' book. Mickey's loyalty to the Westside regime withered. He wanted a career on the streets where whether free or incarcerated, he'd be relevant.

The guards called an early go back, Mickey found a spot in line behind a short Hispanic man. He'd seen the Hispanic man and Rabbit chat it up on the rare occasions that Rabbit went out to the yard. Mickey never saw the Hispanic man speak to nobody else. He avoided the baseball field where the Latinos played softball. The short man walked the yard's perimeter trying to be invisible, in a world where everybody is being watched. Mickey admired him, least he had the nerve to cut the umbilical cord, which is what Mickey wanted to do with the Irish but tolerated the braggadocio lies for the free drugs. The chain gang loco motioned out the yard to the cellblocks.

An annoying drill bell sounded the new morning awaking prisoners out their dreams to a harsh reality. A pigeon soared the tier, landed on the rusted bars of Mickey's cell. Pigeons were the prison's pets; some jailbirds grew so accustomed to inmates, they ate out their palms. Mickey climbed off the top bunk, crumbled two slices of bread and scattered the crumbs on the tier floor. He wobbled to the cracked sink and flicked on the fluorescent light and felt the same wave of envy he did every weekday. Rabbit still in bed, turned over. As the oldest inmate, Rabbit didn't have to do shit. He was on the warden's special payroll. Rabbit got paid more state dollars for spiraling on a mattress than Mickey did sewing state clothes in the state shop. Mickey brushed his teeth, dressed in greens and went to work. The morning's dew condensed on the patch of green grass. A sea of prisoners silently walked to their daily duties. A quiet nod of understanding the stress of facing a brand-new day without freedom. They all understood the demons that kept you up late at night. The silence was necessary, a moment of silence for another deceased day. A few inmates refused to let prison break their spirit. They attacked every new day with so much optimism and excitement, you'd think they slept the night at the Sands

Casino. Lockjaw was of the free-spirited, he high stepped the walkway dishing out "Good mornings" and "Rise and shines." Lockjaw came to terms with his life sentence, the day a Rochester judge handed it to him.

"Mickey Mouse!" called the pencil slim double-murderer. "Lockjaw, how's it going?" Mickey said.

They tapped fists.

"Not good, daddy. I searched the seven seas for you in that yard last night. Then I saw you cooling on the benches and you know the rest. Them some mean looking white boys."

"You could've came over to talk, Lockie Bear." Mickey named him that after the pimp, Hoggey Bear, on the *Starsky and Hutch* sitcom, Lockjaw always wanted to be a pimp. He just wasn't any good at it.

"Naw, I thought it be best to wait for the morning. I need some fresh state pants for my visit."

Working in the state shop created a hustle for Mickey, stealing state clothes out the storage room and selling them to the jail's high rollers. The high rollers wouldn't be caught dead wearing the same state pants twice.

"I'll get them to you this afternoon," Mickey said. Lockjaw glazed a ten-spot on him.

"Starch'em good, Mickey Mouse. My bottom bitch is coming baby." Lockjaw high stepped on, irritating grumpy inmates with his pleasantries.

"We know who you are, amigo. It's time to charge you rent, consider it a contribution to the Cuban political fund." Felix laughed, his teeth a combination of yellow and mud brown. He pinched the tip of the blade in the man's fleshy cheek, a droplet of blood trickled down the man's chin.

"This isn't necessary. Why can't we talk like gentleman and come to an agreement?" Felix's Cuban partner cornered the little man off, breath spewing homemade prison wine.

"What's the big words for? You want to prove you're smarter than us?" Tito increased the pressure on the man's neck.

"I'ma stick my dick in you first, then my knife!" Tito's partner laughed while groping his crotch. The dryers in the laundry room hummed from loads spinning in the heaters.

"I'll give you what you want," said the little man. Mickey entered the laundry room holding Lockjaw's pants in a net bag.

"Pay us no mind, amigo," Felix said. Mickey saw the terrified look on Rabbit's friend.

"Get the fuck off him," Mickey said, tossing down the net bag. "Mind yours. This is Latino business."

Mickey pulled his shirt out his pants.

"We got a fucking superhero." Felix tossed the shank between his right and left hand.

"I 'ma curve you up and play pin the tail on the donkey." Felix's partner banged the little man's head on the cinderblock, knocking him cold out, then he weaved toward Mickey, fist high, chin low.

He's a boxer, Mickey thought. Cuba bred fighters. The Cuban's muscles flexed, showing off what free weights can do. Mickey threw to left jabs; the Cuban easily weaved them off and punched Mickey in the kidney. Mickey stumbled, the Cuban smirked, waving him back to the action.

"Knock this motherfucking Mick out!" Felix screamed. Mickey erased the pain and anger; the way Henry taught him.

"Fight brains, Mickey, not emotions."

The Cuban weaved up and under an imaginary rope. Mickey danced on the balls of his feet. When the Cuban came close, Mickey faked a right, and kicked the Cuban's shin. The boxer, surprised by the kick, dropped his guard for a second. Mickey's left fist lined the Cuban up for a crushing right hook. The Cubans' eyes fluttered, Mickey landed two more lefts, didn't matter, he didn't feel them. The Cuban went down and Felix charged. The shank's ass wrapped in medical tape, the blade sticking out under Felix's pinky. He swung, Mickey ducked catching Felix's wrist with the reflexes of a rattlesnake. Felix's five fingers sprung out, the blade fell right into Mickey's palm. Mickey stabbed Felix in the shoulder. The Cuban shook free and fled the laundry room like a refugee, hollering for the guards.

CHAPTER 6

Harlem, NYC. "1984" Four Years Later

Chuckie and Claire celebrated Thanksgiving at the Freeman's brick house in Yonkers. Tracey was pregnant, the turkey was cooked so the meat fell off the bone and the Detroit Lions defeated some team Chuckie couldn't remember. As Chuckie navigated Claire's Volkswagen back to Harlem, Kurtis Blows' "Christmas rapping" played in the cassette player. Chuckie bopped his head, while Claire slept, her head tilted on the headrest. On the drive back to the city Chuckie recognized the drastic change. A crime wave flooded NYC, crime statistics tripled in every category. There were more murders, robberies, burglaries, and assaults reported in the city's history. The NYPD commissioner had no explanation for the crime spree. A population of zombies ravished the city, their skin ashy white, teeth bright yellow. There'd been three burglaries in Chuckie's apartment building in a two-week span. The zombies attempted to loot Watt's Furniture department store, but Chuckie and some co-workers fought them off. At Claire's hospital, babies were being born malnourished, smaller than two palms placed together.

Chuckie pulled up the emergency brakes, after switching off the ignition. He held Claire close, walking down Bradhurst to their tenement building. A line of zombies scratched and fidgeted near an abandoned building.

"What are they waiting for?" Claire asked Chuckie.

"It ain't free lunch," he said. The zombies' glassy gazes fell on the couple. Chuckie and Claire sped the rest of the way.

"Why can't we do something? This is our community and it's burning to ruins," Claire asked, still a pampered suburban girl who thought she could save the world. She looked into the mirror above the dresser, unhooking the loops to her gold earrings. Chuckie surfed channels on the television, with the remote control.

"That's the mayor's problem, Claire. We should stay inside unless we absolutely have to go outside; and when we do go outside, go together." Chuckie laid on his belly over a pillow. Claire stroked her black hair with the thick teeth of a pink comb.

"That's so selfish, Charles. Those are our people not animals in the wild. At Howard, you used to talk about helping the community. Now you're only concerned with yourself," Claire said, tears gliding down her beautiful ebony face.

Four years of marriage prepared Chuckie for these situations. He learned through trial and error to handle Claire delicately.

"We'll go to City Hall and file a complaint or we can drive up to the Governor's mansion," Chuckie said to appease Claire. She wiped her tears on her sleeve.

"We can go on our day off this Thursday," she said cheerfully. "Thursday isn't good for me. I'm going to the Kurtis Blow concert at the Coliseum," Chuckie said, laughing as George Jefferson swaggered through the deluxe apartment in the sky.

"You and this stupid hop-hip…this is a real issue, bigger than a stupid Kurtis Blow concert," Claire said.

"Why you always putting down Kurtis Blow?" Chuckie asked. "Does he mean that much to you? I'm sorry, Charles." She laughed. "It's not funny, Claire. I love hip-hop. Yeah, hip-hop. Not hop-hip. You don't give it a chance."

"I think grown men spinning on their heads is immature."

"You want me to sit through them boring operas at Lincoln Center." "Opera has survived centuries. Hop-hip won't survive this decade." Chuckie blocked Claire out for the entertainment of *The Jefferson's*.

Claire stood between him and the television, hand on her hips. "Chill out, you killing my vibe," he said.

"You're an educated black man, and those are the words you chose to use to express yourself? 'Chill out,'" Claire mocked him.

Chuckie muttered to himself.

"You should hang out with my friends at the hospital," she said.

"I'm not chilling with those yellow backs at your job. For what? Get invited to their country clubs to play eighteen holes of golf and soon as we're gone, they're talking about us. I'm a black man born in the slums of New York City. A college degree isn't going to change that"

Claire pulled the pillow from under him and flung it out the room. "Why'd you do that?" he asked.

"Because that's where you're sleeping tonight, Mr. Yellow Back!"

Chuckie's wool pea coat was Velcro for the snowflakes falling over Broadway. It was six o'clock in the morning and he cursed himself jerking the keys to the furniture store in a frozen lock. The lock finally cracked, the gate lifted, and Chuckie's back ached from the night on the sofa. He stomped the snow off him onto a welcome mat, and hit the main light switch. The departments of the store lit up seconds apart. Chuckie hung the pea coat on the coatrack, headed to the bedroom department and dozed off on a king-size. At a quarter past eight, Chuckie's assistant manager Lala woke him up. Lala was a pretty Puerto Rican girl from the Soundview section of the Bronx.

"What time is it?" he asked.

"Too late for you to be sleeping on the merchandise and you left the gate up, you're lucky the zombies didn't steal the store."

"Where's Teflin? He's on the schedule for seven o'clock," Chuckie said. "No show, no call, he did the same thing yesterday," Lala said, smacking on a stick of chewing gum.

"When Tof gets in, send him straight to my office," Chuckie said.

"Honey, I'm home!" Tof shouted. Lala broke open a roll of nickels on the cashier drawer.

"Your days are numbered fat boy," Lala said. Tof danced up to the register.

"You miss me, baby?" he asked, playing in Lala's hair. "Hell no! Get off me." She slapped him hard on the chest. "I like my women feisty. I 'ma have to tie you up."

"You might need a loan to buy the rope because your ass is halfway out a job. I'm not a fortune teller, but I foresee your fat ass back on the unemployment line." Lala tilted her head back in laughter.

"No, you'll be seeing my fat ass in the newest Cadillac, while you beat your feet on the streets," Tof said.

"Take your butt to Chuckie's office."

"Don't be hostile, Lala. I'll beep the horn so you can glance at all the fly girls riding with me."

Lala smacked Tof again. This time on the back as he headed to Chuckie's office.

"Boss man, you wanted to see me." Tof entered the office without knocking, like he always did. Chuckie gestured to the empty seat by his desk.

"What time did I schedule you to be here this morning?" Chuckie asked. Tof plucked some lint off a colorful sweater and said.

"My fault Chuckie, but I came here to tell you something." Tof's attitude pissed Chuckie off.

"Bad enough the salesmen think I cut you the most slack. Then you show up to work late two days in a row without calling. What am I supposed to do?"

"You don't have to do anything because I quit," Tof said. "You quit? You can't quit!" Chuckie screamed.

"Sorry, Chuckie, but I'm going into business for myself."

"You're quitting to start Telfin Furniture Incorporated," Chuckie joked. "Nah, more like 117th Street Incorporated, you see this?" Tof went inside his pants pocket and came out holding three nuggets that looked like white aquarium stones. "What is that?" asked Chuckie.

"That's what got everybody on the street losing they mind. Niggas isn't washing they ass, the broad you always wanted to fuck growing up, she'll blow on your dick all night for one of these rocks." Tof put them on the desk. Chuckie picked up a nugget and examined it.

"This little rock got the zombie's ripping up Harlem?" Tof went in his other pants pocket for a fat knot of mix bills, then threw the money on the desk.

"This shit is called crack. In the streets of Harlem, crack is better than gold."

"Why call it crack?" Chuckie asked.

"It makes a crackling sound when the fiends smoke it in a pipe. Niggas don't pray to Jesus no more, Chuckie. They pray to crack," Tof said.

"You're quitting a steady-paying job to sell crack to you own people?" "Hell yeah! That's eight hundred cash on your desk. Made it in one hour selling crack. I'd have to bust my ass in this store for months to get that much cash, Chuckie. Fuck this furniture store, we'll be partners. In a year, we'll make millions selling crack."

"I'm not dealing this shit to my people, I get my money the honest way. I'm legit"

Tof cleared Chuckie's desk of the cash and merchandise.

"Alright bro, keep getting Mr. Watts' money. If you need me, I'll be on 117th Street where the Dessie Club used to be," Tof said, terminating his services to Watt's Furniture Department Store.

Elmira, NY. Elmira Correctional Facility

The Department of Corrections sentenced Mickey to two years in solitary confinement for stabbing Felix. The incident cost him a two-year hit at the parole board. Mickey's first week in "the hole" he slept up until every chow. A week later, he'd pace the dark gloomy cell, occasionally smashing a fist into the brick wall. A month in solitary confinement, Mickey was having lengthy conversations with a roach. He cried like a baby when he accidentally crushed the roach, rushing for the toilet. The hole's four walls stole many criminals' sanity. To some doctors, solitary confinement is the worst form of punishment you can inflict on a human. It's in a human's nature to interact and communicate. To strip a human of human contact is like clipping a bird's wings. In the hole, thoughts creep up from every angle. You'd picture your memories vividly. You'd remember the precise piece of clothing you wore on a day years ago. You'd smell the fragrance of an old lady friend lingering. If the memories weren't nice, they'll torture you night after night. A prisoner's worst enemy inside solitary confinement is fantasy, because fantasy is just a taxicab ride away from insanity. Mickey wanted to escape the pitfalls of solitary confinement so he focused on reality. He started doing sets of pushups before breakfast and shadowboxed after dinner. He read the books Rabbit sent with the guards. He read them mainly because there wasn't anything else to do. The days flew by when Mickey mastered this routine. Then the day came when a guard cracked the cell and said.

"Pack up Tansy. You're back on the mainline."

Thirty-six cartons of Marlboros were on the bed in Mickey's cell back in population. He didn't unpack, instead he began raking his brain for the culprit. Rabbit was the first axed off the list. Elmira's oldest inmate died while Mickey was in the hole. Mickey's paranoia conjured up a plot that the Cubans were rocking him to sleep for a revenge attack. That plot crumbled when Mickey received a kite from the leader of the Cubans stating that there would be no retaliation for the stabbing of a rat. That axed out the Cubans. Mickey found his benefactor in the general library.

"Did you get the cartons I sent you?" Mickey looked over the book he was trying to read. The short Hispanic man sat down at the round table. "You left the smokes!" Mickey said too loud for the librarian's liking. She put her index finger against her lips. They nodded in compliance. "I haven't opened a single carton. Not until I found out who they belonged to."

"They belong to you," the short man said, his skin bronze like the Aztecs', black hair, slicked back and a beak for a nose. Mickey wouldn't put him a day over thirty years old but those gray eyes seemed older. They'd seen more than his young body was willing to tell.

"Thanks for helping me in the laundry room, Mickey."
"How do you know my name?" Mickey asked.

"Rabbit and I were good friends. Rabbit spoke highly of you. Excuse my manners my name is Enrique Sanchez Vargas." He stuck a hand out for Mickey to shake.

"Nice to meet you, Enrique." Mickey shook his hand.

"I see Rabbit has rubbed off on you." Enrique touched the hard book cover to Marcus Aurelius' *Meditations*.

"I want to figure out how he found so much peace in words," Mickey said.

"The peace wasn't in the books, Mickey. It lived in Rabbit's heart. Do you have a lot more time to do?"

"I lost my board for the stabbing so the max I'll be here is fifteen years," Mickey said.

"I have eighteen more months owed to the State of New York," Enrique said.

"That's enough time for us to become friends." Mickey shrugged. "More than enough." Enrique smiled.

A field of stars sparkled in the pitch-black sky, the moon shined in its thinnest cut slice. Inmates packed the recreational prison yard for the softball game between the blacks and whites. The white ballplayers called themselves White Lightning, the blacks were the Negro Leagues. Mickey and Enrique stood a good distance from the ball game and its profanity. They were on the empty basketball courts between the free throw and three point line. Mickey chain-smoked Marlboros, looking up at the stars. Enrique wore a green skull cap and a green state coat. The odd couple of the jail, an Irish and Latino together wasn't usual in the yard. Mickey and Enrique continued to build their friendship. Mickey did the talking, blabbing on about the Westside, bank robberies and Uncle Tom's hairpin trigger. Enrique listened unable to catch Mickey in a lie. Enrique was impressed.

"You want to know why Felix and the boxer attacked me in the laundry room?" Enrique asked.

"I did two years in the hole for it" Mickey tossed a cigarette past the free-throw line and pulled out another.

"Felix found out who my relatives are in Mexico." Enrique waited for Mickey to put fire to cancer.

"My family is very important south of the border." Mickey blew out the match, flinging it by the old cigarette.

"Yeah, your people politicians or something?"

"No politicians. My father is Miquel Vargas, Co-founder of the Tijuana cartel," Enrique said.

"Cartel?"

"International drug traffickers" Mickey pulled off Enrique's skully hat. "You mean to tell me, for eighteen months, I'm playing bodyguard to the Prince of Mexico?" Mickey laughed and extended his hand with the hat high in the air. Enrique leaped twice to get the hat back on his head. "Don't play, Mickey. It's freezing." Enrique said through cluttering teeth, fitting the skully back on.

"I'm no prince, my father's old school. Family or not, you have to prove yourself,"

"That's what this prison term is, proving yourself?" Mickey asked. "I got arrested in the Bronx with a trunk full of cocaine. The drugs weren't mines, belong to my cousin." "You took the rap for him," Mickey said. "I did the time for her."

"A girl?" Mickey asked.

"You told me stories about your Uncle Tom's deeds in Vietnam. My cousin Isabella did that and more before her seventeenth birthday," Enrique said.

"A girl?" Mickey couldn't fathom the thought.

"My responsibilities in the cartel will increase now that I've proven myself. I can put you in a position of power."

"Put me in power," Mickey said.

"Have I ever lied to you? Maybe you want to continue pledging your loyalty to Matches. A leader who disowns his own people."

"I don't want nobody selling me wolf tickets if you can do what you say you can do, do it," Mickey said.

"You can't comprehend the things I can do"

Times Square, October "1985" Eleven Months Later

Mickey rode a Greyhound into Times Square's Port Authority, a free man for the first time in nine years. "The deuce." The new nickname for Forty- Second Street, underwent a complete makeover. The taxis were sleeker and the neon lights advertised 25-cent nude shows. A blue scaffold held up one side of the Port Authority building. Mickey stood digesting the city. He studied the modern day pimp in the fancy European cars.

Mickey felt like a newborn, helpless. One pimp sensed fresh bait on the line.

"You chasing the dragon or wanting something pretty to hump on?" the pimp asked.

"I'm fresh out the pen, man. And this town is moving too fucking fast," Mickey said, wearing the suit he got arrested in.

"You're fresh home. I remember when I first came home. How long did you do?"

"Nine years," Mickey said.

"I did seven, Welcome home. Where you headed?"
"48th street and Tenth Avenue," said Mickey.

"Get in the car, I'll give you a lift."

Mickey buzzed the intercom's buzzer.

"Who the fuck is ringing my bell!" Tom screamed.

"Your nephew." Mickey wanted to get in the building before someone recognized him in the outdated suit.

"Numb nuts! When did you get out?" Tom asked.

"Can we talk upstairs?" The door buzzed, Tom was on the third floor landing, him and his Fruit of the Loom underwear.

"Welcome home, Mickey." Tom bear hugged Mickey and carried him into the apartment.

Mickey rocked inside a rocking chair old enough to buy liquor. Tom flamed up two steaks. The apartment was exactly the same. It was easy to tell Tom hadn't had a successful year since 1976. Tom brought the steaks out on a dinner tray along with some Irish whiskey.

"Matty and that damn girl are pushing out babies twice a year. Eddie doesn't leave 36th Street, nobody's making any money." Tom held a fork and steak knife, chewing while talking.

"Matches is in the can for tax evasion. Snapps and JB still have a stronghold on the Westside, but these independent crack dealers are opening up on every corner." Tom was thirty pounds lighter, grayer, and still addicted to heroin.

"I watched a T.V. special in prison on the crack epidemic," Mickey said.

"The T.V. version is watered down. Crack washed the neighborhood down the drain. All the old-timers left for New Jersey or Long Island."

"Where's Chuckie?" Mickey asked.

"He's doing great. Last I saw, Chuckie had a pretty black girl, nice knockers on her. Luis retired from the bus depot, got him a house in Yonkers. All the smart ones are gone. I'm the idiot sticking around Hell's Kitchen."

"Jackie?" Mickey asked.

"Talk of the town, Jackie Sr. blew a fortune on some young arm candy. He's living in Boston too ashamed to show face. The banks have changed, Mickey. New technology, cameras, silent alarms, dye packets. It's harder to pull off a job." Mickey looked at the ancient apartment.

"I'm back Tom. Things are going to get better."

Hell's Kitchen Pier 84, 24 Hours Later

"Where is this guy, Mick?" Cold winds flew off the Hudson River, on a cold October day.

"He'll show." Mickey said, dressed for the weather.

"Can you call Pamela please, Mickey? She's bugging Mary to death." Drug abuse deteriorated Matty's athletic build, muscles turned to flab.

"Nine years I rotted in a cell. I'm home 24 hours, she can't live without me" Mickey wasn't thrilled to rekindle the flame. A white Rolls Royce entered the pier's parking lot. Matty whistled, "Rolls Royce, who's your friend, Mickey?" Enrique emerged from milk white leather seats.

"Finally, you're home," Enrique hugged Mickey. He wore a full-length black leather jacket and a white pair of Nike sneakers.

"This must be Matty. A friend of Mickey's is a friend of mine. Where's your car?" Enrique asked.

"We don't have one," Mickey said, embarrassed.

"No problem." Enrique popped the trunk and pulled out two Bloomingdales bags.

"You're still riding with the shit in the trunk?" Mickey asked.

"I have immunity." Enrique knocked on the diplomatic license plates before slamming the trunk. He handed the bags to Mickey. "It's five kilos in each bag. I want a hundred grand for the package." Enrique walked to the driver's seat.

"Wait, you're not giving us a ride, you expect us to walk with this shit?" Mickey held up the brown bags.

"You ever heard of Jesus Malverde?" Enrique asked. "Jesus who?"

"He's a saint used to be a bandit. We pray to Jesus Malverde using three stones and a red handkerchief. I prayed over the package, you'll be fine."

Enrique rolled away in the Rolls, leaving them standing in the parking lot.

Hell's Kitchen, N.Y. Matty's Apartment, "1985"

Eddie opened the door with his niece on one hip, her arms tightly around his neck.

"Say hello to Uncle Mickey."

The girl buried her head in Eddie's neck. Eddie led Mickey to the kitchen. Marie watched Mickey curiously, until Mickey crossed his eyes and stuck out his tongue. She laughed and ducked behind Eddie's shoulder. Three more girls busied themselves in Matty's kitchen. A set of three-year-old twins played with Barbie dolls on the kitchen floor, a baby girl sat up in a highchair denying every spoonful Matty tried to feed her.

"You have to eat," Matty said. The baby cried louder.

Mickey saw the mountain of cocaine on the kitchen table.

"Matty, what the fuck are you doing? Where's Mary?" he asked. "She's at work. I'm babysitting," Matty said, proudly burping his youngest cub.

"Why are the girls in here with the drugs?!" Mickey screamed. One twin girl stood up and chewed on her pink nightgown.

"They're babies, Mickey. They don't know what that stuff is," Eddie said.

"What about fumes?"

Mickey opened the kitchen window. "Matty, at least take the kids out the room."

"Alright, shut up already," Matty felt offended that Mickey was questioning his parental skills. Matty took the girls, Eddie rolled up both sleeves.

"Time to work," Eddie became a certified street pharmacist while Mickey was away. Eddie dropped a pinch of coke in a glass of water. "This is how we find out how much the coke's been stepped on. The pure coke will dissolve and the garbage will float to the top." Most of the cocaine dissolved in the water.

"This is A-1 shit Mickey. We can hit this one on one," Eddie said. "Slow down, Eddie. What's a one on one?" Mickey asked.

"Turn this kilo on the table into two kilos," Eddie said, spreading the coke around with a plastic paddle.

"Mickey, pick up the solid rocks of coke and put them in a bowl to the side." Mickey did as he was told. Eddie weighed out a kilogram of lactose on the triple beam scale. Then, he sprinkled the lactose over the cocaine spread out on the table, spraying it with acetone.

"Now we mix it up," Eddie said, using two plastic paddles. Mickey mixed up the cocaine and lactose and spread it out again. Then, Eddie mixed it up one more time for good measure.

"Rub those big rocks we put in the bowl through the strainer, Mickey, and dust it over the mixture." Mickey did it and Eddie mixed it up some more.

"Test it." Mickey scooped up some coke on a fingernail and sniffed.

"This shit is dynamite," Mickey said.

"It's finished, we'll use the compressor to rock it back up. Customers love when the coke comes in big rocks. They think it hasn't been stepped on." They bagged the kilos into four half-kilo bags and sealed them.

"Now we repeat this process nine more times" Eddie said. They turned ten kilos into twenty kilos. The average kilo of cocaine sold for $20,000. Mickey planned to sell his coke for $18,000 a kilo. He'd pay Enrique the $100,000 for the package and pocket $260,000. Mickey divided the 458s into two factions, money and muscle. Eddie and Jackie would be the moneymakers, Tom and Matty was the muscle.

CHAPTER 7

Fort Lee, New Jersey. April 1986

Sam Mitchell parked a black Chevy Caprice horizontal in Snapps' driveway, blocking in two Lincoln town cars. The red brick Victorian house provided an easy commute for Snapps to Hell's Kitchen. The brothers met in the driveway, Snapps wearing a red smoke jacket, black chinos, and black moccasins.

"How was the ride out the city?"

"Caught the Yankee game traffic on the George Washington Bridge," Sam said. The younger brother looked older. Snapps, seven years Sam's senior, raised him after their father died in an accident working on the docks. The Mitchell boys were always close, their only fallout happened when Sam decided to become a cop. Snapps, a full-fledged member of the Lucky Charm mob, banned Sam from the Westside. Matches saw an advantage the crew could exploit by having Sam in the bureau, so he helped reconcile the brothers' broken relationship.

"JB's in my dining room, hurry up. He's a millionaire but he's still a kleptomaniac." Snapps and Sam walked inside the house pass the stone lions.

"The flowers really add life to the room," JB said, complimenting the host.

"I have my florist deliver a few dozen every morning. In our line of work, people only enjoy flowers at funerals. I enjoy them while I'm still breathing," Snapps said.

The dining room had a polished oak table and four hand carved chairs. Sam holstered a .45 to sit comfortably. Snapps settled in on JB's right. With Matches doing time in Leavenworth, JB was appointed the acting boss. He looked identical to Matches, only he had both eyes and a red birthmark on the left side of his face, shaped like the state of Texas.

"You know why I'm calling this meeting?" Snapps said. "Fucking crack dealers destroying the Westside," Said Sam.

"The crack dealers are chips off the iceberg. They're unorganized criminals lunging rocks at the penitentiary. Mickey's crew is organized. They present the biggest threat to our rule on the Westside," Snapps said.

"I talked to Matches on our last visit. He asked me what happened to Mickey. He used to be such a good kid," JB said.

"Mickey's harboring feelings. He thinks we abandoned him in prison.

Says he's independent," Snapps said.

"If the men cry, what the hell are the babies going to do? Tell Mickey, suck it up," Sam said.

"Did you talk to him, Snapps?" asked JB.

"He's ignoring me. Mickey's too busy riding around in that new Mercedes Benz."

"New Mercedes? What happened to the Volvo?" JB asked, thinking of the money the mob was missing.

"I see that redhead he's screwing driving it. And that Mercedes, is top of the line, Mickey dropped a pretty coin on it," Snapps said. "How much money are they making?" Sam asked.

"Maybe a quarter million dollars a week and that's a wild guess, because there's Jackie selling coke in Boston," said Snapps.

"Why don't we kill the bastards?" said the FBI special agent.

"I don't want Mickey dead. I want the fucking cocaine operation.

"Who's their connection, Dominicans?" JB asked.

"I doubt it. I see Dominicans on 36th Street buying kilos off Mickey. If you want Mickey's cocaine, you have to get rid of Tom. He's the real killer. The rest of them can't stand without their backbone," Snapps said.

"Get rid of Tom Tansy?" JB questioned.

"Mickey will be a scared puppy without Tom's protection. We sink our teeth in while Mickey's mourning and distraught, before he knows it, we'll sweep the connection right from under him," Snapps said.

"Do it. Whack Tom and take over Mickey's operation. I'll talk to Matches on my next visit to Leavenworth," JB said.

Harlem, NYC. April "1986"

The horn to Tof 's red Jeep Wrangler snapped Chuckie out a funk on 145th Street in Bradhurst.

"Why you standing on the corner looking spaced out?" Tof asked Chuckie when he got inside the Jeep.

"One of them days, arguing with Claire. That's why I wanted to get out the house, relieve some stress," Chuckie said. Tof pumped up the volume on Eric B and Rakim's "Eric B is President."

The warm night brought out the neighborhood watchers. The Wrangler braked for the traffic light and Chuckie let loose.

"I think Claire's having an affair." Tof lowered the music, a gold four finger ring spelling "Tof " in VVS diamonds shined on his right fist.

"She's coming home late, working late, spending most her free time down at the hospital," Chuckie said. Tof wore a fat gold rope chain with a medallion of the African queen, Nefertiti; more VVS diamonds filled her tiara.

"Told you that was coming, Chuckie. Everybody in the city is getting paid. You the only dude broke on that honest Joe shit," Tof said as they crossed over the 145h Street Bridge into the Bronx.

"Claire's a beautiful, successful black woman. Love kept her around this long. If you ain't making bread, that girl's gonna leave you," Tof warned. Chuckie stayed quit. His self-esteem hit an all-time low. At twenty-seven, he was still flipping furniture and Tof had blown up flipping crack on the streets.

"I don't have any proof but I feel our marriage is slipping away. If she's cheating, you think I should divorce her?"

"What works for me doesn't' work for you. Don't base your life's decisions off what other people would do," Tof said.

"I thought you wanted to go clubbing tonight?" Chuckie asked, looking at the tenement building Tof parked beside.

"I have to drop something at my stash house. That's the price you pay rolling with a ghetto superstar," Tof joked, opening the Jeep.

"By the way, nice ride. When did you get it?" Chuckie asked. "Last weekend. It's the '87' edition. Ain't it fly?"

"1987 edition, we still in 1986," Chuckie said.

"Catch up, Chuckie. We moving fast on these streets." Chuckie continued venting inside the kitchen of Tof 's stash house.

"I'm at a standstill. I'm running as fast as I can and I'm not getting anywhere," he said. Tof poured baking soda in a huge mayonnaise jar. A pot of boiling water cooked on the stove's front burner. Chuckie kept on, not thinking of the consequences he'd face if Tof 's drug den was to get raided by police.

"I went to Howard University dreaming of becoming an executive but I'm the manager at a dead end job. I'm nowhere near accomplishing my dream."

Tof crushed a block of cocaine and mixed it in the jar along with the baking soda.

"Quit the furniture store and do something you love doing," Tof said. "I quit my job, Claire's definitely leaving me."

"You thinking like a cat dick nigga, Chuckie. You deserve to be happy.

If Claire won't allow you to chase your dreams, it's her fault for chasing you away." Tof placed the jar in the boiling water, the mixture in the jar caked into a foam, rising to the top of the jar. Tof asked Chuckie to pass him some ice cubes out the freezer. "I got dreams," Tof said.

"You do?"

"I don't always want to be a motherfucker selling drugs. I 'm going to open a strip club." The foam began shrinking in the jar to a yellow oil. Tof dropped the ice in the jar, and spun the ice-cubes around. "I'm flying in exotic strippers from all over the world to slide down my poles. I'ma call it 'Club Gunnieboi,' sounds French, don't it?" Tof smiled.

"Ghetto French," Chuckie said.

"I already got the paperwork and permits for the strip club. In a year, Club Gunnieboi will be up and running." Tof drained the water from the jar inside a strainer. "This is going to make my dreams come true." Tof showed Chuckie the freshly manufactured crack. "Chase your dreams, Chuckie, because a life without dreams is a life not worth living," Tof said.

"How did you get so smart?" Chuckie asked.

"In the game I play, a week is six months. I'm 107 years old in hustler years."

Tof laughed.

"You lived in Hell's Kitchen, right. I hear there are some Irish boys on the Westside pushing serious weight. I'm copping off them through a third party, who's charging an arm and a leg. I'm hoping you know these white boys so I can boot the middleman," Tof said.

"Maybe an old-timer named Snapps," Chuckie said. "These Irish boys are around our age."

"I haven't been to Hell's Kitchen since my parents moved. I have no reason to go downtown. My man Mickey's locked up," Chuckie said.

Hell's Kitchen, N.Y. May 1986

Tom smelled the rain coming under gray clouds on Ninth Avenue. He limped down the avenue with the aid of a wooden cane to the fruit stand.

"Hola, Mr. Tom," said Lisa, the fruit stand owner. She greeted all her customers on a first-name basis.

"This day wasn't lovely until I saw your face," Tom said, squeezing the red tomatoes for ripeness.

"Come to my house for dinner. I'll cook you a special dish," he said.

Lisa's customers blushed. She was accustomed to Tom's flirtation.

"Mr. Tom, I'm happily married," she said, a Colombian woman in the back half of her forties but a pretty woman indeed.

"What your husband doesn't know won't hurt him," Tom winked. "Mr. Tom, go!" she shouted playfully bagging Tom's tomatoes. "But I haven't paid you yet."

"That's ok, Mr. Tom. Mickey paid me enough to cover your tab for a year," she said.

"Fucking showoff. Mickey knows how I feel about you. He's just like his father, never could see me happy. Did he flirt with you?" Tom asked. "No, he only wanted to pay your debt and between us," Lisa put her hand gently on Tom's broad shoulder and whispered in his ear, "I prefer older men."

"Mi amor," he said, kissing her hand.

"Now go." She directed Tom back to Tenth Avenue. Tom limped off whistling, his next destination, 44th Street for his beloved heroin.

"Where's my boy at?" Tom asked a Puerto Rican teen nervously looking down Tenth Avenue. "Go let Macho know Mr. Tom's on the block, I'm his best customer."

"Macho's not around, I'm filling in for him," the scared teen said. "Well, give me a bundle and this better be Macho's shit. If not, I'll shoot this fucking block up. Ask about me, everybody in this neighborhood knows me, Mr. Tom," Tom said. The kid handed Tom ten glassine bags in exchange for a hundred-dollar bill.

Tom convulsed on the rug, foaming out the mouth. The dose he shot up burned out his veins, Lady Heroin had an ironclad hold on him, and she refused to surrender. Tom's life flashed back to the plot in Londonderry on a rainy windy day in the backyard of a stone house. He slammed belly-first into the grass, mud-stained his tiny bare chest, and orange suspenders clinging to hand-me-down trousers. Mickey laughed watching Tom struggle up from the body slam he performed. Mickey, before he knelt over and died inside a prison hospital, before he dedicated everything to the Irish Republican Army, Mickey before him and Tom sailed to America. Tom's six-year-old self shouted, "Come on, pussy!!"

Tom wondered if Mickey would let him win the fight or beat him mercilessly. Mickey's trousers depended on one suspender, the other broke. He was bare-chested and breathing heavy. The brothers circled, sizing each other in their fighting stance. Mickey dropped his fists and with it, his fighting spirit.

"What's the matter?" Tom asked. Mickey went grave. "I told you to look after little Mickey," he said.

"I did look after little Mickey, I protected him," Tom said eagerly. Mickey pulled on Tom's small arm, riddled with needle marks.

"No, you didn't. You're dead." Mickey turned away.

Hell's Kitchen, N.Y. 10 Days Later

Matty missed three of Eddie's calls that evening. He pressed the pause button on the Toshiba VHS player to answer Eddie's fourth attempt.

"Hello," said Matty, Rocky Balboa froze mid-knockout.

"Jacob Javits Center, twenty minutes." Eddie disconnected the call. Matty wanted to call Eddie back and chew him out but everyone seemed to be acting strange since Tom's death. Matty, tipsy off the whiskey consumed at the funeral, decided to check on Eddie.

The Jacob Javits Center was a federal building being constructed on the Westside of Manhattan. The multimillion-dollar government-funded project was a goldmine to the organized crime factions of New York. The Lucky Charm crew profited the most from the federal work site, because it was in their territory. Matty packed a .44 Magnum under a Lawrence Taylor Giants Jersey.

"A guy who's been shooting dope twenty years suddenly overdoses?" Eddie asked, appearing from behind the 120-ton caterpillar DII crawler, holding a German shepherd on a green leather leash. Matty bent to pet the dog.

"London, hi boy."

Orange cones separated the street from the construction site.

"It don't add up, so I did some investigating," Eddie said, pulling on the leash to curb London's enthusiasm. "Tom's usual dealer mysteriously disappeared the day Tom overdosed." Cars wisped by in the left lane.

"Eddie, I didn't come out in the middle of the night to listen to you talk in riddles. Get to the point," Matty said. Eddie ignored Matty, letting his words build to a steady climax.

"I found the dealer after the funeral, name's Macho. He says the day Tom overdosed, two carloads of men rode up on him, put pistols to his mid-section and told him to take the day off."

The hairs on the back of Matty's neck stood up.

"Macho saw a purple Lincoln town car on the street. There's only one purple Lincoln on this side of town," Eddie said.

"Do you know what you're hinting at, Eddie? A full scale war!" Matty said.

"I drove Macho to the Lucky Charm Pub. He identified Snapps' Lincoln as the car."

"Why would Snapps want Tom dead? They grew up together." Matty asked.

"Those old farts aren't happy about the money we're making. To them, we're still snot noses. They only respected Tom, so they kill him and it's open season on us," Eddie said.

"That motherfucker, Snapps! At the funeral today he was crying over the casket, following Mickey everywhere and he's the one who pushed the button,"

"The LCC don't respect us, they want our cocaine spots." Eddie said. "The Lucky Charmers are powerful and connected to the Italians."

"The old-timers bombed first, It's own us to fight or flee," Matty said.

Vinnie's Bar, Harlem, N.Y. May 1986

Bullet guzzled a 40oz of malt liquor in the backroom of Vinnie's bar. A ceiling fan spun over broken stools and mop buckets. Bullet stood under the fan, trying to catch a drift. The heat matted down his high-top fade, his black t-shirt pasted to his buttermilk skin.

"It's Africa in this motherfucker." Bullet fanned himself with the sweaty shirt. Bino rapped to himself in a small mirror. He was short and dark-skinned, his fade cut low, a red Houston Rockets shirt matched the fat red laces in his white shell-toed Adidas.

"I'm speaking to the mops, huh?" Bullet said, then Floss stepped in. "Is it crowded out there?" Bullet asked.

"It's ten people in the bar, including Vinnie." Floss said.

"Someone please explain why we keep performing in this hole in the wall!" Bullet shouted.

Because if we weren't, we'd be playing at your moms house"Bino said.

"Least the fans work at my momma's house."

"I invited some cuties from my high school to the show," Floss said. "Fuck you and those hoes!" shouted Bullet.

"Fuck you! I'm trying to cheer your miserable ass up!" Floss screamed. "Say, I won't bust you upside your head with this fucking 40 oz."

Bullet guzzled down the beer suds, preparing for launch-off. Bino got between them.

"You'll can't be fighting every damn show. We a rap group, act like it," he said.

Bino and Bullet lived in the William McKinley housing projects in the South Bronx. They rapped at local parties, so eventually the two MCs battled for bragging rights. The battle lasted three hours, the audience declared it a draw and a mutual respect was born. Bino met Floss at Park West High School. Floss, tall, light-skinned guy with silky wavy black hair, was the ladies man of Park West. Bino naturally gravitated to the playboy. Floss lived in a middle-class neighborhood in Hollis, Queens and had good hardworking parents. A fortunate kid who loved being around the unfortunate. That's why he turned down five Catholic schools to attend Park West High. Floss DJ'd parties at the Hollis YMCA. After hearing Bino's rap verses, Floss brought Bino to record at his home studio. They recorded four tracks but both agreed the songs were missing something. The next day, Bino showed up at Floss's studio with Bullet. They laid down a rap track titled "Sky Chiefs," a declaration for their love of weed. They didn't form the rap group, their music did. What the three did decide on was the name Sour Boys, because they were nothing sweet.

Chuckie ordered a vodka and cranberry juice. On the bar's television, The Knicks blew a fourth quarter lead to Isaiah Thomas and the Pistons. "Last Night, Bird broke the Knicks for a triple double," Vinnie said.

Vinnie's bar was two blocks and an avenue over from Chuckie's apartment. A knight's move on a chessboard. It's where Harlemites came to listen to music, blow on some reefers and snort a little cocaine. The bar could squeeze in a hundred heads, but that only happened on a Superbowl Sunday. On Friday nights, Mr. Vinnie let the local musicians perform on stage.

"Who's performing tonight?" Chuckie asked.

"A rap group, call themselves the Sour boys," Vinnie said. "They any good?"

"You'll have to tell me; I don't listen to rap enough to be a critic." The beat dropped to the Sour boy's single.

Chuckie nodded unintentionally to Floss' production, uninterested until Bino rhymed the song's first bar:

"They call me Bino the sky chief because I stay in the clouds, High off the Buddha, feet on the ground, I hear about a sucker chiefing a pound, I maneuver like an intruder, without making a sound." Bullet left the bar, smoking a weed joint.

"That show was dope, fresh, all of the above," Chuckie said.

"Thanks, man. That's an everyday thing for us. We'll be back next Friday." Bullet inhaled the weed smoke.

"I'm Charlie Free," Chuckie said using the name Tof christened him with. "I'm Bullet."

"How old are you?" asked Chuckie.

"I'm seventeen, my partners Bino and Floss are sixteen."

"You under any management?" Chuckie didn't have a reason for asking the questions, he was working on impulse.

"Bino's older brother used to manage us until he robbed the pizza delivery man, now he's managing a year on Riker's Island."

Bino and Floss stumbled out of Vinnie's, Bullet hit the weed an offered it to Chuckie. Floss saw the stranger smoking and asked, "Yo Bullet, Who your man?" If Bino had asked, Bullet would have taken it better but Floss did and Bullet hated Floss.

"Mind your business, this is my uncle," Bullet said, lying, but seeing Floss look stupid was worth it.

"Charlie Free," Chuckie introduced himself.

"Sorry Bullet, I didn't know dude was your family," Floss apologized. "Nah, fuck that! I'm out here talking to my uncle about" "Management." Chuckie plugged in. "Yeah, management, looking out for the interest of the group and you accusing me of aiding a freeloader. Fuck this Uncle Free, we out."

"Thanks for going with the script," Bullet said, around the corner. "Ain't nothing, why you so hard on homeboy?" Chuckie asked. "Floss is a rich kid who wants to be down, I hate perpetrators." "The boy can rap," Chuckie said.

"And he makes dope beats, I can't lie." Bullet smiled "What's this management talk?"

"I'm a manager, it's what I do for a living," Chuckie said, part-truth.

"Your rap group has the potential to get a recording contract. I want to help you get that contract."

"You manager any other groups?" Bullet asked.

"I did manage a band called the Stones but the lead singer got killed." "Damn, you need us more than we need you," Bullet said.

"Yeah, it's true."

"We'll do this, Charlie Free, you can manage us, but we're not signing no contracts. If you can do what you say we'll sign, if you can't hit the road."

"What about Bino and Floss?" Chuckie asked.

"I'll get them onboard, but since you're my new manager, I need carfare. Floss was supposed to pay my way home." They both laughed and slapped fives.

Waldorf-Astoria Hotel. New York, NY

"This is my treat, something to get your mind off Tom's death," Snapps said. Snapps and Mickey dined at the five-star restaurant inside the Waldorf- Astoria, Snapps dressed dapper in a two-thousand-dollar Armani suit, hand painted tie, and the ice-cube diamond pinky ring. Mickey grabbed the neck of a bottle of Dom Perignon, pulling it out a silver ice bucket. "Thanks, Snapps. I needed this. I've been hibernating in my condo for two weeks." The restaurant's pianist played Mozart's "Sixth Symphony" on a grand piano.

"Anything to help, Mickey, Tom is family. This is the most time we spent since you've been home," Snapps said, pricing Mickey's diamond and gold presidential Rolex at twenty large, another three for the white Canali suit he wore to dinner.

"I'm not around as much. I'm on the road a lot," Mickey said.

"No explanation needed, you're doing well. Matty and Eddie are flashing more cash than ever. Is it safe to say you're in the seven-figure tax bracket?" Another innuendo at Mickey's financial status. Mickey brushed it off.

"I can't complain," Mickey said.

"I respect your independence Mickey, but once a Lucky Charmer always a Lucky Charmer. Tom's dead and soon the wolves will be circling your drug empire" Snapps said.

"The wolves are already at my coattail. I need to protect my business. Can you help? I'll pay you." Snapps' plan was executing perfectly, stealing candy from a baby.

"Mickey, your LCC, of course we'll protect your business. How much money we talking?"

"Twenty-five thousand dollars a month. I'll pay this month's payment tonight," Mickey said.

"Twenty-five thousand is good for starters. Give me a list of the crews giving you problems," Snapps said.

"Tom's dead and everybody's approaching me with a handout." "That's done. Nobody fucks with the LCC. We're new partners; hope you don't mind me asking. What's the empire worth?"

"Three million dollars a month," Mickey said. Snapps' fork fell on the plate.

"Three million dollars a month!"

"My biggest problem is counting the cash," Mickey said. "Who's your connection?" Snapps whispered.

"The Mexican cartel."

"The shit's coming directly from the cartel." Snapps laughed and smacked a thigh. "You sneaky bastard, Mickey. A rich, sneaky bastard. Where's the twenty-five thousand, in the car?"

"No. It's in the neighborhood," Mickey said.

A valet attendant drove Mickey's black Mercedes Benz 560 SEC coupe outside the Waldorf.

"You want to drive?" Mickey asked Snapps.

"I've never drove a Mercedes. I'm a Lincoln man," Snapps said. "It's a new era. The best cars are made in Europe," Mickey said.

"It does drive smooth, glides on the concrete," Snapps said at the wheel, watching the downtown traffic. Mickey's thoughts went to the night Snapps gave him the Mark IV, a gift for slaying Fast Ricky. That night resembled this one, beautiful.

"The money's on 36th street," Mickey said.

"This building hasn't changed since your father lived in it," Snapps said once they got there.

Mickey shut the door behind them, after they walked inside the tenement building.

"It's where I stash my money." Mickey followed a few feet behind Snapps as they approached the stairway.

"Smart, Mickey, bet nobody knows this building better than you. What floor is the money on?" Mickey wheeled back to the entrance, not flinching when Matty's gunshots erupted in the hallway. The morning papers mentioned the homicide in a small write-up.

"The body of James "Snapps" Mitchell, a resident of Fort Lee, New Jersey was found last night in the hallways of building 458 West 36th Street in Hell's Kitchen. Mr. Mitchell was shot multiple times in the head and torso. The shooter has not been identified as of yet. No witnesses have come forward. James Mitchell is survived by a brother, FBI Special Agent Samuel Mitchell."

In the aftermath of Snapps' murder, the police were clueless on suspects, but Sam Mitchell knew Mickey's crew were the culprits. Sam was dead set on avenging Snapps' murder. The nerve of them little rascals, thinking they can kill a Westside giant. Sam kicked in every apartment and pub, Mickey frequented. He raided Mary's apartment on Eighth Avenue, harassing her over Matty's whereabouts. He blitzed Eddie's and Matty's parents' apartment on 36th Street and Pamela's condominium on Central Park West. The 458s went to the mattresses, dropping out of plain sight. Sam Mitchell took his frustrations out on Macho, beating the dealer to death. The

Lucky Charm mob was blowing more steam than an overheated teakettle. The mob funneled the word on the wire to all the street crews, Mickey and the Hart twins were dead. Sam would not rest until he stabbed Mickey's head on a stake. A vow he'd carry out even if it took the rest of his natural life.

CHAPTER 8

Harlem, N.Y. January 1987

Claire wasn't a drinker but she was drunk nonetheless. A half- empty bottle of white wine, or half-full depending on your outlook, readied her for a confrontation with her lying spouse.

Claire cupped her streaming tears in jittery palms. The teardrops fell on the bank statements, proof of Charles' deception. He'd withdrew over two thousand dollars out their joint account and maxed out two credit cards. He'd done all this and hadn't mentioned anything to her. Why didn't she detect the change in Charles? The partying, acquiring of bad habits. Claire knew why, she focused all her energy on furthering her career. In the midst of that, her marriage lost its priority on her list of priorities. The million-dollar question, where did he spend the money? A question Claire didn't have the courage to ask without the wine in her system. She was afraid that the answer would be another woman and her heart couldn't take it. Charles accused her of cheating but she remained faithful. She thought Charles' insecurity was a bit cute, it showed he was still attracted to her, enough to be jealous. She may have spoon-fed Charles' curiosity by wearing a blouse a bit too tight, but she wanted to keep him on his toes. Did it backfire? Claire cupped her face again and sobbed louder.

Chuckie tiptoed in the house at five a.m.; the house lights came on where Claire sat in the dark. "Why are you sneaking in your own house?" she asked. Charles saw the wine bottle and braced for another argument.

"Please, not tonight. If you want to argue, I'm staying at Tof's house," he said, intoxicated himself, after a night of clubbing.

"You better not leave this fucking house!" Claire shouted, leaping out the chair like lightning struck it. She walked to him in pink silk pajamas. "What's this! Explain this?" She threw the bank statements at Chuckie's feet. Sooner or later, Chuckie expected this day to come. The Sour Boys recorded their demo at a professional recording studio. The cost bled out Chuckie's accounts.

"I spent a little money, no biggie."

"No biggie? You splurged our cash and maxed out two credit cards." "I'll put the money back. I'll pay everything back," Chuckie said. "With what, Charles? You don't have no job. I called Watts Furniture.

They said you quit on Saturday." "Why you calling my job, woman?"

"It's not your job no more. We sleep in the same bed every night. Who are you? I don't know my own husband."

"Who am I? The man you've avoided for the past year, that's who I am!" Chuckie screamed.

"Who are you spending the money on, another woman?" Claire asked.

"No, I'm paying for studio time to record a rap demo. I quit my job to manage my rap group fulltime," Chuckie said.

"Our money is paying for a rap demo?"

"I wasn't happy at that furniture store. This rap group is what I want.

It's what I love," Chuckie said.

"I can't believe you quit your job. How are we supposed to pay the bills?"

"This is my dream. If you don't want to be a part of it, maybe we should divorce," Chuckie said.

"You're ready to throw our love away for a rap group, and your crack dealing friend. Is that weed you smoking eating away your brain cells?" Claire trembled from anger, fear, and rejection.

"I'm chasing my dreams and I want you to be a part of them," Chuckie said.

"I want no parts of hop-hip. I'm a grown woman, you're a grown man.

Act like one!" she screamed.

"Claire, I want us to separate. I need time to think," Chuckie left the apartment and the wine bottle shattered against the door.

March "1987"

Pamela paid the toll for the Triboro Bridge, her second time crossing it. Mickey taught her to watch the mirrors for tails, a lesson never learned. She swerved the white Volvo, trying to lose a tail she couldn't spot. The driving wrecked her nerves, driving cautious, obeying traffic laws, she was being the model citizen, because if the police pulled her over, she'd be missing for a very long time. Pamela Hogan was born in Hell's Kitchen. Her and her younger sibling Mary jumped rope on 8th Avenue waiting for their awful smelling father. He lugged garbage for a living in the smell of contaminated waste settled permanently in his paws. The creator went for a special paintbrush when he stroked the masterpiece of Pamela Hogan. Pamela realized at a young age that she was beautiful from the way people treated her different, from the extra pieces of candy she'd get at the candy store. Pamela learned then that her looks could get her anything her heart desired and she desired it all. As years passed, Pamela developed into a beautiful woman who embodied class and confidence. A socialite who convinced others she was born in Camelot, not the ghettos of the Westside. She'd enter a party and the men shoved each other to be in her graces. Pamela bedded the world's most powerful men.

In California, she seduced the governor. The fling lasted six months before the press caught wind. The Governor wrote her a personal check and sent her back to New York. Pamela's condo on Central Park West was courtesy of the taxpayers of California. She looped her cowgirl rope around a new sugar daddy, back in NYC. Mr. Datsun owned a franchise of car dealerships. The fifty-year-old millionaire hired Pamela as a secretary but she only went to work to collect a paycheck. Pamela had it all, a closet full of fur coats, diamonds, and a showroom of luxury cars to choose from. Then, Mickey came home. A Venice Beach fortuneteller warned her of a love that knew no boundaries, a man she would love endlessly. Pamela never got over Mickey in that short time they spent together. When Mary told her Mickey had been released, Pamela dropped Mr. Datsun. She dropped everything. It wasn't easy getting Mickey back but no mortal could resist a creature so flawless. A love that knew no boundaries, that's why she travelled in a Volvo packed with machine guns and cocaine to a Bronx hideout. She paid the toll, but didn't pay attention to JB's henchmen tailing her Volvo.

Castle Hill, Bronx. 30 minutes later

"Can we fuck her first then kill her?" Rocco asked.

"Get your mind out the gutter. This is business," Georgie said. Pamela switched into the apartment complex on wedge heel sandals wearing a pink sundress. Georgie rested black Ray Ban shades on his forehead.

"She does have a great ass."

The Castle Hill Street was dark and Georgie's dark blue Buick Riviera blended in.

"This is where those cowards are hiding," said Rocco.

"I'm betting on it. All those fucking U-turns in and out of boroughs wasn't for nothing. She shook us yesterday but not today." Georgie had a head twice the size of his body, spiked black hair, and diluted green pupils.

"It's ten grand a piece for the Hart twins and twenty for Mickey?" Rocco asked.

"Forty thousand is at play and your mind is on banging the broad." "Forty-thousand we can get some hookers, a room at the New Yorker and smoke crack for weeks." Rocco smiled.

"Fuck the partying, it comes down to respect. We kill Mickey, I'll be the top Lieutenant."

This wasn't Georgie's first outing. Four other men died on the wrong side of Georgie's gun. This contract meant everything. Georgie and Mickey were competitors in the gangster triathlon since high school and every Olympics, Georgie stood on the second place podium. When they were neck to neck for induction into the LCC, Matches blessed Mickey with the Fast Ricky contract. Mickey became the youngest Lucky Charmer and Georgie got another silver medal. In the decade of Mickey's absence, Georgie enforced the LCC's reign. The more he killed, robbed, and extorted, Snapps was always there to say,

"Mickey would've done a better job." Georgie's jaw clenched at the mentioning of Mickey's name. When Mickey went independent, it cleared the roadblocks on the path to the Westside throne for Georgie. Mickey didn't perish, instead he conquered Manhattan's drug trade, but the tide turned. When Mickey whacked Snapps, the door of opportunity opened.

London licked Pamela's ankles.

"It took long enough," Mickey mumbled on a Marlboro. He was shirtless, a tattoo of Popeye the sailorman on his chest.

"I wanted to be sure I wasn't being followed," she said, snatching off the black wig and throwing it at him. Mickey checked the shopping bags, smiled widely, and kissed her hard on the lips.

"Good job, baby," he said, running into the living room. "My Mexican got these for us." He was gripping a black Uzi submachine gun. "Jackie, say hello to Pamela, the lady who kept you waiting most the night."

"Nice to meet you," said Jackie.

She almost knocked him off his feet. Luckily, Mickey didn't catch it. The living room was set up like an army barracks, there weren't any windows, just four cots and a twenty-seven-inch color T.V. Matty did the cooking, Eddie met drug customers at a diner down the street, and Pamela helped Mickey transport the drugs from the various stash houses.

"You hungry, Pam?" Matty asked, slurping up a spaghetti string. "No way I'm eating that crap and Mary needs money for the girls," Pamela said.

"Mickey! Mary needs money for the girls!" Matty screamed, then annihilated the bowl of spaghetti, watching Iron Mike Tyson pound on James "Bone crusher" Smith.

"It's ten keys," Mickey said, dropping the bricks on a cot.

"That's $225,000 for the package." Jackie couldn't keep the redhead out the corner of his eyes.

"Hey, you paying attention?" Mickey asked.

"Yeah, Mick, $225,000. It's the same every week," Jackie said. "Alright, pack this shit up. Eddie, walk Jackie to his car," Mickey ordered.

"There's Eddie Hart." Rocco leaned closer to the dashboard for a better glance.

"Who is he with?" Georgie asked.

"Jackie the Butcher, what do you want to do?"

"That's ten thousand on heels." Georgie pulled a .38 revolver out the glove compartment, Rocco had a .44 Magnum.

"Is there a price on Jackie the Butcher too?"

'He's a freebie. You go first I'll be your cleanup hitter," Georgie said.

Eddie had an Uzi zipped in a sky blue windbreaker. London yanked him forward, scratching the gravel. "Who's the dame?" Jackie asked.

"Mary's sister, Pamela. She was out west so you never met her," "What's a classy girl like that doing with a thug like Mickey?" Jackie asked.

"Get those stupid thoughts out your head, Jackie. Pam's Mickey's girl and Mickey is the boss."

"Mickey's your boss. I got my own crew in South Boston."

"You wouldn't have shit if it wasn't for Mickey. Your old man tricked your fortune on that young broad, remember?"

"Fuck you, Eddie, Don't ever speak bad on my father!" Jackie screamed.

They both froze seeing Rocco holding a gun so heavy he could barely lift it. The blast, the flash; Jackie grabbed the side of his head after realizing a piece of his ear was blown off. Jackie took off running, holding the ten bricks of cocaine for dear life. Rocco put the Magnum on the $10,000 mark. London leapt forward and attacked Rocco, biting down on his arm with a thousand pounds of pressure. Eddie struggled to free the Uzi out his windbreaker. Rocco screamed louder as London chewed harder. Finally free, Eddie sprayed the street with the Uzi and ran for cover but Georgie's .38 hit him in the back. Jackie's car flew past in the middle of the street as Georgie pumped shot after shot into Eddie's body.

Washington Heights, September "1987"

The construction crew hammered down the wooden panels to the small stage. The Chrome poles gleamed, the zebra stripe sofas designated for the VIP lounge arrived that morning. A master electrician set the perfect lighting. More workers unloaded cases of liquor. The graffiti crew outside spray-painted the banner for Club Gunnieboi.

Tof and Chuckie auditioned exotic dancers for the club's grand opening. "She's a keeper," Tof said, watching a stripper in red lace lingerie dance on the large stage.

"You've kept every dancer we've auditioned. You can't hire every stripper," Chuckie said.

"I see a special quality in all the dancers." "What's that quality, ass and titties?"

"Stripping is an art form. You should appreciate the fact that these goddesses are sharing their God-given talents," Tof said. He had on his signature Kangoo hat and four finger ring.

"Everything you said breaks down to ass and titties."

"You got the love bug, Chuckie. We around all this ass every day and you're drowning over Claire." Tof gave Chuckie a bedroom in his four- bedroom flat on Riverside Drive. Tof paid the bills, Chuckie maintained the huge apartment and dedicated himself to getting the Sour Boys a record deal. Major record labels didn't want to sign the teenage rap act; one label wanted them to change their image. They thought the rap group would become more marketable in spandex and rhinestone cowboy boots. Chuckie refused to sell the group out for a quick buck.

The Sour Boys stuck to their origins, the streets. Major record labels didn't see the raw talent in the Sour Boys. The boys signed Chuckie's management contract anyway. They respected Charlie Free and loved hanging with Tof; knowing a crack kingpin increased their street credibility. Wherever the Sour Boys performed, audiences connected to the young rappers. That's what encouraged Chuckie to push forward. If the people loved the Sour Boys, he had something. The people paid for albums, not music execs. Chuckie wanted to launch an independent record label, fuck the majors! He'd do everything himself and reap the rewards. It was easier said than done. He wasn't working and Tof 's every dollar was tied up in the strip club. Tof already helped Chuckie out by signing the Sour Boys to a six-week contract to perform at Club Gunnieboi.

"I'm not drowning over Claire. I'm drowning because no major label wants to sign my rap group," Chuckie said. A new nude dancer hit the stage.

"This one's from Indiana, calls herself Coco," Tof said He hadn't listened to a word Chuckie just said. Chuckie couldn't afford to be mad. Tof was the Sour Boys' only paycheck.

"The problem with Coco is I think her right breast is bigger than her left breast," Tof said. Coco wrapped herself around the stripper pole.

"If you tilt your head to the left, they'll even out," Chuckie said. When Tof tilted left, Chuckie knew he and the Sour Boys were in trouble.

Manhasset, Long Island, "1987" Mickey's Mansion

Eddie flipped the turkey burgers grilling on a skillet, with a metal spatula. He laid slices of cheddar cheese on the burgers and heard the running car in the driveway.

"Matty's home!" Eddie screamed, alerting the house to his twin's arrival. It became the new custom, whenever somebody left the nest. Eddie's attention went to Matty's legs. He dazed on everyone's legs because the Castle Hill shootout took his legs. Georgie paralyzed Eddie from the waist down. The first cops arriving at the scene handcuffed Eddie while he bled out. Eddie asked himself every day, did the NYPD's carelessness help rot his limbs. Mickey posted Eddie's bail and after some physical therapy, Eddie checked out of the hospital. They drove him straight to the Long Island mansion. Mickey spent $1.6 million on the southern-style mansion but the price tag came second to the gang's security. A ten- foot wrought iron gate protected the property from intruders.

A high-tech security system had every square inch of the mansion under surveillance. It was a beautiful white two-story house with two tall columns outside supporting the roof. In the back of the house was a patio, swimming pool, basketball court and a six-car garage. The inside had marble floors and oriental carpets. In the living area was a grand piano, red drapes over the windows pulled back with gold ropes. Exquisite paintings hung in the hallway leading to the movie theater. On the other side of the mansion was a plush dining room, two bedrooms and a big kitchen full of the latest appliances. A semi-circular staircase led upstairs to four more bedrooms. Mickey's bedroom was the size of a small apartment and the whole room was mirrored: walls, doors, and ceiling. Eddie rolled to the foyer in a wheelchair.

"Hi, Crip, I thought you'd be out dancing," Matty said, patting Eddie's head. He had a complete arsenal of wheelchair jokes.

"Why are you so happy?"

"I got some information that might end this war," Matty said. "Want a turkey burger?"

"Yeah, extra cheese." Matty dropped the Corvette keys in a glass tray and followed Eddie to the kitchen.

"What's the hot info?" Eddie asked, slapping a greasy burger between two slices of Wonder Bread. Matty killed off a third of the burger, in one bite.

"I've got a location on JB, this Friday night." Matty said.

"It's a secret poker game some Italian named 'The Pen' throws every year. He invites mafia big shots into the city to play. This poker game goes on for days, the purse can hit a half million dollars. Matches and JB get invitations every year. A source of mine knows this year's poker game location," Matty said.

"Where?" Eddie asked.

"An apartment on President Street, in Brooklyn."

"If JB is at the mob's poker game and we kill him, it may mean repercussions," Eddie said.

"Those fucks put you in a wheelchair. Fuck the Italians and their repercussions," Matty barked.

1746 President Street, Brooklyn, Saturday Morning

Frank "The Pen" Pensa was nicknamed The Pen because he wrote incriminating conversations down on legal pads, fearing federal wiretaps were listening in. Once the business concluded, he'd set the papers aflame. Frank's association with the Traumanti crime family went back to the late 60s, when the family's powerbase thrived in Brooklyn. Francis Pensa, a Brooklyn boy through and through, raised in Bay Ridge, idolized Brooklyn wise guys like Jimmy Stallone and "Tony T" Traumanti.

Tony T once lived on Pensa's block and rose to the top of the mafia's volcano. A poor immigrant turned multi-millionaire, you couldn't tell a teenage Frank Pensa crime didn't pay. Frank started out as a wheelman for Jimmy Stallone's crew on the Brooklyn waterfront. Jimmy was a tough capo entrenched in the old school mafia doctrine. Jimmy earned money but Jimmy craved the violence more than anything. Tony T called on Stallone's crew for murder. Frank became Jimmy's favorite shooter. By the mid 70s, Pensa has successfully fulfilled fourteen murder contracts. Frank's killings and Jimmy's sponsorship couldn't get Pensa a button. The Mafia books were closed for new membership for most of the 70s. The bosses decided to open the books in '77 and Frank Pensa became an official Traumanti crime family soldier. In the mid-80s, the Traumanti crime family power base shifted uptown to East Harlem.

Anthony "Tony T" Traumanti and four other New York mafia bosses went down in the famous "Commission" Case. The Brooklyn Don, Tony T received a one-hundred-year sentence. The richest Traumanti family member took charge, Vincent Salerno. Frank Penza despised the uptown East Harlem crew. They were more money-oriented and seldom got their hands dirty. When the Pleasant Ave boys wanted someone whacked, they called on Brooklyn. Frank's bread and butter was gambling and extortion. The poker game he threw annually became a racket in itself. This year's poker game was held at Frank's cousin's apartment on President Street. Frank's elbow touched the green felt on the poker table. A stack of thousand-dollar chips next to him, he spread apart the best hand of the night, a Four of a Kind. They'd been gambling for a day straight and Frank just climbed out the red. He'd won the last two hands and had this one in the bag. The knights at the round table were Sal Green, a Jewish racketeer out of Williamsburg, who owned a minority stake in a Las Vegas casino. Alleycat Torrio, acting boss of the Demeo crime family, ran Brooklyn. JB Volpe, from the Irish mob. The Volpe brothers were making millions from the Jacob Javits Construction site. The last knight at the round table, Richie De La Rosa, consigliere of the Maranzano crime family. De La Rosa masterminded the window inflation scheme. The five families charged the City Housing Authority a two-dollar inflation for every housing window they installed. The City Housing Authority installed ten thousand windows a week. Frank won the hand and JB decided to quit.

"Cash me out, fellas," JB said.

"The game just started," Pensa said, not wanting to see that Jacob Javits' money leave the poker table.

"I've lost enough money to put my daughters through college." Georgie put a camel hair overcoat over JB's shoulders.

"What did you lose, $50,000? There's over $150,000 in the next pot," Pensa said.

"I'm gone, Frank. Georgie, get the car."

Georgie beamed up a crack rock in a glass steam on the metal staircase. The monkey crawled on his back during the poker game. Georgie tried to look normal, to not show the signs of addiction. Now the crack rung bells in his eardrums. Georgie rode the high out the tenement down to the abandoned lot where he parked JB's green Jaguar. A 120 lb. Rottweiler chained to a gate guarded the poker player's cars. In the lot besides the Jaguar were two Mercedes Benzs, a Ferrari, and a Lincoln limousine. The grass grew ankle high and a collection of hubcaps hung on the fence. The dog barely budged when Georgie breezed by.

"You're some guard dog," Georgie said to the half-dead beast. The lot stood between a cleaner's and a hardware store. To the deep end of the lot was the backfire escape of another tenement. Georgie unlocked the jaguar, started up the V8 engine and pushed a button to open the sunroof. He moved the rearview mirror over to the right and saw the face of Mickey Tansy.

"Looking for me Georgie?" Mickey's hand pinned Georgie's head to the headrest, the other swept across Georgie's throat with a switchblade. Georgie's reflex opened the car door. He crawled out gurgling on his own blood. Mickey sat in the drivers' seat, put the car in reverse. The car's tire bumped over Georgie's body.

JB stood outside alone on a Brooklyn corner holding an alligator suitcase containing tens of thousands in cash. He wore a black fedora, chewing on a smoking cigar.

"Where are you, Georgie?" he said. His pupil used to be reliable until crack fried Georgie's senses. JB tolerated Georgie's shortcomings because with Matches serving time in federal prison and Snapps in a cemetery, there weren't many tough guys left on the Westside.

"Finally," JB said seeing the Jaguar stalk slowly down the block. JB stepped off the curb and the car's passenger jumped out. JB's cigar fell to the ground when Matty cocked the hammer on the Colt .45.

"Hell's Kitchen is ours," Matty's words. Then, he put the pistol to Texas on JB's face and fired shots.

CHAPTER 9

Boston, Mass. November 1987

Jackie sold cocaine to mid-level African American dealers in South Boston and the Roxbury area. His feelings for blacks hadn't changed, Jackie put money above everything. He filtered cocaine proceeds into his legitimate enterprises. Jackie was back in the butcher business and mapping out a blueprint for a construction company. Jackie hated one black dealer to the core of his heart, Victor Washington. The Queens native relocated to Boston after dropping a body on 107th and Guy brewer. Victor's story began as a smalltime dealer selling grams of coke on a Queens corner. His business philosophy of "Have mine or be mine," took him off the corner and into the upper echelons of the Boston drug game. Victor being Jackie's biggest customer insisted on dealing with Jackie directly. Jackie checked in the Howard Johnson in Roxbury. The perfect location, off a main highway, no traffic, and the manager had a don't ask, don't tell policy. Jackie and Victor conducted business in the Howard Johnson several times. Jackie preferred to stay hands-off letting lieutenants deal the powder, but Victor was too big a customer to lose. In front of suite 302, you heard the television airing an episode of *Wheel of Fortune*. Victor welcomed Jackie into the suite.

"Mr. Jackie, on time as always," Victor said. An Asian woman was on the double-sized bed, her hair wet, the hotel's terrycloth robe slightly open on her moist body.

"I'm tired of putting everything I'm doing aside to come here and pamper you," Jackie said.

"Mr. Jackie, you're getting paid for this and paid well. Lose the 'you're doing me a favor attitude.'" Victor wore a white Fila velour suit and white Fila sneakers and a gold cable chain attached to an anchor charm the size of a dinner plate. Jackie put the steel briefcase on the bed. Victor's date cut open a kilo and tested the product on her tongue.

"My man. Mr. Jackie four keys at 35 g's a piece, that's what?" Victor asked, taking out a gym bag with rolls of $100 bills done up in rubber bands.

"140 grand."

"Yeah, 140 g's." As the cash flowed out of the bag, the room door flew off its hinges.

"DEA!!!"

The Asian woman on the bed jumped up and aimed her gun at Jackie. "Sorry, but I can't do no time. Better you than me," Victor Washington said, getting escorted out of the suite by agents.

Jackie's arm went numb from being handcuffed to the bedpost, tears stained his cream Armani wool blazer.

"You're on audio and video selling four kilograms of cocaine, save yourself. Where'd you get the drugs? Who are you working for?" asked the Asian woman now dressed in street clothes.

"Mickey Tansy from Hell's Kitchen," Jackie said.

Hell's Kitchen, NYC

A sign went up outside the Lucky Charm pub on 48th Street and Tenth Ave, "Under New Management." JB's body hadn't been buried yet and the 458s planted their flag in the crown jewel of the Westside. The surrounding crews paid homage to the new king of Hell's Kitchen, Mickey Tansy. The 458s inherited the name "the Lucky Charm Crew." He who inherited the Lucky Charm bar inherited the name. Westsiders began bringing their problems to Mickey. If a daughter ran away, they expected Mickey to find her. If a tenant needed rent money, Mickey paid the bill. Mickey learned fast, heavy is the head that wears the crown.

"Where's the party at tonight?" Mickey asked the Hart twins, sitting in Matches' old office.

"Being on the lam for so long, it feels good to be back in the swing of things," Matty said, putting on Matches' worn boxing glove autographed by middleweight great, Sugar Ray Robinson.

"It's a hot new strip club uptown in Washington Heights, Club Gunnieboi," Eddie said.

"You're keeping tabs on strippers?"

"Fuck off, Matty. I know the guy who owns the joint. He's a customer of ours, funny cat," Eddie said.

"If he spends money with us, we spend money with him. Tell E.B. to wash the cars. We're partying uptown tonight," Mickey said.

Washington Heights, Club Gunnieboi

Tof built it and they came; the hustlers that is. They came from Atlanta, Baltimore, and Philadelphia. In stretch limos and full-length black Sables. Inside the club, drug crews barred no expense on outdoing each other. There were champagne wars to see who'd buy the most bottles, wars over the best jewelry, which crew arrived in the most expensive fleet of cars. Tof was parlaying outside Gunnieboi when Mickey's entourage arrived. "Hi, Fat boy," said Eddie Hart with his head out Matty's yellow Corvette.

"It's my favorite white boy. You finally took me up on my invitation," Tof said.

"Yeah, it's fifteen of us, so I need the best seats in the house." "Whoever's in VIP, kick their asses out!" Tof spoke to the bouncer next to him. The bouncer hurried inside the strip club.

"Welcome to Club Gunnieboi, the greatest show on earth!" Tof said, escorting Mickey's entourage inside.

The gang of dealers who got evicted from VIP gave Mickey hard stares. Mickey wasn't concerned, Eddie sat on two .40 caliber pistols stashed in his wheelchair. The crew lounged on the zebra stripe seats, getting lap dances, Matty from a blonde.

"This is heaven on earth," Matty said, smacking the dancer on the ass.

Money fell like confetti all over naked bodies.

A waitress appeared, Mickey unzipped a Fendi man-purse.

"This should cover the champagne," he said. The waitress inspected the cash, all hundred dollar bills.

"How much is this?" she asked. The money hardened her nipples. "Around $18,000, I'm not sure, sweetie. I hate counting money," Mickey said.

"I want to introduce you to somebody," Tof said.

"I'm sick of meeting people. I think I've met every drug dealer on the Western hemisphere," Chuckie said.

"This is the big guy, my Westside connection," Tof said. "Hell's Kitchen, Westside?" Chuckie asked.

"Yeah, you probably past him on the street or something, I don't know?"

"This is the last damn time, Tof," Chuckie said.

"Eddie, this is my ace boon coon, Chuckie." Eddie pushed two 36- DD's breasts aside to see Tof's buddy.

"Chuckie! Get the fuck out of here!" Eddie yelled.

"Eddie, what, what happen?" Chuckie asked, realizing Eddie sat in a wheelchair.

"You know each other?" Tof asked, excited.

"I got burned a couple times by a loaded pipe but I'm still kicking and screaming. Well maybe not kicking." Eddie laughed.

"I didn't know. I would've visited," Chuckie said.

"You didn't know because you never come to the Westside. Mickey's looking everywhere for you."

"Mickey's home?" Chuckie asked.

"The cocksucker's in VIP," Eddie said and spun the wheelchair around. "Follow me, Chuckie."

Later that night, Tof 's Riverside Drive Apartment

Tof rubbed blue chalk on the tip of a black pool stick, Chuckie racked the pool balls setting the black eight dead center.

"It's crazy. Mickey's the connection," Tof said, breaking the rack, a striped nine fell in a side pocket.

"I gave up on Mickey after he missed his first board. I thought he'd max out. It's good to see him home," Chuckie said. Tof read his next shot, the Nefertiti Medallion hit the side of the pool table when he set up for it. The queue ball knocked a three-ball inside the corner pocket.

"Is Mickey as big as they say?" Chuckie asked.

"He's the King Kong of cocaine. If you get me inside his loop, Harlem will be mine."

"Mickey invited us to his house party on Saturday. I'll talk to him and he'll give you whatever you want." Tof bridged the five-ball over the four, into a side pocket.

Chuckie hung his pool stick over his shoulders, the best spot for it because Tof was running the table.

"Where's the party?"

"At Mickey's mansion in Long Island. Mickey has a mansion." Chuckie laughed.

"Why don't you ask Mickey for the money to start your record label?

I promised to help but Mickey can do ten times what I can," Tof said. "The last time I saw Mickey was in 1976. You think I'm the type to hound a man for money just because he has it?" Chuckie said. "Opportunity is opportunity. Lose the foolish pride."

Chuckie laid the unused pool stick on the pool table. "I'm not asking Mickey for shit, end of discussion."

Manhasset, Long Island. 1987. Mickey's Party

"Why are you hiding at your own party?" Pamela asked Mickey. He turned from the balcony's view, set his Moet & Chandon bottle on the railing, and took her in his arms. They wore matching white linen, Mickey a short-sleeved button up and pants. Pamela, a dress and red Prada heels. He pecked at her neck with soft kisses. She instinctively felt for the emeralds in her earlobes. The $125,000 set of earrings were a birthday present from Mickey.

"I think you love those earrings more than me," Mickey said. Pamela kissed him back.

"I do."

"Growing up on 36th Street, my mom couldn't afford a television and now there's nothing I can't buy," Mickey said, looking over the festivities "This is a long way from Hell's Kitchen, but it's about maintaining the wealth. That's why you should invest in Jackie's construction company," Pamela suggested.

"I've dodged Jackie since he got here."

"That isn't nice, talk to him. It's your party, Have some fun." "Jackie's asking stupid questions. He's annoying," Mickey said. "Well, Chuckie is downstairs; I saw him on my way up. I know you want to talk to him."

"Yeah, I do want to talk to Chuckie," Mickey said.

"Come on." Her arm wrapped around his lower back. His arm fell on her shoulders. They walked down to the party together.

"I can see me in this car already, this mansion. It's made for a young player," Bullet said, breathing on Mickey's red Porsche 911 inside the six- car garage. Bino rubbed a chrome rim on Mickey's black Mercedes Benz 560 SEC, and Floss couldn't decide which Corvette he liked the most, Mickey's white Corvette or Matty's yellow Corvette with the black stripe down the middle.

"Master your craft. Stay in the studio and you can have this and more," Chuckie said, looking inside Pamela's gold Mercedes Benz 560 SL.

"Charlie Free be for real, rapping ain't getting us this shit. Name a rapper living this good," Bullet said.

"What about LL Cool J, he's getting paid," Chuckie said.

"I partied wit LL Cool J at club Gunnieboi. I got more money than that nigga," Tof said, leaning on the white Volvo.

"Thanks, Tof," Chuckie moaned.

"I'm just being honest." The last automatic garage door opened. "Enjoying the party?" Mickey asked walking inside.

"Not more than these fly ass cars," Bullet said. "Good. I'm stealing Chuckie for a minute." "Yeah, take Mr. Do Good," Tof said.

"This is incredible, Mickey. You're living it up," Chuckie said while they walked into the main house.

"How's the family?" Mickey asked.

"My dad retired. He's up in Yonkers. Mom goes to work part time at the hospital to get out the house and my little sisters all have kids, but none of them are married,"

"Even baby Belinda?" Mickey asked.

"They're all whores," Chuckie laughed. "Did you bring Claire?"

"We're separated, things weren't going right," Chuckie said. They continued up a stone ramp to the entrance of a second-floor bedroom.

"From the letters you wrote me in jail, I could tell you loved her," Mickey said.

"Back to you Mickey, the Irish Scarface. Linen suits, Rolex watches." "You like this watch?" Mickey asked.

"Only because it's worth more than my whole life," Chuckie said.

"Keep it. I've got two more." Mickey slipped off the Rolex and put the heavy gold watch in Chuckie's hand.

"I can't, Mickey. It's your watch."

"It's a present and if you don't accept it, I'll feel insulted," Mickey said. "Then shit, thanks." Chuckie buckled on the Rolex. Mickey unlocked the room door.

"Eddie says Tof told him you need cash for some music company." "No, Tof 's rumbling off at the mouth," Chuckie said.

"Why would he tell Eddie that if it wasn't true?" Mickey walked inside a walk-in closet.

"Tof's smoking that chronic. We got some good weed uptown." Mickey dumped a Louis Vuitton duffle bag on the carpet.

"Open it," he said. When Chuckie did, his heart shot down to his nutsack.

"It's a little over a million and a half or a little under. I hate counting money," Mickey said.

"Why are you giving me this?" Chuckie asked.

"So you can start the music company, idiot" Looking at the green, Chuckie was speechless.

"I was supposed to give this money to Jackie. Pamela wants me to invest in Jackie's construction company but lately, Jackie's giving me the fucking creeps. I'm giving you the money, Chuckie. You're smart, finished college, and you really love music."

"Thank you, Mickey. Thank you," was all Chuckie could say.

115th street Pleasant Avenue, May 1988

The East Harlem hut was temporary. Cold pizza and crushed beer cans attracted roaches. A transmitter and headphones sat on the vinyl seat of a three-leg wooden chair. The missing leg, replaced by the support of a broken sheet rock wall. Two clotheslines of electric cables waist-high squared the living room like the ropes of a boxing ring. Wet photos attached to the lines with clothespins hung drying. Sam Mitchell poked the camera lens through a broken piece of the blinds covering the window. He snapped shots of Pleasant Ave, mainly of the Lion's Den Sports and Hunting Club. When African Americans migrated to Harlem, the Italians moved away. Those stubborn Italians who refused to leave stayed east near the Harlem River. Vincent Salerno was among the Italians who refused to leave. Vincent's headquarters, the Lion's Den, was a storefront where Salerno and friends played gin rummy and plotted the biggest crimes in the country. Sam snapped away at the Lion's Den in a slumlord's building leaning worse than the Pisa. No agent in the New York Field Office took the risks Sam did. He risked his badge breaking into the Lion's Den and planting an illegal bug in Vincent's office. The bug was inside a lamp on the office's minibar, a strategic location. Sam heard Vincent liked to talk business over drinks. Vincent's crew barbecued out in the sun on Pleasant Avenue. A four-door Buick parked and a short Italian with a barrel for a neck got out and kissed Vincent on both cheeks. Sam searched the Traumanti family tree on the wall and matched the Italian's face to a photo. At the bottom of the pyramid under the rank of soldier, was Frank Pensa. The Don and the soldier went inside the Lion's Den. Sam put on the headphones and switched on the transmitter. He heard a muffle, a door close, and then Pensa's voice.

"It's an honor to be in your presence, Godfather. I have the utmost respect for you and all the boys on Pleasant Ave." Sam pictured Vincent sitting in his custom barber chair, legs crossed, offering a ring for Pensa to kiss.

"Frank, you were loyal to Jimmy and Tony T. Now I want you to pledge your loyalty to me," Vincent said.

"Yes, Godfather, you have my undivided loyalty."

"You don't have to call me Godfather, Vinnie's fine." The transmitter made static in the headphones. Sam slapped it and Vincent's voice cleared up. "Did you handle the problem for me?"

"I talked to the Irish kid Mickey at the Lucky Charm bar. He tells me whatever arrangement we had with Matches is done. He's the new boss and he answers to nobody." Sam pressed harder on the headphones, hearing Mickey's name.

"The Lucky Charm crew has answered to the Traumanti family since Lucky Luciano organized this whole thing. This kid thinks he can break tradition?" Vinnie asked.

"Mickey is a lunatic that's wired up on cocaine," Pensa said.

"A fucking junkie is king of the Westside. Matches heard JB got murdered, falls dead a month later. I read a *New York Times* article on that. People who are so close that when one dies the other's in perfect health, then bam! They die too," Vincent said.

"They whacked JB at my poker game. Gave my reputation a black- eye," Pensa said.

"Kill Mickey. Do it so the message gets out to any other young hotshot," Vincent said.

"Yes, Godfather."

"Stop calling me that and before you go to Brooklyn, have a taste of my shish kebabs." Sam heard them leaving Vincent's office. He ejected the cassette tape, the voice of America's biggest crime boss ordering the cold-blooded murder of a rival. The wire was illegal but the Director of the FBI could push past the yellow tape for the biggest shark in the ocean. This would get Sam that big office in the J. Edgar Hoover building. Sam stomped on the cassette tape with his boot. The image of Mickey's skull at the bottom of the Harlem River with eels swimming out his eye sockets meant more than any promotion.

Tof 's Riverside Apartment

$1,486,140 in cash packed the Louis Vuitton duffle bag. One million, four hundred eighty-six thousand, one hundred and forty dollars of blood money. Chuckie planned to do some good with the ill-gotten gains, hoping it would wash the money clean of its sins. Chuckie founded Dessie Stone Records. Dessie for the old nightclub on 117th, Stone in honor of Uncle Steve's band. Chuckie paid top dollar for studio time at Daddy's House Studio, a premiere studio in Manhattan's Tribeca section. The Sour Boys recorded their debut album titled *The Sour Life*. The album consisted of twelve tracks, Chuckie's brown bags of cash got the Sour Boys' beats from hip-hop's best producers. Floss produced four tracks, Bino and Bullet lyrically slaughtered every track. Chuckie negotiated a distribution deal with a Michigan company called Top Pay Records, to distribute *The Sour Life* LP nationwide. The deal allowed Chuckie's independent label to keep 85% of the profits their records generated. Chuckie put a lot of cash into marketing. He realized having a buzz on the streets gave The Sour Boys credibility in the rap world. Chuckie bought the group three brand new Nissan 300 Z's in a variety of colors, along with mink coats. The teens went everywhere in the cars like Chuckie knew they would. The sparkling new cars, new jewelry, and raw talent left a lasting impression all over the city. Top Pay Records sent Chuckie the first copy of *The Sour Life* LP. On the album cover, the Sour Boys were standing on the hood of Tof 's white 7 series BMW, wearing thick gold rope chains and mean mugging the camera.

Chuckie was playing the album when Tof asked, "Have you seen my car keys?" Chuckie grabbed the keys off the stereo and tossed them to Tof.

"You listen to that record so much I can recite the words to every song and Top Pay just sent you the album yesterday," Tof said.

"You played the great adventures of Slick Rick until the tape popped." "Slick Rick's the ruler, the Sour Boys are just peasants," Tof said in a MC Ricky D accent.

"Shut the hell up. Where you off to?"

"The Lucky Charm to talk to Eddie, why? You want to roll?" Tof asked. Chuckie grabbed a custom Gucci jacket designed by Dapper Dan.

"Yeah, I want Mickey to hear what he helped create."

Tof took the Westside Highway to Hell's Kitchen, he pushed the 7 series BMW to speeds up to 90 mph, they got downtown in a zip. On 48th Street, Eddie was on the sidewalk wearing a Mets jersey talking Yankee history.

"Who won the Most Valuable Player award in the '78 World Series?" he asked the boys on 10th Avenue.

"Reggie Jackson," one of them said.

"Nope, Bucky Dent." Eddie saw Tof 's BMW and rolled over. "Where's Matty? Chuckie asked.

"Who?"

"Matty, your twin." Chuckie got out of the BMW.

"I don't know anybody by that name. I don't have a brother." Matty must've owed Eddie money. He always disowned Matty until he paid up.

"Where's Mickey?" Chuckie asked.

"Mickey's in the pub." Chuckie left Eddie and Tof to their business. "Chuckie, what's good baby?" Mickey flipped through the jukebox's record collection and settled on Al Green's *Not Tonight* Chuckie handed Mickey *The Sour Life* cassette.

"This is the record? That's great. The boys look tougher than me," Mickey laughed.

"You have to hear it. It's a rap classic," Chuckie said. "If you say so. I'm more a rhythm and blues man." "No! You have to hear it Mickey,"

"Ok, we'll listen to the tape in my car. This bar isn't the rap kind of crowd." Mickey clicked the safety off a nine-millimeter berretta. "Italians are trying to muscle in on my turf. Got to carry a piece to be on the safe."

The Sour Life LP was giving Mickey the worst headache. Chuckie blasted the music in the Porsche 911, rapping along to every song. When Mickey thought he survived the listening session, Chuckie flipped the cassette over to the other side.

"Side B, It's better than Side A." Mickey wanted out. Tof and Eddie came out the Lucky Charm together.

"Fat boy!" Mickey screamed. "Me and Fat boy need to talk for a minute, Chuckie."

"OK, when you finish, I'll let you listen to the B side," Chuckie said, stepping out the car so Tof could get in.

"What's shaking Mickey?" Tof asked.

"I couldn't stand no more of that fucking rap record. My head's throbbing, you got an Aspirin?" Mickey asked.

"I live with that motherfucker. He plays that record so much, I hate it already. Chuckie's really passionate about the music. He and the Sour Boys are going to do great things," Tof said.

"I hope they sell millions of records and make me plenty of money, so long as I don't have to listen to a single song," Mickey said. A woman's scream sat Mickey up out of a slouch position. He looked out the car window at two barrels pointed at the 911.

"Get out!!!" Mickey pushed Tof into the passenger door. Frank Pensa shot two handguns until they both emptied then Frank dashed towards 47th street, where Gene his partner had a stolen car ready and running.

Club Gunnieboi, Washington Heights. January 1989.

Chuckie's Light Brown MGM leather outfit collected dust standing in the remains of Tof 's dream. The neighborhood's drug addicts stripped the club of its glory. What the addicts couldn't steal, they destroyed. It seemed ironic to Chuckie how drug fiends destroyed a drug dealer's dream. A breeze whirled through a broken window into the empty club. Chuckie staggered around drinking a bottle of Hennessy VSOP. He rode in a Lincoln Limousine uptown after abruptly leaving the celebration. The party would miss Charlie Free, but who cared about what Charlie Free missed? He missed Claire, who constantly appeared in his thoughts. Her silk pajamas, arm folded over her breast, left leg fidgeting and those famous words, "Why you sneaking in, Charles?"

He missed Tof, whose body rested in a graveyard on 155th Street and Amsterdam Ave. All Chuckie had to remember him by was the Nefertiti gold rope chain. He missed Mickey, for months Mickey lingered in a coma, doctors itching to pull the plug. Bino, Bullet, and Floss provided the crutch for their mentor to fall on. Chuckie's therapy was promoting *The Sour Life* LP. The hard work paid off, the Sour Boys opened up for Run- DMC in thirty U.S. cities. Rap magazines gave Chuckie's group rave reviews. *The Sour Life* hit stores November 5th, 1988 and sold 143,000 copies its first week. The album surpassed 500,000 sales that morning, the reason for the Sour Boy's celebration at the Time- Life building. Chuckie reached the pinnacle of his life but felt defeated. The three people he loved most couldn't share in his success. A rattle near the large stage made Chuckie twirl around, probably a rodent but Chuckie wasn't taking any chances. Wearing Tof 's chain and Mickey's Rolex, he'd be a crack fiend's dream. Chuckie laid the Recording Industry Association of America certified Gold Plaque for *The Sour Life* LP on the stage. He splattered some Hennessy on top of it and stumbled out to the limousine.

On a steel beam high above the tallest skyscraper in New York City, Mickey sat naked and shivering. The presence of night or day couldn't be told high up on the beam. A permanent light, shined like a car's high beam on a deer crossing the road. Mickey looked down on the ant farm that was New York City.

"What are you doing up here, numb nuts?" Tom wore a lumberjack shirt, hardhat, blue denims, and a tool belt. There weren't any tools on the belt just dismembered body parts. Tom walked the beam and sat facing Mickey, his short legs on either side of the steel beam. Mickey faced the sky or the light; he wasn't sure which it was. Tom didn't mind him being naked. "Where's my clothes?" Tom twisted the top off a Thermos cup, poured a shot.

"Drink some." The drink instantly warmed Mickey up and made him unashamed of his nakedness.

"Good coffee," Mickey said.

"That wasn't coffee. It's blood. Nothing gets you up like the taste of blood and you need some getting up," Tom said.

"Where are we Tom? Am I dead?" Mickey asked.

"This is where you go when life wants a divorce and you're dodging the clerk serving the divorce papers. You're not dead, Mickey. I am," Tom said, swinging his legs off the beam.

"You're not fully committed, those people over there are dead." On a billboard's steel railing thirty yards away, Big

Mickey and Rita slow- danced to a lover's tune. The billboard advertised State Farm life insurance, a coincidence?

"That's my mom," Mickey said.

"Your father, too. They get on that billboard every night and dance together. Every night for eternity," Tom said. "It's time you wake up. You've slept long enough."

"How long?" Mickey asked.

"So long, I'm sick of watching over your ugly mug."

"If I go who's going to keep you company?" Big Mickey dipped Rita, spun her, and pulled her in close.

"I've got Gwendolyn." She appeared on one end of the beam in a floral dress. Tom stood up

"I'm fine, numb nuts. So wake the fuck up."

Mickey woke up in a hospital with a tube down his throat. He moved one arm and machines sounded. A female nurse rushed inside his room and crossed her heart three times. Mickey couldn't understand what she said, something about God, then Spanish, and then more God. She began disconnecting him from the machines. More people entered the hospital room. Mickey's heart pumped faster, the machines he was attached to verified it. An Asian woman stiff-armed the nurse for a bedside position. Then she showed her badge. She spoke and Mickey understood.

"Mickey Thomas Tansy Jr., you're under arrest for trafficking cocaine"

CHAPTER 10

Boston, Mass. June "1994" Five Years Later "The Ward Estate"

Jackie tossed and turned on satin sheets, damp with perspiration. Light from the moon filled the gaps in the loose drapes, illuminating the bedroom. A buzzing sound lingered out a power drill. The drill's tip rotated over Jackie's eyeball.

"You fucking rat," Mickey said, pressing the drill's trigger. A rusty steel vice grip held Jackie's head in place. Matty winded the cam, tightening the vice.

"Sold you pals out for your corporations," Mickey force-fed Jackie a mouthful of dollar bills. The act was an assault on his taste buds. Jackie tried spitting out the currency. One bill spiraled slowly to the ground. The vice grip pushed inward, raising Jackie's facial features upward.

"The Witness Protection Program couldn't afford to pay for your plastic surgery, leave it to Mickey."

"Jackie! Jackie!"

A moment later, Jackie familiarized his surroundings, the master bedroom. His wife stood beside him, not a vengeful Mickey Tansy.

"Take this," she insisted. Jackie chewed on some pills, washing them down with ice cold water. The glass mildly quenched his thirst.

"Bring me some more," he said in a hoarse voice. Jackie waited for her to leave the room, grabbed a robe laying on a nearby chair, and wiped the sweat away. His heart slowly returned to its normal pace. Six long years and the nightmares still warred on Jackie's peace of mind.

The taped conversations he recorded solidified the DEA's investigation. Jackie's microphone and transmitter caught hours of drug deals in the Lucky Charm Pub, where the words coke, blow, and kilo were as common as shit, fuck, and cunt. The one language everyone shied away from was called homicide. On the many attempts Jackie tried inquiring about Hell's Kitchen's bloody civil war, he got nothing.

"Leave that to us. Focus on the business," Matty suggested drawing an invisible line between the money and the muscle. Jackie heard of the killings going back to Fast Ricky, but by hearsay not from anyone directly. The federal agents contained enough evidence to bury the Lucky Charm gang without the murders. Jackie aided the DEA up until the arrests of the '458s' founders and eleven associates. Matty and Eddie Hart copped out to ten years a piece for their leadership roles in the drug ring. Mickey plead guilty to drug trafficking and money laundering, he copped a plea to twenty years and federal prison and a two million dollars fine. The Feds confiscated the Lucky

Charm Pub, the Manhasset mansion and eight luxury cars. They also seized twenty-three kilograms of cocaine and approximately $3.8 million in cash. The prosecutor exonerated Jackie from all charges in exchange for his testimony. Jackie got to keep his legitimate businesses. He signed out of the Witness Protection Program and relocated to a plush suburb in Massachusetts.

Jackie walked a long corridor to his home office and searched the messy desktop for a business card. Jackie Sr. passed along the card during the DEA's takedown, knowing Jackie Jr. could use the extra protection. The card was under a copy of the *Wall Street Journal*. Jackie picked up the phone and stuck a finger in the third hole on the dial. The plastic dial wheeled right, then returned to the 3 marker. The old fashioned phone coordinated with the office's retro designs. On the second ring, a gruff voice answered, "Special Agent Sam Mitchell."

"Another episode, this one worse than last time." Sam let out an inaudible sigh, frustrated that he hadn't found a way to bill the bureau for countless hours of psychotherapy.

"What's the problem?"

"Mickey Tansy and Matthew Hart drilling my head to a fucking sawhorse."

"This is the first episode in over a year. What triggered it?"

Sam unscrewed a wooden reed from the mouthpiece of a saxophone. "My wife's father is sick. I'm sneaking back and forth to Hell's Kitchen."

Sam fully disassembled the instrument. His around the clock schedule left no time for life's pleasures.

"Hell's Kitchen is the cause of your mental anguish." "My in-law is practically on his deathbed."

"Stop worrying. Mickey is finito, the money he didn't leave lying around, the IRS tracked to offshore accounts. A rookie fresh out of law school is handling his appeal for pro-bono work." Sam laughed.

"Does he have any chance of winning the appeal?"

"Not with a guilty plea. Relax, Mickey won't be home for another fifteen years."

"You're right. It's those trips to Manhattan," Jackie said.

"That's exactly what it is. Oh, I can use some tickets to The Jets vs. The Dolphins."

"Not a problem. I'll have my secretary send you four tickets." "Thanks, kiddo." Sam disconnected the call.

"Thought you'd be waiting in the bedroom."

"I had to make a phone call."

Pamela rubbed a glass of cold water against Jackie's forehead. Her voluptuous body shaped a silk purple nightgown.

"You're burning up," she said. Jackie reached for her hand, the one with the four-karat diamond wedding ring. Pamela pulled the plug on Mickey mentally during the weeks she visited a vegetable. Agents stormed their Manhasset Mansion at a quarter past dawn. A crew of agents escorted Pamela off the 4-acre property with just a change of clothes. She lost everything, the possessions she acquired before Mickey were considered the spoils of a queen pin and abruptly seized. Pamela went back to what she knew best, seducing rich men. This time around in her thirties and without the wardrobe of a Prima Donna. Pamela found it harder to court a man of her stature. Then her knight in shining armor appeared in a white Maserati instead of a horse. The neighborhood knew Jackie testified against the Lucky Charm Crew. Pamela loved Mickey but Jackie gave her a way out. He saved her from a life of second-class living. She did what she had to, Jackie provided a lifestyle she'd grown accustomed to. The coup de grace, Jackie's companies were legitimate. The Feds could never take away her godly possessions.

Midtown Manhattan. C.I.M.G Offices

James "Big Jim" Morrison office topped the 76th floor of the Chrysler Building, offering exceptional views of Central Park. Big Jim built a custom miniature golf course in the spacious suite to fight off bouts of boredom.

"I want Charlie Free over here at C.I.M.G," Big Jim said.

"It's a complex situation. Charlie Free sells boatloads of records independently. We can't just entice him with a big check," Josh Stevenson said, Big Jim's personal assistant.

"I want those acts on my label!" The golf club hit a pink ball. The ball bounced off a windmill's blade.

"We'll need more than money to sign Dessie Stone. Charlie Free wants full ownership of his masters." Josh gave Big Jim a list of Chuckie's demands.

"What do you suggest?" was a question Big Jim often asked Josh. "Give Charlie what he wants. Worst case scenario, he signs with Sony Music Group." Big Jim leaned against a glass sculpture of the Sun god Apollo. A collage of gold and platinum plagues covered the walls.

James Morrison chaired the Continental Island Music Group, the most prolific major record label in the music industry. C.I.M.G stretched two continents and owned assets worth billions of dollars. James descended from a long lineage of leaders. The elected president of the United States was Big Jim's fourth cousin, and he shared kinship with two former U.S. presidents. Big Jim was schooled at the most prestigious boarding schools. He graduated high school at the age of sixteen to attend Oxford University as a Rhode's scholar. At six-feet seven inches tall, Big Jim looked like an extraterrestrial compared to the other nerdy students. His Aryan bloodline produced the sandy blonde hair and blue eyes. Big Jim's appointment to Vice President of C.I.M.G came through a family friend. Fifteen years later, the Board of Directors voted Big Jim Morrison Chairman of the Continental Island Music Group.

"I'll make Charlie Free an offer he can't refuse." Josh squinted at the small numbers on his mobile pager.

"What's that?" Josh asked, clipping the beeper on his ostrich belt. "Twenty million dollars and ownership of his masters. We'll take twenty percent of the profit for distribution fees," Morrison said.

"Nobody in the music industry has that kind of deal," Josh said. "That's why I called it an offer Charlie Free can't refuse." The pink golf ball dropped inside the black hole.

Chuckie weaved a bright red Ducati motorcycle on the Westside highway, wearing a black helmet and black Vanson leather jacket to protect him from the wind. The weatherman predicted heavy rain in the forecast. That didn't stop New Yorkers from taking to the town. The spirit of New York City in 1994 made thousands of tourists change zip codes. The New York Rangers won the Stanley Cup finals, led by team captain Mark Messier. The Knicks were in the NBA finals for the first time in twenty years. The orange and blue posters read, "Go! New York, Go!" Kids fought over who was Hakeem "The Dream" Olajuwon or Patrick "The Beast of East" Ewing. On the music scene Wu-Tang Clan's 36 Chambers sound tracked the fury of the inner-city youth. Chuckie missed the ball completely on that play. Who would have thought a nine-man rap-group would conquer the rap world. The previous summer Chuckie discovered four black girls from Baltimore called the Sparks, their debut album reached number 7 on Billboard's Top 200 Albums chart. The Sour Boys remained Dessie Stone's cornerstone artists but the tension between Floss and Bullet reached new heights when the two exchanged shots outside Daddy's House Studio. Chuckie had to book two separate recording sessions just so the group could record a single track. A young music prodigy gave Chuckie the upper hand in negotiations with major labels. A twelve-year-old name Devante Ross could sing, write, and play nine musical instruments. Major labels launched a bidding war to sign the young prodigy. Chuckie's recruitment skills didn't win over Devante's parents. They trusted Dessie Stone simply because Chuckie graduated from their alma mater, Howard University. The major labels called when the Sour Boys released three critically acclaimed gold albums. The calls increased when the Sparks caught fire in route to platinum sales. Now with Devante Ross, the major labels slept outside Dessie Stone's offices. Chuckie remembered begging these same record labels to sign his teenage rap group, the tables had turned. Dessie Stone Records had kidnapped the music industry and held it hostage at gunpoint. Chuckie lifted the Ducati's front wheel, gliding towards the Chrysler Building to collect a king's ransom from Big Jim Morrison.

East Tremont, Bronx. Two Weeks Later

Thin vines from green plants sprouted across the red bricks of the Booker T Washington grade school building. Four yellow school buses clogged the street with smoke from exhaust pipes. A few parents actually were happy to pick up their children, most were pissed at the Board of Education for cancelling the afterschool program. Chuckie left the car idle, contemplating whether to drive off.

"What am I doing?" he asked himself. Three days earlier, Lala's car broke down and she called Chuckie for a ride to work. Chuckie was turning the steering wheel around the school's corner when he noticed a familiar face on a different body. The face stirred back from a gated playground, purple barrettes clipped to the tips of her long braids. At three o'clock, Chuckie happened to be on the same street. The face on the little girl belonged to Claire. Mother and daughter ordered vanilla ice-cream cones from a Mister Softee ice cream truck, then disappeared hand-in-hand up the steps to the train station. Chuckie almost approached Claire but his insecurity won out.

"She's probably got a boyfriend. She's got a daughter, might have three kids waiting at home. This is stupid." Chuckie still showed up the next two afternoons.

"That's my car, the white one," a kid said, referring to Chuckie's SL600 Mercedes Benz "Nope, that's my car. I changed my mind," another kid said. "You can't do that. You already picked the blue car!"

"I can do whatever I want. You ain't my leader," said the second kid. "Let's fight for it" Kenny got clubbed with a right to the head. The heavy textbooks in Kenny's backpack pinned him to the floor.

"Yo shorty, chill out." Chuckie stopped the first kid from pummeling Kenny.

"He cheated! I picked the car first!" The weight from the backpack kept Kenny on the pavement.

"So what, you ain't my leader!" Kenny's last act of defiance. "Listen up." Chuckie lifted Kenny up. "It's none of y'all car, It's mine. I got it by spreading love not fighting my homeboys." The boys sucked their teeth.

"Want me to show you how to get a nice ride?"

"I already know how to get a nice ride, bust some dope moves on the street."

"You're wrong, I didn't bust no dope moves for this car. I worked hard for it," Chuckie said.

"What do you do?" Kenny's attacker asked curiously.

"I own a record company, ever heard of the Sour Boys, that's my rap group. Every black man in a nice car isn't slinging dope." Chuckie flipped through his bankroll for two twenties.

"Don't spend it all on candy."

"Thanks! What's your name?" Kenny asked. "Charlie Free."

"Is that you, Charles?" Chuckie turned to find Claire and her smaller version hiding behind her dress. "Oh my god! What are you doing here?"

"I…I was enjoying the weather. Who's that hiding behind you?" Claire smiled heartily.

"This is my daughter, Mia. Say hello to Charles." Mia stayed behind her mother.

"She's really shy," Claire explained. "She's beautiful."

"Thank you, I read about your big deal in the newspaper, congrats. I thought you'd be in the East Hamptons not East Tremont." Mia pulled Claire when Mr. Softee's theme music blared past.

"Mommy, the ice cream truck is leaving," she cried.

"I'll get you some tomorrow," Claire said. Mia cried instantly. Chuckie knew where she got it from.

"There's a Baskin Robbins in Parkchester. I can drive you over," he offered.

"Alright, I don't have nothing planned." Mia wiped her tears away.

"I got the call from the army and didn't have the strength to get out of bed." Claire was telling the tragic story of Mia's father, whose heel activated a landmine in Desert Storm.

"Everything happens for a reason. It's God's plan," Chuckie said. "That's what everybody says. It's hard being a single parent, and maintaining a career." Mia's toy pony galloped up Chuckie's back. "I think Mia likes you, Charles."

"Everybody loves Charlie Free." Chuckie tickled Mia. "I guess you proved me wrong with hip-hop."

"It wasn't a right or wrong thing. I just wanted to chase my dreams." Chuckie shrugged.

"Does it feel good living out your dreams?"

"It's cool but lonely. I'm always asking myself, are the people around for me or what I can do for them?"

"With twenty million dollars, I can handle being lonely," Claire said.

"A lot comes with having money is what I'm saying."

"A bunch of groupies I bet." Claire wished that comment hadn't slipped out.

"They're around but I don't go for the one-night stands. It's the quickest way to a lawsuit. Look at Tupac Shakur, a night of pleasure led to a rape case."

"There's some trifling people in this world," Claire agreed licking ice- cream off a cone.

"You're smart, Charles. You'll be ok."

"Smart gets you so far in this game. I need a queen to command my castle." Chuckie moved closer.

"Quit it, Charles. You still studying those Dolomite tapes?" "I'm serious, Claire." They were close enough to brush noses.

"I got a five-year-old daughter. You think you can handle that?" "It's enough room in the castle for a princess." Mia pretended she wasn't listening.

"Who's to say I want you back anyhow?" Claire snaked her neck.

"You kidding! 'Is that you? Oh my god!' Almost stampeded a brother." Chuckie popped the collar on his Karl Kani button-up.

"Yeah right! I, I, I was enjoying the weather. That car tends to stand out," Claire said.

"What you trying to say. I got the only white Mercedes Benz in New York?"

"No, I'm saying you're the only one in New York with a white Mercedes Benz with C. Free on the license plate." Claire burst out laughing, Chuckie did too.

"I'm guilty as charged. Law enforcement at its best, baby," Chuckie laughed.

"You know; I get Sherlock Homes on your ass." "Please. Don't remind me,"

"I don't know Charles. You're not the daddy type."

Chuckie scooped Mia up.

"What? I love kids." Claire fanned her wrist. "Say that a year from now, mister."

"You forgot? I just signed for twenty million. We can hire a nanny."

CHAPTER 11

MTV Music Video Awards, New York, N.Y. September"1999" 5 Years Later

I want to thank god first and foremost. My mother, brother, the entire McKinley Projects posse. My seven kids, Daddy loves you.

My former group the Sour Boys, hold on a minute. Dessie Stone, my record label and Charlie Free, matter of fact, get up here, Charlie," Bino said, holding a silver moon man for Best Rap Video. The camera zoomed in on Chuckie in the fourth row.

"Come on, I'm not leaving the stage until you get up here, Free!" MTV producers urged Chuckie to the podium. Bino was threatening to cut short the next performance. Claire pushed Chuckie down the aisle.

"What's the fuss about?" Mickey banged a sawdust paddle on the Ping-Pong table. Milwaukee Magoo straightened his coke bottles lenses.

"The Music Video Awards, Some black guys and baggy clothes, your serve," Milwaukee said.

"Game!" Let's run it back for double to nothing," Magoo said. "I'm done. I think you enjoy beating my ass."

"I'm turning pro again, when I get released."

"Magoo, you're fucking seventy years old," Mickey said. "And could still whip the whole jail including you."

Mickey had awoken from a coma to a world of confusion. The "DEA" showed no compassion for his medical condition. He appeared in a federal courtroom five days later in a wheelchair with months, worth of overgrowth. His fight for his life coincided with the fight for his freedom. He didn't recall much from the next several months but slowly a walker replaced his wheelchair. It seemed every milestone he achieved in physical therapy, the courts countered with a legal attack. Jackie fucked the gang with no Vaseline. The raid at the Hell's Kitchen stash house wiped Mickey out of millions of dollars. The government found his offshore accounts in the Cayman Islands. Mickey faced natural life, if convicted at trial. The months ticked away with his legal team. What began as an all-star team of three battle-tested lawyers narrowed down to one disgruntled lawyer. If going to trial became inevitable, it would've been none. The cash coffers were empty. There wasn't any money to pay anybody. The twenty-year sentence sounded like forever after being home just a few years from a ten-year prison stretch. To Mickey, numbers beat letters any day. When alphabets attached to your bid, it meant only one way out, a wooden coffin. A person that becomes accustomed to incarceration knows the less people in your bid equals less stress. A man trying to police a marriage with twenty years might come home looking forty years older, if the stress didn't kill him first. Felons learned how to block out the world in order to return to it.

The last time Mickey saw Pamela was the day he got shot. He learned about the wedding from Matty's wife. A block of dry ice described Mickey the best, cold enough to burn. His anger seesawed from Pamela to Jackie.

Pamela, whose loyalty served one master, the almighty dollar. Jackie, who bamboozled the 458s and openly practiced deception. The hot flashes of rage inflicted Mickey sporadically. The image of their bloody bodies served as an antidote to his murderous fevers.

"I'm the guy usually in the background, so this is awkward. I want to thank my parents, Claire, my wife, and my daughter Mia. Um, that's it. Oh yeah, RIP Tof, and Free Mickey Tansy." Chuckie raised Bino's moon man in the spotlight to a standing ovation.

"Mickey! He said your name! He said your name on national television!" screamed Magoo. Mickey glimpsed up at the television. He marveled at Chuckie on the widescreen, then, Mickey laughed out loud.

"What's so funny?" Magoo asked.

"Thinking about the return on my investment," Mickey said.

London, England

In a hollow room, hundreds of wax candles aligned in the shape of a star burning brightly. Ten bodies formed around a marble portrait of the sun, with twelve signs of the zodiac encircling the flaming star. The marble image was carved along the floors of a London cathedral. The droopy white cowls attached to the bib-like scapulars hid their faces. The tenth person wore a scarlet cowl and scapular. He stood inside the center of the sun, at the helm of the gathering. He raised a fist with a platinum skull and crossbone ring; two rubies sparkled from the eyes. The rest raised fists wearing identical rings. The red rubies symbolized the lodge's duty. They called themselves "the Watchers," bearers' of the hidden truths of the universe, passed down generations since the great catastrophe devoured the city of Atlantis. The Catholic Church provided a smoke screen to disguise "the Watchers" true worshipper, the first king of Babylon, Nimrod. The shining sun in the marble was the ruler's iconic symbol. The Watchers, known as the Priory of Scion, created a secret society in 6th century France. They served the Merovingian bloodline, the dynasty of kings who claimed to be direct descendants of Jesus Christ.

"The Priory of Scion has prepped you for leadership roles in the quest for world dominance. The blue bloods of the Aryan Nation the descendants of Christ and the Merovingian kings." The scion in the center of the sun clutched a large golden grail.

"Tonight you'll drink the blood of the goat and forever be linked through brotherhood!" A priest led a goat past the scions on a string and quickly dismissed himself from the ceremony. Peter Rothkid slid a poniard from under the scapular, the slim dagger had a crucifix wielded to its handle. The goat moved nervously trying to break through the tightly knit circle. The superior general lifted the poniard.

"In the name of Nimrod, lord of the sun," Rothkid sliced the goats' jugular vein with one swift motion, blood squirted over the marble sun, then poured out the goat in a steady stream. Rothkid filled the grail with blood.

"The 29th degree is four from the thirty-three required to be elected Superior General. One of you chosen nine will lead the Priory of Scion, when I'm extracted from my physical being. I wish you the best." Peter Rothkid passed the golden grail to the first Scion in line. Big Jim Morrison drank the blood of the goat and kissed the ring of the Superior General.

New York, N.Y. December 31st, "1999" New Year's Eve

Chuckie and Bullet staggered down the gangplank of the USS Montana. The Continental Island Music Group rented the gigantic vessel for special events. Tonight's party served two purposes, the welcoming of the new millennium and Charlie Free's appointment to President of C.I.M.G.

"It's freezing, how far is your car?" Chuckie slurred. His Versace shirt made of Egyptian cotton sailed with the winds.

"The richer you get, the more you complain about everything," Bullet said.

"Because I'm supposed to be in my warm party not freezing for God knows what."

"I picked you up a present. I know it's your life dream to become an executive of a major corporation. I wanted to give you something special." With Bullet, nobody knew what to expect. His ego played the biggest role in the Sour Boys breaking up. The rap group separated after five studio albums. Bino stayed with Dessie Stone and released a succession of number one records on the Billboard charts. Floss signed to a major label, but his solo career went into a free fall when the album flopped terribly, but he recovered on the keyboards as the go-to beat maker for a new generation of rappers. The music industry never heard from Bullet again. He traded recording studios for street corners. When money got low, he'd hit Chuckie up for some cash loans. Chuckie thought Bullet wanted a loan tonight.

"The world really must be ending tonight if you're giving gifts," Chuckie joked.

"Santa Claus crossed me off the naughty list." Bullet reached in his car and gave Chuckie a gift-wrapped box.

"Here you go, Mr. President." Chuckie gently unwrapped the gift. "Free, tear the fucking paper off. That's the high maintenance shit I'm talking about."

"Ok." Chuckie trashed the paper and opened the wooden box. An 18-karat white gold Harry Winston watch with a diamond bezel.

"Wow," Chuckie said.

"The jeweler said its nine karats in the bezel."

"Thanks, I wanted a Harry Winston for my watch collection," Chuckie admitted.

"I saw you with every watch but a Harry Winston, that's why I got it." "This cost some change. You put out a record I don't know about?"

Chuckie asked.

"My rapping days are over. Leaving that to Bino and Floss."

"I haven't seen you in months. You show up at my party with this expensive watch," Chuckie grilled.

"I'm chilling, Free."

"I appreciate the gift but if you did anything illegal to get it, keep it."

"Free, get off your high horse, Remember I know how Dessie Stone Records got funded."

"Then you know what happen to my two best friends."

"It's not like that, Free, something came up. They say scared money don't make money," Bullet said.

"I raised you, I don't want you going that route. Money isn't everything" "It's your day and we out here fussing.

Enjoy the gift, let's get back to the party." Chuckie put on the watch. "This does fit a President don't it?"

"We gone have to upgrade once you take the chairman seat from Big Jim." Bullet palmed Chuckie's head.

"That'll be the day," Chuckie said.

San Francisco, California. March 2000

Big Jim steadied the Mossberg 12-gauge shotgun while four bloodhounds sniffed through the woods of Northern California. The orange reflectors on Morrison's vest warned off other hunters in the 2700-acre forest. Two belts of shotgun ammunition crisscrossed his chest. A snapback cap with "shoot to kill" framed in bull's eye covered Jim's head. The forest turned shades of orange in his wraparound Oakley shades.

"Get going, Charlie. The hounds are on the trail." Chuckie was bent over, hands on kneecaps.

"Go ahead, I'll be right here." Big Jim doubled back, picking up Chuckie's rifle off the ground.

"First rule in hunting, stay armed at all times."

"That thing weights at least ten pounds." Chuckie anticipated the hunting trip would be a disaster. A city boy hunting deer in the woods of California. Big Jim insisted on going hunting and nobody told Big Jim to go fuck himself. Big Jim whistled out and the hounds sprinted back to their master.

"You want to call it quits, Charlie?"

"Yes, yes," Chuckie said, moving his head up and down.

"We hiked at least four miles in this forest. I got mosquito bites over my arms. I live in a penthouse. I'm not cut out for this shit."

"Alright, let's had back to the castle." Big Jim turned the Mossberg on a bloodhound. The shotgun blast levitated the dog six feet.

"My record still stands. Now we can leave, Charlie." Chuckie had already passed out.

The stone castle towered over the forest, overseeing thousands of acres of government land off-limits to the public. The property named Pearl Grove looked camouflage under San Francisco's fog. It was a secret resort for the Priory of Scion.

Big Jim forked at the chunks of lumber burning in the fireplace. The sparks danced off the wood turning to ash on the navy blue carpet. A warm washrag was on Chuckie's head, he asked, "What's this room called?" "The leather room, hence the entire room is decorated in Italian leather. It's the second largest room in the castle. The largest is the dark room located under the great lounge. The dark room is the superior general's office." Big Jim served cups of coffee on small porcelain saucers. "This shit is too deep to comprehend." Chuckie blew at the steaming cup.

"You saying a small group of people run the world from this bad ass castle?"

"We run the world, not from this particular castle. We have castles that would put this one to shame."

"This some James Bond shit and not Roger Moore James Bond. I'm talking Sean Connery, original 007," Chuckie said. Big Jim unbuckled the belt of shotgun shells.

"It's things I can tell you that will send you to an asylum."

"Who killed the Notorious B.I.G?" One of Chuckie's eyebrows overlapped the other.

"That's minor stuff, the Watchers don't get involved in small stuff. I can tell you who killed President Kennedy. The conspiracy theorists will say the mob but we killed Kennedy. The presidency ballooned John's head. He forgot who really ran the show."

"Why me?

"Because your name came up. The lodge wants you, Charlie. Think of the possibilities. You'll accumulate enough wealth to last your family ten generations." Chuckie envisioned living in a castle half the size of Pearl Grove.

"The power we have is endless. Can you imagine telling a king what to do?"

"Martin Luther the only king I knew," Chuckie replied. "We killed King too."

"A good man like Brother Martin." Big Jim kicked a boot off.

"King screwed half the females on the church's congregation," Jim said, rubbing at the dead skin between his toes.

"Killed the Reverend for some pussy?"

"We killed King because he preached world peace. That's against our agenda. The Watchers use war to instill fear in the masses. Fear is the greatest form of control."

"You're right about that," Chuckie said.

"You made C.I.M.G more money than anybody else in the last six years. This is my reward, a lifetime of security." Chuckie punched the springs to a gold pen.

"Where do I sign?"

"It isn't that simple, Charlie, with anything worth having, you have to give up something to get it."

"Oh, you want some money. I left my check book in my luggage." "We don't want your money."

"What do you want?" Chuckie asked. "A blood sacrifice."

"What you got a blood lab in one of these big ass rooms", call it the "blood room?" Big Jim wasn't amused.

"I'm talking a human sacrifice, Charlie. To become a scion, you have to sacrifice someone you love." Chuckie wasn't laughing now either. "You're not joking, are you?"

"What's a life for a lifetime of happiness? It's a hundred dollar down payment on a Lamborghini. It's a win-win situation," Big Jim said.

"Who is it?" Chuckie asked, tired of beating around the bush. Big Jim turned to the fireplace.

"It's Claire."

Chuckie jerked quickly right, then left. "What?!?!"

"I know Scions that killed their own mothers to join the lodge. Claire's not your flesh and blood."

"She's my wife!" Chuckie screamed.

"Get a new wife. Charlie, this is the biggest opportunity you'll have in this lifetime. Don't let your love for Claire fuck it up."

"I'ma act like I didn't hear you say that, Jim. I'll be in my room packed and ready to go!" The doors slammed.

"He knows too much for a civilian." Big Jim ate green grapes from a wooden bowl in the dark room. Peter Rothkid sharpened the poniard's blade on a smooth block of stone.

"It's always those who can't part with a loved one even if you offer them immortality," Rothkid said.

"We can have our people at Langley dispose of Charlie. Have it look like a motorcycle accident?"

"It's two ways to skin a cat, we leave Freemen alone. When the time's right, I'll call Rupert over at the New York

Post. In a few years, Charles Freeman, shining star, will fade to black," Rothkid said.

CHAPTER 12

Monaco, coast of France. June 2007, 7 Years Later

The white Azzura berthed on the Mediterranean Sea cost Chuckie $3 million. It used to be a nuisance paying that big a bill but a swipe of his American Express Black Card transferred ownership of the fifty-seven footer. The Azzura in the U.S. commanded attention from yacht lovers but in Monaco on France's Mediterranean coast, 150 footers were the main attraction. A group of bikini-clad blondes tanned on the sun deck. The gold bottles of Louis Roderer's Cristal littered the upper deck. Chuckie roamed topless in bright yellow Nautica swim trunks, three platinum and diamond necklaces banged against each other on his neck. The priciest designed by Jacob & Co. contained 224 Asher-cut diamonds.

"Anybody see Mickey," Chuckie asked. Another blonde hand-chopped Matty's hairy back.

"Mickey's in bed. He doesn't know how to enjoy a vacation." Matty's voice vibrated from the massage. The two bedrooms down in the lower deck came with personal bathrooms. Chuckie opened the lock with a card key.

"Hi, Chuckie."

"On a yacht in the South of France is where you sleep the days away." Chuckie turned on the TV.

"I ate prison food for eighteen years. Forgive me if my stomach doesn't agree with the sushi." Mickey said. Chuckie smelled the vomit in the waste bin.

"I'll have my butler change the trash."

"I'm forty-nine, fucking body is breaking down," Mickey said. Chuckie sprayed the air freshener.

"Speak for yourself, I'm forty-nine and in the best shape of my life." Chuckie picked up a DVD off the mini fridge. Mickey's blonde hair went gray at the wings. He put on a blue and yellow shirt, left it unbuttoned, his potbelly on display.

"I'm violating my parole. I'm not supposed to leave New York and I'm in Paris."

"Monaco," Chuckie said.

"Whatever, damn private jets fly you everywhere you don't want to go" "Where'd you get this?" Chuckie held up the DVD.

"The hotel in Monte Carlo, a kid gave it to me." "The Hotel de Paris?" Chuckie asked.

"That's it." The "Crack" DVD provided a gritty insight into urban street culture. The DVD documented exclusive interviews, infamous rap battles and upcoming music artists. Chuckie put the compact disc in the DVD player and skipped to the fourth scene.

"It's your boy, Bullet, reporting live from Third Avenue in the Bronx." The camera focused on the street sign.

"Isn't that the kid used to follow us around?" Mickey asked.

"People asking what up with Bullet. What he doing? I'm in the streets. I'm not on MTV shaking my ass for record sales. I'm in the mix 365." Bullet posed next to hardened criminals. "Critics say you're the Sour Boy that fell off. Bino's is on everybody's top five greatest rappers list. Floss is producing hits worldwide," the interviewer said.

Bullet directed the camera to the 2007 Bentley Continental GTC. "I'm pushing a Bentley. That's falling off? Pop the trunk." The camera zoomed to the back of the coupe.

"You see that? Two hundred thousand cash, that's light. Yesterday I had half a million in this car." The sunrays shined on Bullets' platinum and diamond Cartier watch.

"That's another hundred thousand on my wrist. This isn't industry money; this is in the streets money."

"They should wear signs saying we're drug dealers," Mickey said. Chuckie pressed pause on the DVD remote.

"I put all my time and energy into that boy. He ain't nothing but a knucklehead."

"If he's selling drugs after being around us, he deserves what's coming. Smart people learn from other people's mistakes." Life's experiences tamed the wild beast in Mickey Tansy. The twenty-year sentence broke Mickey down. Mickey lost the killer instinct.

"When are we leaving? I have to water my plants." Mickey turned Chuckie's old Madison Avenue penthouse into a horticultural experiment.

"That's why you have a maid. Let Susan water the plants." Chuckie threw an ace of spades playing card over Eddie's king of the same suit.

"Susan's a retard I should've fired a month ago." Mickey collected the book.

"Everywhere we go, you're spoiling the party," Eddie said tossing out a 7 of clubs.

"That's a fucking lie," Mickey said.

"It's the truth. In Brazil, you complained about your allergies. In London, it rained too much. In France, it's the food." Matty beat Mickey's deuce with a joker. The umbrella in Matty's drink was a mini to the one blocking the sun from the card game.

"I have food poisoning and I'm playing cards on the ocean. I should be in bed."

"You're a broken record Mick, Chuckie gives you $25 million dollars and the keys to a Manhattan penthouse and you're only happy when you're watering tulips," Eddie said.

"You do a punk ass dime and think you can get off telling me what to do?" Mickey collected another book.

"At least I came home with my balls, more than what I can say for some people." Mickey threw the cards in Eddie's face.

"Ah, what the fuck!" Chuckie screamed, pushing Mickey from the game. The wind blew most of the playing cards overboard.

"That's the old Mickey I know." Matty chuckled.

"Bullshit, the old Mickey would've killed that rat bastard Jackie!!" Eddie said, rolling away.

Manhattan, NYC 3 Months Later

A slender Latino waited in the two-man phone booth on 28th Street and Second Avenue. Josh Stevenson unhooked the telephone in the unoccupied booth; Josh faced a Starbucks coffee shop. The Latino kept his back to the sidewalk.

"Who is he?" The Latino asked.

"Mickey Tansy, recently released from a twenty-year prison term." Josh passed a manila envelope under the booth.

"This is some 4X6 photos of Tansy."

"What's Tansy's relationship with Charles Freeman?"

"I haven't dug that deep but Mickey Tansy used to be a heavyweight on the Westside," Josh told the private investigator.

"He's a fighter?"

"No, Tansy's a drug-dealer. Got rich dealing cocaine in the 80s." Josh turned into the booth when two cops exited the Starbucks.

"Tansy lives in Freeman's penthouse on Madison Avenue. He's a homebody, buys lots of gardener equipment." "Anything else?" The Latino asked.

"The government confiscated Tansy's cash but he's spending money, lots of it. It's Freeman's money. The two are inseparable. That's why it's vital you dig out the connection."

"In a week, I'll have all the pieces," the P.I. said.

"A week is all you got, and if the shit lands on Charlie Free, you got a hefty bonus too,"

Englewood Cliffs, N.J. Chuckie's Mansion, Four Days Later

The police had the house sealed off with yellow caution tape. The call came forty minutes earlier; somebody burglarized Chuckie's home. Chuckie and Claire flew to Miami that morning to celebrate their anniversary. Chuckie called Mickey personally, saying his seventeen-year-old daughter was home alone. Mickey stepped out the smoke gray Aston Martin DB9 Volante. A group of cops huddled on the lawn helping themselves to a box of Dunkin Donuts. Mickey walked twenty feet from the officers, then limboed the yellow tape.

"Excuse me, sir!" a patrol officer screamed.

Always a damn witness, that's why I'm retired, Mickey thought. "

Mickey started sprinting to the teary-faced teenager, with the patrolman in a close second. Two detectives reached for holsters, seeing the two men running in their direction.

"He's a trespasser!" screamed the patrolman.

"It's okay, he's family," Mia said, stepping forward.

"Are you sure?" the patrolman asked, wanting to repay Mickey for the chase with a bullet.

"I'm positive. He's my father's best friend." Mickey resisted the urge to stick his tongue out at the patrolman.

"Next time, show my tape some fucking respect." The patrolman walked away. A black cop wearing a beige suit introduced himself as Detective Reed.

"It's a standard burglary. The thief encountered the young lady and ran off," Detective Reed said, giving Mickey a firm handshake.

"He looked Spanish, but I'm not sure. I locked myself in my room, I thought he wanted to kill me," cried Mia.

"He escaped over the back gate. The surveillance camera didn't pick up any good footage. He knew all the camera angles." Detective Reed led them inside.

"The young lady told us her parents flew to Miami this morning. I'm guessing the burglar knew about the vacation and planned according to the house being empty. That's why when he encountered the young lady, he aborted the heist. She scared the burglar more than he scared her." Detective Reed stopped by the shell-shaped staircase.

"The burglar has to be somebody associated to Chuckie, if they know about his anniversary," Mickey said.

"Exactly, or one of Mr. Freeman's associates employed the burglar." Mickey surveyed the house.

"What did he steal?"

"That's the puzzler. There's ledgers missing from Mr. Freeman's office.

Other than that, nothing." Detective Reed shrugged.

"You didn't hear any loud noises?" Mickey asked Mia. "No, I was listening to Lil Wayne on my iPod." "Little who?" Mickey said.

"I recently took my sixteen-year-old to the guy's concert," Detective Reed confessed.

"Why steal worthless ledgers and leave a watch collection worth millions," Asked Mickey.

"That's what my men are working on. Does Mr. Freeman have any known enemies in the music business?"

"I wouldn't know. I'm just coming back around." "What's your name?" Detective Reed asked.

"Mark Raymond." The detective looked from Mia to Mickey.

"Ok, whatever. The burglar stole Mr. Freeman's financial ledgers from years dated 1987 to 1989." The years registered in Mickey's memory.

"Holy shit," he said.

Madison Ave, Manhattan. One Week Later, Mickey's Penthouse

"Why steal those books?" Mickey questioned, curling a dumbbell. "Coincidence, maybe the burglar heard Mia and snatched the first thing in sight," Chuckie said, running uphill on a treadmill.

"My drug money started Dessie Stone Records. Those ledgers can prove it and you're not concerned?"

Chuckie hit the pause button on the treadmill.

"What about your reputation? This hits the newspapers, it'll destroy everything." A loud clap from a thunderstorm rocked the penthouse. Chuckie rested on the weight bench, raindrops rained against Mickey's glass fortress. The weather outside fitted Chuckie, dark and damp. In public, he appeared unfazed by recent events, but he'd fallen to pieces. The burglary sparkplugged a series of suspicions and Big Jim was at the center, for years Chuckie lived in fear of retribution from the Watchers.

"I fought hard to protect my family and my empire. They found my Achilles heel. There's some major shit going down and I know too much about it. I'm marked for death," Chuckie said.

"Who marked you for death?" Mickey asked.

"Jim Morrison, the head of C.I.M.G," Mickey laughed. "You're scared of that square?"

"Big Jim's a part of a secret society, they've killed presidents. Imagine what they'll do to us." Chuckie stared in space.

"Secret society? Next, you're sighting UFOs. Those young rappers are fucking you up."

"It exists. I swear on my Uncle Steve." Mickey knew Chuckie wouldn't lie on Uncle Steve.

"Those people really exist."

"They offered me a percentage in an oil company worth $250 million."

"Why didn't you take it, stupid!!!?" Mickey yelled.

"They wanted to kill Claire!!" Susan busted in the weight room. "You call, Mr. Mickey?"

"No, I'm talking to Chuckie," Mickey said.

"Yes, you screamed Susan. I heard you from the kitchen. What do you want?" Mickey exhaled loudly.

"We're out of Ben & Jerry's ice creams. Can you go to the grocery store?"

"Sure, Mr. Mickey."

"She's worse than having a wife," Mickey said when Susan left. "She's eager to please. That's all."

"They wanted to kill Claire?" Mickey continued.

"I love Claire more than I love myself. No way could I do it." "Damn, we're talking $250 million."

"How do you sound, Claire's my wife," Chuckie said.

"Let's say, hypothetically speaking, three years down the line, we find out Claire's fucking the mailman. What would you do?" Mickey asked.

"Kill her."

"Claire's dead and you're out of $250 million." "Mickey!!!"

"You know those years in prison fucked me up. You did the right thing, standing up for Claire."

"If Big Jim has those ledgers, I'm dead. My career, my contacts, twenty-five years of work, gone," Chuckie said.

"We're old Chuckie. We lived our lives. Let's sail off in the Azzura, buy a fucking island. They can shame us but they can't touch us," Mickey said.

CHAPTER 13

Central Park Zoo, NYC. October 2007

It's written in stone. Freeman's company started from unaccountable income. I'm betting 10 to 1, it's Mickey Tansy's drug cash." Big Jim thumbed Mickey's photo.

"We have to prove it. These files are twenty years old. More than enough time to let the dope money drip dry." Josh closed the ledgers on Tansy's pictures.

"How do we know Freeman's not laundering drug money right now?" "Give Charlie some credit, he's no idiot," Josh said.

Big Jim bit a red candy apple and said, "He has to be going nuts over these missing ledgers." The pair leisurely strolled the Central Park Zoo. "Once Rupert at the New York Post gets this, it's the end of Charlie Free, the music industry will blackball him," Morrison's teeth crushed the candy apple coating.

"Let's hold off on giving this to the press," Josh recommended.

"We have to destroy Charlie ASAP. He's a snake. I'm not letting Freeman slither out of this pit." The cream Calvin Klein collection suit with the Brunello Cucinelli pocket square fit the chairman snugly. His height bewildered the zoo's children more than the glass specimens.

"It's too early. More research on Tansy won't hurt. It gives us a better perspective on who we're dealing with."

"We're dealing with street scum and his black friend who created a record company off of other people's misery. It's great press if I say so myself," Big Jim smiled narcissistically. Josh was a foot shorter than Big Jim. A pulled hamstring from a tennis match had him limping on a cane. His black Masion Martin Margiela cardigan shadowed a Ralph Lauren Black Label t-shirt. The bad condition of Josh's New Balance sneakers deterred a spectator from believing the black Maybach sedan at the park's entrance belonged to him.

"We can crush Charlie Free completely but it'll take some time." Big Jim's breath fogged the glass enclosing the sea lions.

"How?" he asked.

"Charlie has an associate that's getting lots of attention from the wrong people."

Big Jim jumped shot the candy apple, missing the garbage by three feet. They settled on a secluded bench by a map of the zoo.

"This associate is under investigation by various government law enforcement agencies. I think he'll connect the dots to annihilate Charlie Free. We'll pull some strings with the deputy director at Langley, tell him to put more pressure on this associate," Josh suggested.

"Pressure busts pipes." Big Jim shimmied.

Bronx, NY. 9 ½ Weeks Later

Bullet exited his Bentley on a drug-infested block, opening a log cabin umbrella to shield his mink jacket from the drizzle. He leaped over a cracked curb onto a front lawn entrenched in garbage. A rusty gray 87 Buick rested on four cinderblocks in the lawn. The windows to the house were boarded and highlighted with gang graffiti. Bullet climbed the unsteady stairs to the porch. On cue, the wooden plank blocking the entrance moved to the right. The doorman wore a black durag and dark sunglasses in the candle lit house. He holstered a six-shot revolver and greeted Bullet.

"Sup, homeboy." Three pit bulls chained to the stairwell choked themselves fighting for freedom or a chance to tear Bullet to shreds.

"Where's Jay?" Bullet asked.

"He be be be in the living room," the man stuttered, kicking a leg to finish the sentence. Bullet sidestepped the caked dog shit on the floor panels. In the living room, there were three more armed men with guns and blinded by dark shades. A group of females wearing nothing but panties and handkerchiefs cut up pounds of cocaine on the mixing table. Bullet hired females from his housing projects and paid them a hundred bucks an hour. A twelve-hour shift at the mixing table netted the woman $1200, not bad for a night's work.

"Where's Jay at?" A female pointed a latex hand at the bathroom. Bullet pushed in catching Jay pants down stroking a cutting girl over the sink.

"Oh shit," Jay said, pulling out the chocolate cutie. The female nonchalantly pulled up her panties and went back to her duties at the mixing table.

"This how you handle business, playboy?" "Nah, bro, I needed some downtime." "Downtime," Bullet repeated.

"I got carried away all this ass and coke," Jay said, choosing honesty as his best policy. Bullet went back to the mixing table.

"We almost finished, Sour Boy, I'm working these hoes like mules." "I can tell," Bullet examined a kilo stamped with a red chicken. "We got to be ready tonight, my big spenders are coming in from Pittsburgh." A loud bang cut the convo. The pit bulls barked and Stutter Man screamed, "5, 5, 5 O raiding the spot!" The room panicked. Bullet and Jay ran to a cozy room in the back where the girls sometimes slept.

"Help me kick this board off the window," Jay said. They kicked until it snapped in half. Bullet jumped out the window, a firm hand grabbed his mink jacket.

"Move in, I'll shoot!"

The deputy director at the Central Intelligence Agency observed Bullet behind a one-way mirror. The rap star turned drug czar recanted many statements during his interrogation. The evidence was overwhelming. A bullpen full of robed women fingered Bullet as their boss.

"Who's in charge? Cause you got the wrong man. I stopped at the house to buy some weed." Bullet jerked the handcuffs.

"Save it for the jury. You pissed somebody off, the CIA is here."

The Deputy Director entered the interrogation room. The cops cleared out.

"I'm Robert Laughlin, Deputy Director of the CIA."

"I bought some weed. I don't have nothing to do with them drugs in that house." Laughlin had a drip of sweat on the tip of his nose that refused to fall.

"I don't care if you're innocent or not. I'm here because you're on my radar."

Bullet thought back to flossing on "The Crack" DVD.

"How did I get on your radar? The C.I.A watch street DVDs?" "Charles Freeman put you on my radar." The name stunned Bullet. "What? Charles Free?"

"You play Monopoly. Heard of the Get out of Jail Free card?" Laughlin said.

"Charlie Free showed me the game."

"The past four years your South Bronx drug ring dealt five hundred kilos of cocaine." A fact Bullet couldn't dispute.

"That's a lot of cocaine. Do you know how much time you get for five hundred kilos?"

"Charlie Free don't deal drugs," Bullet said.

"We don't want Freeman for drugs. We want Charles for laundering Mickey Tansy's drug money."

"That's ancient history."

"An important person wants history dug from the earth." Bullet's wrists reddened from the tight restraints.

"I'm not Indiana Jones. I can't lead you to the lost treasures," Bullet said.

"No but you can tie Freeman and Tansy up by testifying Freeman continued to launder Tansy's drug money up until the early 2000s," Laughlin said.

"But Charlie's clean, been so for the past twenty years."

"We'll do some addition, Charles Freeman gets away with laundering drug money, and Bullet does life without parole for engaging in a continuing criminal enterprise. Let's do subtraction, Charles Freeman gets convicted of laundering drug money, Bullet gets ten years."

Bullet did the division.

"Ten years, that's your word."

Paramus Mall, Paramus N.J. December 2007

"I have to try this on, Mr. Mickey." Susan held a yellow dress up to her breast. "Hold my purse, I'll be back."

Mickey's objections fell on deaf ears. Susan ran into the dressing room. They were shopping for a Christmas tree because Susan insisted on celebrating the holidays. Three hours roaming the mall with Susan, Mickey wanted to punt her purse over the mall's artificial waterfall.

"Don't get upset, you'll get used to it," said an old man holding a purse. "You're a newlywed?" he asked.

"I'm not married," Mickey said.

"And you're already babysitting the purse. She has her hooks in you." "She's my maid. I'm not in a relationship," Mickey explained. "Whatever, buddy," the old man laughed.

"Seriously."

"I believe you," the man said sarcastically.

"Fuck you!" Mickey screamed, hitting the man with Susan's purse. "I don't have time for this shit." Mickey rode up the escalators.

Later That Evening

"Why haven't you reached out sooner?" Enrique asked. "Setting my affairs straight took a bit longer than expected."

Enrique's butler was a Chinese body builder who adopted the name Carlos while in Mexico. Carlos' loyalty to Enrique made the 7th degree black belt grunt at anything that stole El Ingeniero's affection. The happiness in Enrique's voice had the slanted eye warrior growling at the phone.

"They say absence makes the heart grow fonder. I tell my children how much I miss my good friend Mickey." Enrique's two daughters bathed in a hot tub inside the manmade cave.

"Twenty years of absence but the nightmare is over."

"Pleasant dreams are now our reality, are we back in business?" Enrique asked.

"I'm retired. An old investment paid off big dividends." Mickey said.

"I'm glad you're prosperous. Come to Tijuana. I want to show you my beautiful country."

"Soon, I'm in need of a favor, El Ingeniero. My friend is having a problem. A certain individual, he claims to be very powerful, is jeopardizing my investment."

The roars in the background were Enrique's pet panthers, not Carlos. "I'll check him out. Do you have a name?" Mickey unfolded a small paper. "James Morrison AKA Big Jim."

"I'll have his life story in the morning."

"Thanks, Enrique. I'll call tomorrow," Mickey said.

"One last thing, I thought you might want it. I have the address to your Informant, Jackie Ward." The phone went silent.

"Hello, hello? Mickey!" The dial tone answered.

Chrysler Building, 31st Floor, Dessie Stone Offices

"The record business is going to hell, music sales plummeted from $14.6 billion at its peak down to $6.3 billion this year," said Dessie Stone Records President, Bino.

"It's the illegal downloading but can you blame the people. It's a recession. Everybody is broke," Said Lala, the Vice President. The Dessie Stone executives crammed the conference room to debate why consumers illegally downloaded more music than they actually purchased. The digital age had record labels everywhere, feeling the crunch. The labels resorted to budget cuts, leaving unestablished artist contracts in the dust. "Every song that's downloaded should be purchased. We have to find a way to regulate this piracy. That's my homework assignment for you guys over the weekend. On Monday morning, we'll meet back here and swap ideas," Chuckie said. The executives gathered their notepads and bottled waters.

"Plans for the weekend?" Bino asked when the conference room cleared out.

"A guest appearance on a late-night radio show. I haven't started my Christmas shopping," Chuckie said.

"Smack a few hundreds in a Hallmark card. That's what I do."

"Seven kids and eight baby mothers. I'll do the same thing," Chuckie laughed. "When was the last time you spoke to Bullet?"

"Last time I saw Bullet, he was acting a fool on some DVD."

"That mean you didn't hear the Alphabet Boys locked Bullet up. They say he dealt a ton of powder." Chuckie slouched back in his seat. "Some of my family members got caught up in that web."

"You, and Floss made good on the opportunity I provided you. Bullet wanted to be Tof," Chuckie said.

Bino loosened his tie.

"There's a bad apple in every bunch, Free."

"It's some distilled vodka in the cabinet. Pour some drinks," Chuckie said.

Bino filled two shot glasses.

"A toast to the fallen Sour boy," Bino said. "To my nephew, may God be with you."

The elevator doors opened, loads of federal agents waving assault rifles, ransacked Dessie Stone Records offices. The agents confiscated the company's files, computers, and CEO, Charles "Charlie Free" Freeman.

CHAPTER 14

Madison Avenue, Manhattan. December 2007

Susan slid towards a payphone on the frosty corner, her rain boots lost traction and she grasped the phone booth to keep from falling. To Susan's benefit, the horrible weather emptied the corner. If a parade of spectators had seen the blooper, she wouldn't have suffered a shade of embarrassment. Her pride was further from her thoughts than summer was from the icy city. At the kitchen sink cleaning shrimp marked the spot where the day catapulted from routine to catastrophic, the battering ram shattered her nerves along with the penthouse door. The federal agents destroyed everything Mickey paid her to upkeep. They left the penthouse in a condition similar to New Orleans after Hurricane Katrina. Susan let two quarters fall down the money slot. The cold air cringed her fingers, she mistook a two for a four and hung up. The payphone released the change, one quarter. The rigged payphone cheated her out of twenty-five cents. On the second attempt, Susan got through. "Yo," Mickey answered.

"Mr. Mickey."

He checked the cellular screen. "Where are you?"

Susan put a hand on her heart to prevent it from lunging out. At any moment, she feared a cop car would jump the curb.

"They come to the house for you, so many of them."

"Calm down, you're speaking too fast. Who's at the house?" Mickey turned down the volume on Lenny Williams' falsetto. "The police. They have a warrant for your arrest."

"A warrant for what?" Mickey asked.

"I don't know but I think they have Mr. Chuckie," Susan said frantically. "What did you tell them?"

"I no tell them nothing. I gave them the old phone number." Mickey changed prepaid cell phones every thirty days.

"I'm scared," she sobbed.

"Go to your mother's house. When I get things figured out, I'll send for you."

"But, what about you, Mr. Mickey?"

Moments like this was why Mickey regretted not keeping their relationship strictly business.

"Do what I say!" He flung the cell phone on the expressway. The Aston Martin maxed out at over 200 mph. Mickey leaned on the gas paddle opening up the V8 engine. He checked for the watchful eye in the sky. A helicopter tracking his movements. Matty's house was two exits away, the last place he wanted to bring the heat.

Westchester, N.Y.

Mickey loaned Matty the money to buy a house in Westchester, N.Y. He didn't expect to get reimbursed and Matty had no intentions of paying the money back. The DB9 crawled the shoveled driveway to Matty's shed.

Mickey left the car running, knocking on a "no women allowed" sign. Matty opened the shed.

"Hurry up, don't let the cold air in." Two small heaters faced a Lazy Boy recliner. A wooden picnic table stretched wall to wall. An iron stove cornered a Whirlpool refrigerator. *The Last Supper* hung above the picnic table.

"The Feds raided my penthouse." Mickey searched the fridge for a cold beer.

"Oh yeah, why'd you come here?" Matty asked, dusting off the recliner's cushion.

"Serious, Susan called my phone on the verge of a breakdown. I think the Feds arrested Chuckie." Mickey bit open a Heineken.

"What the fuck did you do?" Matty asked. "It's a long story" Mickey said.

"You're a fucking saint these days. Why are they bothering you?" Matty asked protectively.

"I spent twenty-nine years of my life in jail. I'm not going back, not for one hour."

"How did they get Chuckie?"

"Chuckie's not the hardest person to find. Who doesn't know he's at the Chrysler Building every day of the week?"

Mickey peeped at the Aston Martin in the driveway.

"I have to get moving. How much cash do you have on you?" Matty opened a tin toolbox.

"Forty grand, used to be fifty but Mary stole ten thousand, my own wife." Mickey emptied the toolbox faster than a pickpocket.

"What's your next move?"

"Tonight a motel until the banks open and I can get to my safe deposit boxes." Mickey's plan formulated with every word.

"Once I get my money, I'm going to Mexico." "I'm going with you."

"This isn't your beef, Matty." "Like hell it isn't."

"What about Mary and this new house?" Mickey asked.

"Fuck this shit, Mary is a trooper. She'll be fine. We'll leave Eddie some money to handle things." Matty grabbed his .45 caliber pistol out the toolbox.

"There's no coming back, no more barbeques with the grandkids." "The boredom is killing me, Mickey. I'm addicted to the action," Matty said.

"Fuck it, come on."

The Chrysler Building, Later That Evening

"Mr. Morrison, any comment on Charles Freeman's arrest?" a reporter asked, pushing through the press mob outside the Chrysler Building.

"It's a tragedy when a person so talented resorts to that magnitude of bad decision-making," Big Jim said.

"Will Mr. Freeman remain the president of C.I.M.G, pending the outcome of the indictment?" another reporter asked.

"The board of directors and myself found it in the company's best interest to terminate Mr. Freeman's contract. I say again it's a tragedy. I lost a business associate and a close friend."

The reporters boxed in Big Jim's limo.

"Charles Freeman is innocent until proven guilty. Doesn't it seem harsh to abandon a business associate and close friend? The ink hasn't dried on the indictment yet," said the kinky-haired mulatto reporting for an independent network.

"That's enough questions for today. Mr. Morrison has an extra workload," Josh said. The chauffer swirled the limousine around the crowd.

"Great job. You were remorseful and that's the key. We don't want to come off basking in Freeman's misfortune," Josh said.

"I wanted to strangle that little jerk off."

"I'll call the networks, get that creep edited in time for the six o'clock news." The limo drove downtown.

"We have an hour before the press conference." Big Jim looked at his Vacheron Constantine wristwatch.

"It's two scheduled for tonight. The more press coverage this arrest draws; the more tainted Charles' name becomes."

"The credit belongs to you, Josh, the mastermind," Big Jim said. "The fat lady hasn't sung yet; Mickey Tansy has gone under the radar." "Tansy won't get far. He's got nowhere to run. Their bank accounts are frozen." Big Jim inhaled the scent of victory. "Can you hear that? It's the fat lady singing loud and clear."

They ditched the Aston Martin for Matty's Honda Accord. Matty found a cheap motel room on New Jersey's Route 4 since his mugshot wasn't on the evening news. He also fetched dinner, two cups of coffee, and eight chili hot dogs from an On-The-Run gas station. Chuckie's arrest made the evening's news coverage. The newsreels showed Chuckie leaving the Chrysler Building in handcuffs.

"The Chase Bank on the Avenue of the Americas is where my safe deposit boxes are. We'll buy some cheap luggage and load it up with cash," Mickey said.

Avenue of the Americas, Manhattan. Chase Bank

Whenever Mickey entered a bank, his natural instinct was to scream, "Everybody on the ground, it's a fucking hold up!" He kicked cocaine cold turkey but the adrenaline high generated from armed robbery couldn't be rehabilitated. Two bank tellers readied their stations for transactions. Mickey let an old woman win the race to the tellers, nobody remembered the second customer of the day. Mickey hadn't robbed a bank in thirty years but naturally he cased the bank. On the inside it seemed sweet, but the bank's location was its best protection. A security guard banged on a coffeemaker. A Glock pistol in his holster, the guard wasn't older than Twenty-five, probably never fired the gun. The bank's custodian waxed the floor. The way he handled the buffing machine, Mickey was sure he wasn't an undercover agent. A young woman wearing old ladies' perfume escorted Mickey to the safe deposit boxes. Mickey gave her his state identification and prayed she went out on a date last night. The way that perfume smelled, he seriously doubted it. The women read the I.D. card and didn't blink. She verified Mickey's name with the deposit box. Mickey and the young woman stuck their keys in simultaneously, pulling the box from the wall.

"Can I help you with anything else, Mr. Tansy?"

"Yes, a quiet place so I can get my things in order." Mickey avoided her eyes. The woman wasn't offended.

"Right this way, Mr. Tansy." She led Mickey to a room the size of a large closet. Mickey opened the safe deposit box. A passport with a photo of him read the name Mark Raymond. Mickey zipped open one of the duffel bags with "I Love NY" stitched on the side. He bought two for fifteen bucks from a Korean in Times Square. Mickey put the passport in the inside pocket of his parka. He picked up a clear zip lock bag from the box. It contained the .32 revolver Tom had given him and the Rolex he'd given Chuckie. Mickey put on the Rolex and put the revolver in the parka's front pocket. The cash was wrapped neatly in ten thousand dollar stacks. Mickey filled both duffel bags. It still wasn't enough to empty the deposit box. The rest of the cash would have to stay. Mickey locked his driver license inside the safety deposit box. From now on, Mickey Tansy no longer existed. He was Mark Raymond. Mickey passed one duffle bag to Matty outside the bank.

"Any problems?" Matty asked as they sped up the street.

"Wasn't enough space to fit all the cash," Mickey said, holding the shoulder straps to the duffle bag.

"Everything's a go. Enrique's waiting at the flight school. Eddie's at the motel." Mickey spotted two cop cars, a blue and white, and an unmarked Plymouth.

"Good, where's the car?" Matty unlocked the door with the remote key.

"You just passed it."

That Afternoon, Newark, New Jersey, December 2007

The Newark flight school trained wannabe pilots how to fly aircrafts. It taught an Al Qaeda suicide bomber how to fly a Boeing 767 into the World Trade Center. The flight school also served as a drop point for the Tijuana cartel's cocaine. The cartel owned a private hanger on the school's property. The hanger housed nine aircrafts, from single passenger planes to Gulfstream jets. A short mechanic with oil stains on a beige uniform transported Mickey and Matty threw the hanger on a golf cart. He drove recklessly narrowly avoiding two collisions. When he parked, Matty wanted to gun butt the son of a bitch. Enrique appeared from behind a Gulfstream 350 with Carlos.

"There goes the man of the hour." Mickey embraced Enrique until his bodyguard made an uncomfortable noise.

"Matty, you lost weight." Enrique patted Matty's belly. Matty was actually much heavier but accepted the compliment.

"Got to take care of yourself." Matty smiled. The salt & pepper goatee seemed to be the only sign of aging on Enrique.

"My pilot is waiting. My personal's chef 's on board." Enrique took a whiff of air and kissed his fingertips. "The food is incredible."

100 Centre Street, Manhattan December 2007

Chuckie read the New York Post in Bino's Audi. He avoided the news during the two-day lock up. Chuckie avoided everything except the floor, the one thing he wasn't afraid to stare at. On the 55th hour, Claire's parents posted the seven-figure bail.

"Two days in a row, you're on the front page. The media's not letting this shit die down." Bino signaled for the right lane. The headlines read "Barely Free," a deliberate shot at the bailout and Chuckie's moniker. A photo of Chuckie and Mickey illustrated the front page.

"I'm dressed like a dealer," Chuckie commented scratching at his day- old beard. He wanted a hot shower and a razor. A toothbrush and some Colgate.

"They shut us down, we can't get access to the office. There's a cop on duty 24/7 kicking people off the 31st floor."

Bino hit the horn with his hand for a daring taxi.

"The projects we were working on are dead, marked as evidence," Chuckie read in the article, the C.I.M.G presidency had been stripped from him.

"Dessie Stone is the last thing on my mind. I'm not trying to relive what I went through these past two days."

"Freedom is first and foremost but what we built is in shambles. All I know is Dessie Stone Records, I've been signed since sixteen." Bino hit the horn again now for a cowboy driver.

"Bullet says I laundered money, they froze my accounts. I'm fighting to stay in Englewood Cliffs and if I lose this case, the mansion is gone too."

"What did Deluca say?"

"If the jury believes Bullet, I'm going to prison. I have no criminal history, no problems with the law. That doesn't mean shit," Chuckie said.

CHAPTER 15

Worth St, Manhattan. January 2008

The law offices of Blake, Deluca, and Kerr employed seventy associates. The firm was a pebble compared to the other colossal law firms in New York. What set Blake, Deluca, and Kerr apart was the firm's co-founder Gary Deluca. The famous litigator defended cop killers, mob bosses, and Wall Street tycoons. A client's race, creed, or profession didn't matter. If they wrote the check, Deluca worked 100-hour weeks. The hip-hop police hand delivered Deluca plenty of clients. The N.Y.P.D unit designed to target rappers, often broke the law to enforce it. The harassed rap stars sought Deluca's counsel. The hip-hop police despised Deluca, hip-hop artist gave him shout-out on rap records.

"Can I get you some orange juice, a donut?" Deluca offered. Chuckie opted for the O.J. The firm secretly called Deluca's office organized mess, files spilled out cabinets, and papers were scattered every which way but if you asked Deluca for a specific case, he'd have it in seconds. Deluca gave Chuckie a bottled Tropicana orange juice, Chuckie wouldn't have accepted it any other way.

"It'll be awfully difficult to convince a jury you're not guilty with such a close associate testifying against you, but it's not impossible. The Feds cut a deal with a guy who dealt five hundred kilos to indict you on money laundering. It's setting free a murderer to get a petty thief!" Deluca spoke with passion, Chuckie loved it.

"What can you do, Gary?" Chuckie asked.

"I can't guarantee victory, but I'll work my ass off. It'll be a plus if Mickey Tansy surrendered to authorities."

"Innocent or not, Mickey's not turning himself in," Chuckie said. "Mickey on the run makes you look guilty. I'm not worried about fighting your case in the courtroom. It's what's going on outside the courtroom that has me worried," Deluca said.

Federal Courtroom, 224 Days Later

The majority of the courtroom pews were filled with members of the press. The rest, family, friends, and enemies of Charles Freeman. A youth being squashed in the last pew was neither friend nor foe to the defendant. The youth sat blessed with the fortune of this being his first-ever court appearance. An incredible feat because most African American youths were being stagnated by the modern day Jim Crow, mass incarceration. A guardian angel guided the youth from cops determined to get every black male fingerprinted. When the youth's mother smoked up the money for back-to-school shopping, his guardian angel took him shopping. When he ran away from home, the angel scoured the mean streets for him. The youth smirked, reminiscing. His cell phone vibrated but there wasn't enough room to answer it. He rather a missed call than a missed seat. The courtroom played a silent version of musical chairs. If anybody read the city's newspapers, they might've recognized the youth from the sports section. The 36 points he scored on Boys & Girls high school to lead Lincoln to back-to-back PSAL titles, his commitment to St. John's University. The youth came to court because he needed to see if the rumors were true. The code remained the same despite the game. "No snitching." Bullet settled in the witness stand. The youth's angel had fallen from the heavens to the depths of hell.

"State your name for the court," said Deluca approaching the witness stand. Bullet answered a few warm-up questions, then Deluca got to the goods.

"When did you meet the defendant, Charles Freeman?"

"1986." Chuckie's laser vision zeroed in on Bullet. The rapper must've felt Chuckie's disgust. He refused to acknowledge the defense table.

"What was your relationship with the defendant?" "Mr. Freeman discovered my rap group."

"Is this around the time you met Mr. Tansy?"

"I met Mr. Tansy a year later, performing at Club Gunnieboi." "Club Gunnieboi?" Deluca quizzed.

"A strip club that doubled as a hangout for drug dealers." "Did Mr. Tansy deal narcotics?"

"At the time, he was the biggest cocaine dealer in New York City." Chuckie turned to Bino in the first pew. His expression said everything. "Did Mr. Freeman deal in drugs?"

"No, but he loved spending drug money." Loud whispers buzzed inside the courtroom.

"Order in the court," yelled the Honorable Judge Renee J. White. "What was the basis of Mr. Freeman and Mr. Tansy's relationship?" "Mr. Freeman was Mr. Tansy's bagman. He laundered drug money through Dessie Stone Records, their record company," Bullet said. "How do you know this?"

"As Mr. Freeman's artist, I witnessed it. I personally transported cash from Tansy's organization to Mr. Freeman up until 2001." Chuckie broke the tip to a No. 2 pencil on a legal pad.

"Is it true you're currently in federal lock-up?" Deluca asked. "Yes," Bullet answered.

"For what?"

"848 Kingpin Statue."

Deluca read from a thick legal pamphlet, "According to federal sentencing guidelines, an 848 CCE carries a minimum of twenty years' imprisonment and a maximum of life imprisonment plus a two million dollar fine, correct?"

Bullet gestured to the U.S. Assistant District Attorney for help. "Yes, but—"

Deluca faced the jury. "Let the record reflect this testimony wasn't given voluntarily, you!" Deluca pointed to Bullet. "Sacrificed a friend, a mentor, you're a despicable dope dealer!"

"Objection!" the prosecutor screamed. Deluca kept on.

"Who isn't man enough to own up to his crimes, so you bring innocent people down with you! No further questions, Your Honor."

Tijuana, Mexico. August 2008

A photographer snapped photos of the bride in a white Alexander McQueen wedding dress. This wedding made husband number six for the Mexican beauty. The first five died under mysterious circumstances. The groom knew of the short life expectancy that came with being Isabella Vargas' spouse. There was nothing he could do, the woman asked for his hand in marriage. To say no meant execution on the spot. Isabella smiled for the cameras; her new husband contemplated who to leave out of his will.

"The United States raised the bounty for you to $500,000. If it increases again, I'll have to turn you in." Enrique held his daughter, sitting apart from the two hundred guests attending the wedding.

"I might've believed you if I hadn't read Forbes Magazine. Your old man and his brother are worth over 4 billion dollars."

"That figure is an estimation. They can't possibly monitor the assets of a drug cartel," Enrique said.

"I'm glad to have such rich friends. Nobody'll turn Judas for five- hundred thousand." Enrique pulled his daughter's hair back.

"There's your five hundred-thousand." Enrique cast his eyes on the diamond in her ear.

"El Ingeniero, my worries are for my friend Chuckie. He doesn't deserve this. He's lived a law-abiding life."

"I've followed the trial on court TV. It's a real circus. They're crucifying your friend. The government doesn't take kind to his form of entertainment. Then with young entrepreneurs turning illegal money to legitimate empires, that's what the government really fears. It was okay when Joseph Kennedy did it during Prohibition but minorities from the poorest ghettos, no way," Enrique said, then observed the groom. "He's scared to death."

"Isabella gives a new meaning to the word black widow," Mickey said. "It gets more ridiculous every wedding. The groom is one of my best lieutenants. Her third husband grew up in the same shack as us.

Isabella falls madly in love. Then a year later, she's asking permission to kill them." Enrique rocked his daughter on one knee.

"At least she stays busy," Mickey laughed.

"Don't think I don't know you're seeing Isabella," Enrique said. "We went on a few dates, no big deal."

"Isabella is very beautiful, but she's poison, Mickey. I fear you'll be husband number seven and when you miss dinner, she'll kill you and I won't be able to do anything because to my father, Isabella's a princess. Doesn't matter how many husbands she slaughters." Isabella left her father's knee for the dance floor. "Don't put me in a position where I have to choose between my family and you. I'll always chose my family."

Later That Same Night

Isabella collapsed on Mickey's chest after a round of sex. Mickey rubbed his fingers through Isabella's short curly hair. The hairdo wasn't for everybody, but complimented her.

"Shouldn't you be getting home to your husband?" he asked.

"He's busy planning our honeymoon." She put a cigarette in her mouth. Many nights Mickey wondered how someone so beautiful could be so ruthless. Isabella pulled her lace panties around her hips. She modeled topless in the mirror, falling spellbound to her own body. What wasn't God-given was implanted by plastic surgeons. Who cared about getting older with doctors so wonderful?

"You should be on your way home. I'm drained." Isabella went in her purse and dabbled some cocaine on a gold cigarette case. "Let's fuck on coke."

"I'm not fucking with that shit, I'm tired," Mickey said.

"It'll give you stamina, you scared?" Isabella snorted a nail full.

"I did enough of that shit. One more line, my heart might explode." "Just a little bit, I promise it'll be worth your while." She cupped her perfectly firm breast, giving Mickey an instant erection. Isabella scooped up more coke with her fingernail, she put the nail under Mickey's nostril.

"Don't be a wuss." Mickey snorted.

Federal Courtroom, September 2008

"The prosecutor sucks dick," written on the bathroom stall kept Chuckie from praying. The artist's remarks may have been ignorant but what the fuck.

"A big fat one," Chuckie mumbled. How can a man talk to God with these conflicting thoughts on his mind? The jury deliberated for six hours before they reached a verdict. Deluca's courtroom theatrics left the jury with reasonable doubt. When the doubt disappeared, the reasoning was left to twelve of Chuckie's peers.

"We, the jury, find the defendant, Charles Luis Freeman, guilty." Chuckie heard Claire's wail over complete pandemonium.

CHAPTER 16

Tijuana, Mexico. September 2009, A Year Later "Enrique's Villa"

Enrique relaxed poolside contemplating his next move. The Guadalajara cartel, his rivals, grew stronger each day, forcing him to stay one step ahead of the competition. He laid in a white beach chair, smoking a cigar with a crystal ashtray propped on his stomach. "Papi, Papi, Mickey's here," Enrique's daughter screamed. Enrique absolutely hated being disturbed during these thinking sessions. She jumped on him, knocking the ashtray to pieces on the floor. "Shit!" his scream frightened the five-year-old.

"Sorry," Isabella said.

"It's ok, princess. You don't have to run everywhere you go."

"Si," she jumped from the chair and ran full-speed to the main house. Enrique laughed. Isabella could melt the coldest heart. Carlos met Enrique by the villa's entrance.

"I know, tell Mickey to meet me in the study," Enrique said, wondering who deserved the six-figure salary, Carlos or Isabella. The study reminded Mickey of waiting in a principal's office, with its huge mahogany oak desk and sculptures of dictators who lived thousands of years ago. The walls were stocked floor to ceiling with leather-bound books. Enrique entered the study with Carlos.

"You're up early. You don't wake up until mid-afternoon." Enrique took a seat on the throne.

"I'm going back to the United States," Mickey said.

"You're a fugitive in the United States and you want to return?" Enrique asked. "I appreciate your hospitality. You've given us the red-carpet treatment but I have business waiting back home."

"In Mexico, the President's on my payroll, you're protected in Mexico. Is this business worth your life?"

"Possibly," Mickey replied. Enrique dismissed Carlos.

"I'm no imbecile. You're going back to start a killing spree." "I'm going for justice."

"What do you want from me?" Enrique knew Mickey couldn't be persuaded.

"Your private jet," Mickey said.

"I'll have it fueled and ready tonight." Enrique walked towards Mickey. "Carlos will pick you up in the morning." The men embraced, Mickey left. Enrique went to gazing on the Pacific Ocean. He knew that would be the last time he saw Mickey alive.

Tijuana, Mexico. Mickey's Ranch

Mickey smoked a joint on his patio. As long as Enrique stayed in power, they were safe in Mexico. He could live off the millions Chuckie put away for him. The things he couldn't live with troubled him the most. He'd have to explain to Matty the vacation was over. Mickey thought of ways to do it. He rolled another joint and headed to Matty's room. "Smoke this. You'll feel better." Mickey offered the weed. "Hell no, you're trying to kill me! I'm fighting a cold."

"It's time for us to go," Mickey said. Matty struggled upright.

"It's about time. I thought you went completely soft. The food is great but I miss my daughters."

"It won't be a family reunion," he said, sighing. Matty's face sat in stone.

"I know when it's time to kill."

Mickey stared at Matty, their minds compatible like night and day. "Fuck it, pass the joint," Matty chuckled.

Mickey drove his Cadillac Escalade to the city to meet Isabella. She was in charge of the most feared cell in the cartel. They claimed responsibility for half the murders and kidnappings in Tijuana. To the naked eye, Gloria's jewelry shop seemed to be your average small business. Those associated with the Tijuana underworld knew the dealings that occurred in the jewelry shop and the bandits knew not to rob it, no matter how vulnerable the old lady behind the counter looked. The old lady buzzed Mickey in. A tall Mexican man walked him to a steel door and knocked in a discrete code. A few clicks and cranks, the steel door opened. Isabella's crew acted as a protection unit for the cartel's drug money. On any given day, there could be twenty million dollars cash in the jewelry shop. Mickey passed the professional pool tables stacked with hundred dollar bills. The constant sound of money machines counting cash banged his eardrums. Isabella chattered on a cell phone at the bar.

"San Diego is finished. I'm counting Texas, I'll be done tonight," she said, then closed the phone.

"This is your last day. Why don't you stay a while longer?" Isabella said, spreading cocaine on the bar's glass surface.

"I wish but my business is urgent," Mickey said. She divided four thick lines and rolled up a hundred-dollar bill. The cocaine froze Mickey's brain.

"I want you to ride with me," she said. "Where to?"

"No place far." They continued drinking shots of tequila and snorting cocaine.

4 Hours Later

Mickey came to in the passenger seat of his Cadillac truck, Isabella at the wheel. He was too high to notice the two goons in the backseat.

"Where are we?" he asked. "Handling something, it'll be quick."

Mickey's thoughts went to the nine-millimeter stashed in the dashboard. He regretted not putting it somewhere closer. Isabella parked and spoke to her henchmen in Spanish. The men left the truck, cocking AR 15's. Mickey contemplated making a move for the pistol on Isabella's waist. The green numbers on the dashboard read 11:26 PM. Isabella sparked a cigar, the goons stopped three houses down and calmly shot the locks off a yellow house. Thus far, Isabella hadn't involved Mickey in her business. They were fuck buddies, not crime partners. Minutes later, one goon emerged from the house and whispered something in Isabella's ear.

"We go inside," she said. Mickey smelled the familiar aroma of gunpowder entering the house. A body laid face down in the foyer. The group leisurely stepped over it, walking to the bedroom. The second goon, pointed his assault rifle at two hostages, a male and a female. They were rope-tied to chairs, mouths silenced with duct tape. The female hostage was pregnant. The hostages cried uncontrollably at the sight of Isabella. She chose her words carefully.

"Jose, I trusted you," Jose's head sunk.

"Where's my money?" Isabella tore the duct tape from his mouth. "The money is in the trunk of my brother's car, a maroon Chevy Malibu. The keys are in his pockets."

Isabella sent a henchman to relieve the dead man of his car keys. Jose's wife tried relentlessly to free herself from the knotted rope. The goon returned holding a sports-bag. Isabella counted the money, not saying a word, nobody did until she finished.

"It's seventy-thousand short," she said and jammed the lit cigar in Jose's eyeball. The heat and pressure caused the eyeball to pop. Mickey heard rumors of her ruthlessness but to witness it numbed him. Jose's wife succeeded at flipping the chair over. Her persistence in erratic movements finally paid off. Isabella handed Mickey her gun and without hesitation said, "Kill her."

Mickey's first thought was to kill Isabella. If he shot her, no way he'd leave alive. He finally understood the purpose of this ride. Mickey put two rounds into the woman's head, then threw the smoking gun on the bed, and walked out. Isabella finished off José, standing between two corpses, she phoned her boss.

"He's good." Enrique hung up.

CHAPTER 17

FCI Jesup Federal Prison, September 2009

All the glitz and glamor of show business vanished for Charles Freeman. He adjusted to prison life. Chuckie paid a prison consultant to ease the transition from mogul to jailbird.

"Please don't fight. You'll end up in the worst part of jail, the box," his consultant advised. Chuckie didn't feel bad knowing Martha Stewart got suckered out of thousands too, for advice they could've received from a wino on a street corner. Chuckie's visitor sat by the vending machine. She wore a gray business suit, her hair in a sophisticated bun.

"Hello," Claire said. Chuckie mustered a smile.

"All visitors, the visit room will be closed in two minutes," the guard said. Chuckie watched Claire leave the visiting floor and felt guilty. He wanted to tell her everything. The Society of Serpents, the contract he feared the Watchers put on her life. Nobody believed secret societies existed. If he started yapping off at the mouth, everybody would think he'd gone insane. Chuckie busted his bunkie masturbating when he returned to the cell. "My fault, Brethren." Bobby tucked the magazine under the mattress. "Wasn't expecting you to come back this soon." Chuckie reentered the cell. "Where did you get the book?"

In federal prison, pornographic magazines were forbidden.

"From Detroit," he said. Bobby was a top enforcer for the notorious Shower Posse. He received a life sentence for his role in numerous murders. Chuckie met a lot of characters in prison, most wanted favors. Bobby seemed different. He wanted nothing and he tutored Chuckie on prison politics.

"If I sleep past 7 p.m., wake me up," Chuckie said.

Later That Night

They finished their evening workout. Bobby wore a Brown hoodie with thick dreadlocks hanging out the sides.

"How was your lawyer visit?" Chuckie asked.

"Claims he's working on my appeal." Chuckie understood the process. "My people in the free world say things are scarce right now. What's your co-defendant's name?" "Mickey," Chuckie answered.

"Word on the streets Mickey has a pipeline, knows some strong people."

Chuckie felt the yard closing in on him. Mickey always came back to haunt him.

"I don't have nothing to do with Mickey."

"All those years you've known Mickey, you never met his connection?" "I don't know shit!" Chuckie's lips quivered. Bobby smiled.

"I'm sorry, Chuckie. I wanted to earn a little money. My fault, Brethren." "It's cool, Bobby. It's cool."

Greenwich Village, Manhattan. October 2009

Umberto's Clam house, the seafood restaurant in Manhattan's Greenwich Village catered to an upscale crowd. This particular Saturday, it was closed to the public. A pack of Italians exhaled cold clouds out of respect for their clansmen. Frank Pensa returned to the crime family after eighteen years in prison. Frank never left the brotherhood, his crew remained strong on the Brooklyn waterfront. Frank arrived in a black Chrysler 300 limo. He strutted into Umberto's Clam house with the confidence of Alexander the Great marching into the heart of the Persian Empire.

Hours Later...

Frank had the corner table, near the fire exit. At the table sat his son Michael, brother Michael, and trusted bodyguard Gene. The crowd departed, leaving Frank's entourage and a few of Umberto's employees in the restaurant. The homecoming party wasn't Frank's concern; the hundred cash-stuffed envelopes were.

"Do you believe this guy, Gene?" Frank asked, visibly disturbed chopping off the end of a cigar with a pocket guillotine.

"I dedicated my life to this thing of ours and for what?"

"Pop, Vincent has that fed beef for the stolen cars," Michael said. "He's the boss of the family. It wouldn't be wise to attend this party; he did send an envelope."

Michael searched for the envelope.

"Right here, Vincent Salerno and family." Frank reached for the envelope with two eager hands. He threw it to the other Michael.

"Count that."

Two Mexican laborers entered Umberto's after taking out the trash. The bartender collecting their per diem from the cash register wished them farewell and dialed a number on her cellphone.

"Hello, Eddie. My guys are gone. It's four of them; I'll leave it open, Ok. Goodbye."

"Thirty-four hundred bucks," Big Michael said.

"I got a fatter envelope from a crack dealer, there's no honor." Frank, still conscious of eavesdroppers, paused when the bartender approached.

Gene already gave him the goods on the foxy redhead.

"Divorcee from Hell's Kitchen. No ties to law enforcement or organized crime," Gene whispered in Frank's ear hours earlier.

"Mr. Pensa, I'll be only a minute. I have to lock the fire exist." "It's alright sweetie," Frank said.

"When you're ready to leave, Mr. Pensa, remember the security code is 1212. The gate locks automatically."

Mickey screwed a thick suppressor on a MP5 submachine gun. "Eddie says it's four of them." Matty nodded in the driver's seat. "They're sitting at the corner table." Mickey put on a black ski mask.

They did a quick sweep of the streets before getting out the vehicle. Mickey leaned against the wall by the fire exist, Matty put a gloved hand on the doorknob.

"On my three. One, two..." Mickey counted. The exit swung open and Mickey rushed in with the MP5. Frank spotted the gunner first but the proximity from the table to the exit gave him no time to react. Mickey aimed at the table and pulled the trigger, nothing. He tried again, the machine gun jammed! Mickey threw the gun at Gene to break his momentum. The MP5 bounced hard off Gene's forearm, giving Mickey time to avoid his tackle. Matty fired a loud cannon. Little Michael fell over with a bullet hole through the mouth. Mickey wrestled Gene, the old man was strong as an ox. Gene pushed Mickey into the wall and retrieved his revolver. Mickey fought for the gun, and during their struggle, a shot went off. Another, boom! From Matty's cannon drowned out the screams. The bullet hit Gene, the hollow point scrambled everything between his ears.

"Take it, take the money!" Big Michael threw wads of cash stained with Lil Michael's blood. Matty shot Michael three times in the chest. Frank Pensa trembled when Matty's hot barrel touched his temple. Then, Frank felt no more. Matty lifted Mickey over his shoulder and ran out the fire exit.

CHAPTER 18

N.Y. FBI Fieldhouse, November 2009

Wayne Robertson bought a cup of coffee and a raisin bagel from a pushcart vendor in lower Manhattan. He needed the caffeine to keep awake. Wayne led the FBI organized crime squad, the only African American to do so. A brown skin man with a wide forehead and high cheekbones. Robertson stood six feet with a sleek build. He was responsible for Traumanti family crime boss Vincent Salerno's indictment for overseeing a stolen car ring. Vincent didn't go anywhere near stolen cars, but he accepted cash tributes which opened the mob boss up for the Rico Statute. The Vincent Salerno indictment raised Wayne's profile within the bureau. Wayne's supervisor urged him to report to headquarters. He rode the elevator up to the eighth floor.

"Are you Special Agent Robertson?" "Yes," Wayne answered.

"I'm Sam Mitchell, come with me." They walked into a small empty conference room.

"We have a positive identification on the blood samples found at the Clam house murder scene." Sam gave Wayne a black & white photograph.

"The man you're looking at is Mickey Tansy Jr." Sam wrote the name on a chalkboard.

"A federal fugitive for the past twenty-two months. In the 1980s, Tansy led a Hell's Kitchen drug ring supplied by a Mexican cartel." Sam wrote Tijuana cartel on the board.

"In 1988, Frank Pensa attempted to kill Tansy for not sharing in the drug profits. Tansy never retaliated, he didn't get the chance to. Drug Enforcement Agency busted him soon after" Sam wrote Charles Freeman.

"Mickey waited twenty years to kill Pensa?" Wayne asked. Sam wrote "Matthew Hart" on the board and dusted his hands.

"It appears so. Mickey Tansy is a suspect in at least eight homicides. His chief enforcer is Matthew Hart, a former high school football star. Hart disappeared with Tansy, twenty-two months ago."

"I remember this case in the newspapers. Mickey Tansy gave Charles Freeman the start-up money for his music company."

"Charles Freeman is in the dark on this one. I have tight surveillance on him," Sam said.

"I'll pass these photos out to my squad," said Wayne.

Hell's Kitchen, N.Y. Eddie's Old Lady Apartment

Mickey's left thigh was wrapped in a white bandage. He slept most the day due to the painkillers, Eddie supplied. Eddie's old lady did a great job cleaning Mickey's wound and stitching him back together.

"It's too much heat in the city," Matty said. They botched the Pensa hit, the moment that old guinea got that shot off. Mickey knew they were fucked.

"Move Mickey, your leg isn't going to get better sitting on your ass," Matty said.

"If your piece of shit gun didn't jam, we'd be camouflaged in the city. You picked a great time to clean your arsenal." Mickey pulled himself up with the broomstick they modified into a crutch. He hopped to the refrigerator.

"What's your plan?" Matty asked. "Boston, that's where Jackie's at."

"How come nobody tells me anything?"

"Cause you're not the thinker, Matty. I don't think I'm one with this plan." Mickey leaned his back against the wall.

"Sometimes, it's better to skip the plan. Do what you do, whatever happens, happens," Matty said.

Washington, D.C. November 2009. J Edgar Hoover Building

Sam Mitchell flipped through a Rolodex on his desk. He developed a large network of informants over his career. To Sam, an old informant could be the missing link to a new case. He dialed a number.

"Yeah, Sam," Jackie said.

"We found Mickey's blood samples at a quadruple homicide crime scene in New York City."

"I thought Mickey fled to Mexico."

"I'm concerned for your safety. Report to Washington D.C. until I get some leads on this situation," Sam said.

"I have a life; I can't leave town at the drop of a hat."

"If you don't come to Washington D.C., you may not have a life period," Sam said, dropping the receiver in the cradle.

Boston, Mass. "The Ward Estate"

"Jackie, is that you!" Pamela yelled. Jackie went up to the home office on the second floor. He tapped in the combination to the safe on a digital keypad. Pamela walked in the office, wearing a white apron over a red Carolina Herrera dress.

"You going somewhere?" she asked, her high heels clicking on marble. "We're leaving town, Mickey's on some killing spree," Jackie said. "Don't be foolish. The Senator lives down the road. Nobody's coming here,"

"Mickey doesn't care if the President lives down the road. He killed four people in a Manhattan restaurant."

"It doesn't mean he's after you. Mickey has a hairpin temper, probably killed those people in the spur of the moment. Anyway, he'll be in jail soon. Mickey is and always will be a bum from Hell's Kitchen," Pamela said.

Jackie stayed quiet.

"Carol's husband owns a security firm. I'll hire extra security, if you're scared," she said.

One Day Later

"That's the second time that toy cop passed," Matty said.

Mickey squinted.

"These houses are too far from the road, I can't read the numbers, drive slowly." Matty nudged Mickey. A red convertible pulled alongside Eddie's girl, Nissan Altima.

"It's her," he whispered.

"It sure resembles her, I haven't seen her in years." They watched the car turn into a circular asphalt driveway.

"The women fetched some groceries out the trunk.

"It's Pamela, I can tell by her walk. We'll come back tomorrow," Mickey said.

The Next Morning, November 2009

Jackie started every morning with a four-mile jog, hot shower, and a wholesome breakfast. Today he had a meeting with some sub-contractors.

"Today I'm working, so don't wait up," he said.

"Should I leave your plate in the oven?" Pamela asked. "I'll stop at a fast-food joint. Who are those guys outside?" "Remember I hired security?"

"I forgot. What's on your agenda today?" Jackie asked.

"I have to wait for the plumber then I'm going shopping."

Mickey wore a green painter's uniform, waiting for Matty.

"Where did you find this bad boy? Got the ladder on top and everything," Mickey said, climbing into the work van. Then he heard a groan, Mickey pulled back the wool blanket, the van's owner was tied up with two black eyes in the back of the van.

"Not a fucking hostage, Matty!" Mickey screamed.

"You said get a van so I got one. We're on a tight schedule," Matty said. "He looks like a fucking raccoon! Did you at least get the knives and ropes?" Mickey asked.

"Even found some brass knuckles, I saw some security guards on post last night. I think they're armed," Matty said.

"No guns, in that neighborhood, a gunshot will draw too much attention. We'll gain entry to the mansion and kill Jackie. Worst come to worst, we cut the guards throats."

The Ward Estate

"You're not on the list," said the security guard standing on the manicured lawn.

"Somebody called Friendly's Painting Service," Mickey said.

"I got plumbers down, nothing about painters. I'll check with my employer." The guard radioed his comrade.

"Sorry to disturb you, Mrs. Ward. Did you schedule an appointment with a Friendly's Painting Service?" Pamela tied the silk belt to her purple robe.

"No, I'm expecting the plumber," she said.

"That's what I thought, sorry for the interruption." Pamela turned away, then she figured what the hell. They're already here and the guesthouse could use a touch-up.

"It almost slipped my mind, I did call a painting service. Show them to the guest house," she said.

The guard gave them a brief tour of the guesthouse.

"Mrs. Ward wants these bedrooms painted over." Matty sidelined the guard with the brass knuckles, leaving him destitute on the carpet.

"Why'd you hit him so fucking hard?" Mickey asked. "He's still alive."

"But he can't talk with a broken jaw. He was supposed to lure the other guards to the guest house." Mickey collected the guard's walkie- talkie and service pistol.

"The other guards are going to be checking for him soon, let's move first." Mickey jogged to the front of the house.

"Excuse me, I'm Jerry the painter. What's your name?" The guard wasn't in the mood for conversation.

"What's it to you?" he replied.

"We could use your help in the guest house."

"Ricky's over there. What the fuck you need me for?" The guard turned to the red stuccos on the roof of the guest residence and Mickey smashed him with the butt of the gun, then whistled. Matty drove the work van to the front of the mansion. They carried both hostages inside the guesthouse. Mickey splashed the unconscious guard with a cup of ice cold water.

"Who's in the house?"

"Mrs. Ward and one guard." The gun slap gave the guard an attitude adjustment.

"Get the guard to the guest house." The guard was more than willing to cooperate. Mickey shoved him the radio.

"Cross Ranger to Lone Wolf, do you read me?" "Cross Ranger, I hear you loud and clear."

"We're having some problems, could use your assistance in the guesthouse,"

"Is everything alright?"

"Everything's fine. Moving some furniture, that's all."

"I'll be there in a minute. Over and out." Matty hid the guards and the painter. Then he waited beside the front door. When Lone Wolf crossed the threshold, Matty swung a haymaker with the brass knuckles. Lone Wolf ducked swiftly, the force behind the swing through Matty off balance. Lone Wolf 's left connected, sending Matty to the canvas. Mickey tiptoed to the action, he pushed the hunting knife deep into the guard's back and brought Lone Wolf slowly down to the carpet.

"Motherfucker!" Matty cocked the gun, shaking out his daze.

"He's already dead, no noise. I'm going inside, stay here," Mickey said.

The mansion's main floor was empty. Mickey crept up the spiral staircase with the hunting knife and the painter's mask on. The master bedroom had a black and gold color scheme with a bathroom off to its left. Mickey gently pushed in the bathroom door and saw a nude body through the blurry shower glass. He grabbed Pamela by the hair and pressed the knife's blade against her throat. Mickey dragged her to the bedroom, Pamela trembled, too shocked to scream. Mickey ripped the mask off, Pamela fainted.

She felt drowsy tied to the bedpost. Pamela recognized the painter's uniform and regretted giving her security the green light.

"Your guards are tied up; nobody has to die. I just want Jackie." "Fuck you!" she screamed. A backhand smacked her. "Disloyal cunt," Mickey said.

"Disloyal, you left me, you Irish piece of shit!"

"When is your husband coming home?" Mickey asked calmly.

"He's working late." She bit down on her lip, feeling Mickey yearning her damp, naked body. "Untie me, Mickey. Where am I going to go?"

Her thighs and pie were on full display. Mickey wasn't stupid. He also wasn't strong enough to stay.

"Mickey, wait."

He backed out the room.

Hours Later...

A surgical glove stuffed with ice cubes cooled Matty's busted lip. Mickey returned to the main house, leaving Matty to babysit. A burgundy SUV rolled up the grooves of the driveway. Its bright headlights lighting up the path. Matty twisted the red knob on the walkie-talkie.

"Jackie's home." No response. He tried several more times; an urge overcame Matty to gun Jackie down right on the lawn.

"No gunplay." Mickey's orders. Matty would wait at least a few minutes. If still no word from Mickey, he'd sack the house, guns blazing.

Jackie pushed the white button on a remote control, activating the garage door and parked his Chevrolet Suburban inside. Pamela hadn't answered her phone all day, which was unusual. Though with the huge developments Jackie had underway they spoke less and less. Jackie put a thick roll of blueprints under an armpit and secured the garage with the remote, never realizing the armed guards weren't on- duty.

Pamela chewed on a block of mozzarella Mickey discovered along with some smoked ham in the fridge. He laid the silver tray with the cold cuts on the nightstand.

"Can I make a call, maybe I can get Jackie to come home," Pamela said.

"Don't insult my intelligence. I put you on the phone, you'll have the National Guard over here." She threw the half-eaten block of cheese.

"I fucking hate you." She pouted. The cheese missed Mickey and hit a headless mannequin.

"Hurry up so I can tie your arm back up."

"Are you going to kill me?" Pamela asked, trying to sound brave, but she wasn't very convincing.

"What do you think, should I kill you?" Mickey asked.

"They said you wouldn't see the light of day again. I left Manhasset with a shopping bag and a subway token. What was I supposed to do?" Tears ran down her pretty face.

"That gives you the right to marry Jackie. The friend who put me a way for a quarter century. What was you supposed to do? Get a fucking job!"

"Is killing me going to make things right?" "It'll make me feel better."

"Just do it! Get it over with!" Her voice echoed throughout the mansion. Mickey ran the sharp point of the knife between her breasts.

"Don't tempt me, Pam. Revenge is one of life's sweetest joys." She arched underneath the soft pinches of the knife.

"Put that thing away, Mickey." She was referring to the knife, not Mickey's hard-on. Mickey slid his forefinger inside her. Pamela's gasps turned to moans when his middle finger slid in next.

"I missed you, Mickey. I missed you so much." Pamela tugged with her free hand at the Velcro patches on the painter's uniform. "Untie me, Mickey." He sliced through the ropes and set her free.

Jackie stared at the two naked bodies sleeping intertwined. He heard a light snore but the bodies were too tangled to determine from who. Then came a beep, either a watch or radio. No, a walkie-talkie laying on the sheets.

The guards, he thought, it was her idea to hire them. Jackie 'approached the sleeping bodies with a single thought: *kill.*

A loud thud startled Pamela out her sleep. On the other side of the mattress, Jackie was punching Mickey. She rolled off the bed, using its spread to cover her naked body. She succeeded at seducing Mickey but the sex was so good, it put her to sleep. Pamela, a few feet away from her brawling lovers, wanted to scream for the cops, but she couldn't. She was at a loss for words. As the two men tried to kill each other, Matty's voice came over the radio that somehow landed by her.

A hard punch sent him to a bending knee. The metal tray collided with his face, sending him back down before he had a chance to rise up. The same rope that was used to bind Pamela was wrapped around his neck. Pamela saw the blood clots surround his pupils as his soul was being slowly squeezed out of him. She refused to watch him die. She managed to crawl to the hunting knife. His back faced her as he yelled incoherent blabber in a killer's rage. She stabbed him in the collarbone, pulled out the blade, and stabbed him again and again.

CHAPTER 19

His impulses fought the self-inflicted punishment of patience. The blue steel he palmed brought serenity to an unpredictable situation. At this precise moment, a plastic Casio watch blurted three audible bleeps, five minutes had snailed past since Jackie arrived. Time to move! The sound of crickets chirping played melody to boots splashing on grass, dozens of sprinklers sprayed water across the lawn. Matty zigzagged trying to ward off a clear shot. He ran to the door Mickey frequented. The distance couldn't've been more than twenty yards, but you'd think he broke the tape to the Boston Marathon. Matty stole three gulps of air from the fog and disappeared into the house.

The nine-millimeter led him up the spiral staircase. Matty, an arm's length behind the gun, let out three breaths followed by a long inhale, breath control. He already searched the main floor. The house was huge, miraculously furnished, yet hollow. The vibe reminded Matty of his parents' apartment a year before they divorced. The walls to the hall were ghost white, with a strip of red marble running the floor from the steps down to the mouth of a small balcony. Matty's gun hand cut through the red velvet with swift wall-to-wall motion. A loud cry came from down the hall. Matty pinned himself against the wall, the nine-millimeter clutched in both hands, its barrel pointed at the ceiling. He slowly sidestepped to the source of the sobs, only leaving the wall to prevent knocking down a few fancy oil paintings. Matty looked over for a split second, glancing inside the room. What he saw disturbed the stone-cold killer. Two bloody bodies lying horizontally from one another. A third person kneeled over one of the bodies, stabbing at it repeatedly. All Matty could think about was Mickey getting butchered. He rotated off the wall and fired a shot into the room.

The bullet's impact bounced Pamela off the bedpost. She fell breast first on the carpet. Her attention locked on the knife until a boot kicked it away, spurts of excruciating pain exploded up her shoulder until her entire left side went numb. A pond of blood surfaced under her wound. She blinked bewildered at the scene, trying to think through hazy clouds in her mind. Then, she remembered everything. The fighting, stabbing, body diced to smithereens.

"Mickey, Mickey," a voice called. Pamela's pond was now a lake. She lifted her head in time to see Matty dash out the room. The clouds returned, this time too strong for her mind to penetrate; she slowly drifted away.

Later That Night

The black armored Lincoln Navigator made a detour minutes from its destination. The loose ends kept reacquiring in Sam's mind. He couldn't function without the knots being tied tight. Sam spent most the night courtside at a Celtic's game, accompanied by a prominent United States Senator. The NBA franchise acquired the "big ticket" Kevin Garnett. So Sam made the Senator dish out the bread for their tickets. If Jackie Ward had answered the telephone, he'd be flying first class on a Delta flight back to the nation's capital. The previous day, Jackie reneged on a promise to check in. Sam rolled down the window, and let the wind sweep a head full of gray hair. The driver clocked the navigational screen.

"We're here, sir," he said. A Friendly's Painting van drove out the driveway. Sam shook in disbelief.

"How could Jackie carry on without a care?" The driver eased behind a red Jaguar.

"These unexpected visits never last long, keep the car running. I might have to shoot my way out the joint." The driver turned pale.

"I'm busting your balls." Sam stepped out the SUV with a devilish grin. In the Federal Bureau, Sam's escapades were legendary folklore. The rookie's reaction wasn't a surprise. In actuality, Sam hadn't fired a live round in years. He gave up carrying firearms to accommodate the wishes of new acquaintances who loved being around tough guys, but seeing tools of the trade brought them too close to the action. Sam ignored the doorbell and knocked on the Oakwood bare-knuckled. The unlocked door moved off its latch. Mitchell wasn't inside ten seconds when he saw blood splattered on the floors. He sprinted back to the Navigator and yanked it open.

"Where's your piece!" he screamed.

"Won't catch me twice," said the rookie, refusing to be the butt of another joke.

"Give me your fucking gun!" Sam demanded.

Lower Manhattan, December 2009

Wayne Robertson squatted on the edge of a mattress hunched over a laptop propped up on a milk crate. His boney fingers mindlessly typed on the keypad. The emails landed nonstop in the inbox column of his MSN account. When Wayne responded to one message, three more flew in. Wayne's extremely organized life got swept up by a category 5 tornado. It wasn't just Wayne in disarray, FBI offices across the country were in damage control mode. The heinous crimes committed in Boston garnered nationwide news coverage. The press ate up the fact that the murders were committed down the block from a U.S. Senator's house. No matter which way you spun it; it spelled bad publicity. The FBI's obsession to save face resulted in more pressure to solve the case. The agency's field commander pushed Wayne through the meat grinder for letting the thugs escape New York City. To add to the list of compounding problems, he had a meeting scheduled with the great Sam Mitchell in less than an hour. Wayne closed the laptop and replaced it with a sandwich from Subways, transforming the milk crate from a desk to a dinner table. The rented room wasn't much bigger than the offices at headquarters. The cramped space fit the loner. The apartment's owner, a Chinese widow charged $600 a month for the back room. The lady drank too much coffee, and thought her pet cat was human but she minded her business. That's what Wayne cherished most about the Chinatown honeycomb. The room was a train stop from headquarters, and within walking distance of a chic sports bar called "Little's." After the sandwich, Wayne showered, dressed in under forty minutes and put a brown suede race hat over a milk dud baldy. Wayne arrived at Little's ten minutes early to find Sam Mitchell chasing Buffalo wings with Miller Genuine draft.

"Waiting long?" Wayne asked, pulling out a chair.

"Half an hour. This is a nice bar, modern with the liquor guns and touchscreens. In Hell's Kitchen we tie metal hangers around our televisions for reception.

"Times are changing, so I try to change with them." Wayne poured a beer into a chilled mug.

"But I'm glad this place suits you, Mr. Mitchell. I come here a lot. The beer is cheap and the crowd is friendly."

"It's ironic you said that, Wayne. That's the reason why I wanted to chat." The Clam house murderers damaged Wayne's squeaky-clean record, and with the massacre in Boston, job security was at an all-time low. Wayne coasted the beer mug and prepared to take his walking papers with some dignity.

"The older I get, the more I stubbornly think time will change with Sam Mitchell instead of vice-versa. The young shall succeed the old."

Mitchell swigged some beer and continued. "I'm no longer going to stand in the way of nature's course. I'm putting you in charge of the taskforce I'm creating to hunt down Mickey Tansey and Matthew Hart. I'm too old to lead the charge. Your new office is next to mine in the J. Edgar Hoover building. No more supervisors. You report directly to me."

The statement left Wayne appalled.

"What, You don't want the job?" Sam asked. "I expected to get fired, not promoted."

"Life is funny that way. You're the best man for the job, Wayne. We're catching a redeye flight to Washington to get you up to date on the case," Sam said.

"I know everything there is to know about the case. The Wards, three guards and an immigrant painter is dead. Pamela Ward bled to death from a gunshot wound. Jackie Ward and one guard were stabbed to death. The other two guards and the painter got their throats slashed.

"Close my friend, but no cigar. The investigators confirmed Pamela Ward stabbed her husband. She was covered in Jackie's blood, her fingerprints on the murder weapon."

"What the fuck, are you for real?!" Wayne asked.

"This case is very complex. Hurry down the street and get your things packed. We'll talk on the flight." Wayne took a few steps then it hit him.

"How do you know I live down the street?"

FCI Jesup Federal Prison

Bobby jotted down bets on a brown paper bag with a broken pencil.

"Pirates over the Indians 4-point spread. Phillies under the Yankees for seven." Detroit sealed the deal with a folded Andrew Jackson.

"Hold on Brethren, this is too much." Bobby learned anything given in jail for free wasn't worth having.

"That's yours, Bobby. If you get Charlie to listen to my boy rap."

"I told you Charlie isn't interested in no rappers. The man barely listens to music. If I did get your boy some airtime, you got to come harder than twenty dollars."

Detroit passed Bobby another folded President, this one a Grant. "This is all I'm given up. We just want five minutes of the man's time. If he isn't feeling Dash, keep the money, you don't owe us a dime." Bobby hid the bills in a skully cap.

"You better not make a fool out of me," he warned.

Detroit banged his chest with an ashy fist, creating a beat. A circle of convicts formed, most of them grinning in anticipation of some free entertainment. They nodded in sync with the human beat box. A tall, skinny brown skin felon wearing a red durag rapped in a raspy voice over Detroit's concoction. Chuckie bounced a blue handball off the concrete, pretending to be unamused. In a twenty-plus year career in the music business, over a thousand aspiring MCs rapped their best verses to the ex- label boss. Chuckie put Dash through a lyrical workout regimen, making him rap fast, slow, without punch lines. For the last verse, Chuckie opted for some classic storytelling. Dash rhymed about getting caught red- handed on the visit floor with two different girls. Nobody could tell if he wrote the verse beforehand or made it up right on the spot, but the crowd approved, some from experience. The handball court cleared. Chuckie and Dash stayed behind.

"You definitely got skills but in this predicament, I can't do much to help you," Chuckie said.

"You're Charlie Free, I grew up listening to the Sour Boys."

"I'm blackballed, no major label in the music industry wants to do business with me"

"Don't sound defeated, Charlie. We inside the belly of the beast. This environment makes you or breaks you and I don't break" Chuckie laughed.

"You're really convinced, I'm your ticket to stardom, huh?"

"Yeah! This is America. Everybody loves a comeback story." Thoughts of a comeback excited Chuckie plus Dash had the makings of a true star. Chuckie played it cool.

"I 'ma do some thinking and get back to you," he said.

"Cool but don't take forever, Charlie Free, because I don't have life and you don't have distribution." Dash spun off.

A wall of cinderblock four feet high and sixteen wide stood between the showers and the stalls. On the shower side, six showerheads hosed inmates with water hot enough to boil tea. Though it was six heads, no more than three inmates ever showered at a time. Two men occupied the shower area, one in shower one, the other in six. That left two through five empty, enough space for them to spot an ambush. Chuckie walked through a steam cloud with a brown towel wrapped around his waist. He twisted on shower three and greeted Bobby in six. Chuckie stripped off the towel and kept on his boxers. He rocked back and forth like a girl trying to catch the rhythm off a double dutch, leapt in the water, and clenched when it scolded him.

"You'll never get used to it," Bobby said.

"We put in the work orders and still nothing. We got to get third degree burns to get a decent shower." Bobby complained about everything, even when it wasn't nothing to complain about. The guards nicknamed him Al

Sharpton. He never passed on an opportunity to fight the faculty tooth and nail.

"Hopefully I won't be around when they fix these blowtorches. I got a letter from parole today. I go to the board next Monday."

"You're due for the board already?" Bobby asked, shoulders slumped. "You don't look the least bit happy" Chuckie said. Bobby's posture straightened.

"No, I'm happy. I got a lawyer visit this afternoon. If everything goes right with my appeal, I might beat you to the front gates."

Chuckie laughed.

"That's great news Bobby! We'll get up on the outside."

"What about Dash? He's counting on you to push him to the mainstream." Bobby asked.

"I can't do much for Dash. I don't have the clout no more." Bobby frowned.

"Everybody thinks you can help the kid except you, Chuckie. Dash is hungrier than a starving pit bull. I don't see why you can't be successful again." The idea of tucking Dash under the wing tugged at Chuckie since the rap cipher.

"It's bigger than hit records, I've got enemies." "With friends like Mickey?" Bobby asked.

"Did you see what they did in Boston? They're on a fucking war path." Chuckie looked contorted. With the parole board coming, he didn't want to venture anywhere near the subject.

"Mickey moved up the ranks to number two on the Ten Most Wanted list, behind Osama Bin Laden. Where are they hiding, Chuckie?" Bobby asked.

"I wouldn't want to remember if I did know. I thought you had an afternoon visit. You should be getting ready. You might miss it," Chuckie said.

Bobby sat on the iron stool, hands folded on a manila folder thick with legal work. The usual pack of smokes and chocolate Payday candy bars were missing from the equation. The other stools in the tank were empty. Bobby lifted the receiver, wiped it down and said.

"It's a pleasure to see you." Sam Mitchell peered over the eyeglasses stuck on the bridge of his nose.

"Cut the bullshit. Do you have some information?" he asked. "Not at this very moment, but I'm working my magic."

"For two years, you've worked magic and I have nothing, Houdini." "When I bring Mickey up, Charles clams up. I don't want to come across too strong. He might get suspicious," Bobby said.

"You've reigned supreme for two years in this jail under my protection.

That's over until you hold up your end of the bargain."

"Why are you doing this, Sam? We got a good thing," Bobby begged.

"You got a good thing. I got the Justice Department breathing down my throat, asking for Mickey Tansy. That's what I hired you to find out. Now I'm asking, where the fuck is Mickey Tansy!?!" Sam screamed.

"More time is what I'm asking for Sam. I can pluck Tansy's whereabouts out of Charles. It's going to be tougher with the motherfucker going to the parole board soon." Sam recognized the envy.

"Fifteen years in on a life beef. I can't imagine the daily stress that comes with knowing you'll take your last breath in this shithole. What if I tell you I can change that? Get me Mickey Tansy and I'll get you out! It'll take one phone call to draw up your release papers." Sam said.

"Don't play with my freedom." Bobby salivated.

"You're the one playing Mr. Wales. You could be playing soccer on a beach in Montego Bay." Bobby killed for recreation in Kingston. For a chance at freedom, he'd slaughter an army.

The following Monday

The tiles shined bright enough to see your reflection. The constant humming from the air condition muffled the shuffle of papers. The damn air condition that cooled everything excepted sweat on Chuckie's forehead. The parole board spent the better of an hour questioning

Chuckie. The questions ranged from the nature of his crime, rehabilitation and remorse. Chuckie answered each question sincerely. The chair of the board appeared to be its youngest member, an attractive female in her early thirties. She stamped three sheets of paper and dismissed Chuckie from the hearing.

Five anxious prisoners sat on a wooden bench outside the hearing room, waiting to be called.

"They showing us some mercy in there?" someone asked. "I can't tell. This is my first board," Chuckie said.

"He's a virgin, shit!" an old timer shouted.

Later in the Day…

Chuckie laid on the cot, covered from head to toe in a green knitted blanket. He could see clearly through the blanket but for those on the outside looking in the cell, Chuckie appeared asleep. It was a defensive mechanism Chuckie utilized whenever he wanted to be left alone. It worked about 50 percent of the time; some guys didn't comprehend when they weren't welcomed. Chuckie replayed the scenes from the parole board. Tonight, he'd call Claire and confess to wrecking her homecoming party. Chuckie was about to roll over when he saw an outline of a body outside the cell bars. The person stared obsessively, gritted their teeth and murmured something to themselves, then disappeared. It seemed harmless but something within told Chuckie, something wasn't right.

"Watch Bobby," said his subconscious.

CHAPTER 20

Los Angeles, California. May 2010

A bell 430 helicopter touched down in the helipad, on the roof of the Hilton hotel. Its propellers rotated the California heat above a sweltering Josh Stevenson. As the blades slowed to wind speed, Josh approached the aircraft. A female French model a week over the legal drinking age hopped out. Big Jim stood on the guardrails, arms spread wide.

"Josh!!" he shouted, jumping from the helicopter into his best impersonation of the salsa.

"This is not the time for fun and games," Josh said.

"Don't be so uptight. I just renewed my membership with the mile- high club." The model kissed Big Jim on the cheek.

"The American Music Awards is honoring you with a lifetime achievement award. This is a monumental event in the life and times of James Morrison, yet you arrive with another blonde bimbo, where's your wife?" Josh asked. The young arm candy sucked her teeth.

"Excuse us for a second, sweetie," Big Jim said. She crinkled her perfect face at Josh, the Grinch, trying to steal her Christmas.

"Why must you be so rude? She's sensitive, this one," Big Jim said when she walked off.

"This is business. At the rate you're going, she'll be replaced by morning. Her feelings will heal with the complimentary breakup gift," Josh said.

"The award show is three days away and Maggie is flying in with the kids tomorrow night. It's plenty of time to indulge in business and pleasure." Big Jim looked to the pouting teen waiting impatiently.

"With all the publicity I scheduled this weekend, you should be working. I'm exhausted from planning your fucking after party."

"I run the biggest corporation in the world of music. I should be able to unwind sometimes," Big Jim said.

"No, I run the biggest corporation in the world of music," Josh thought. "About the after party, is everything squared up?" Big Jim asked.

"I rented a mansion on Mullhound Drive and sent out two hundred invitations to the world's richest and most famous."

Santa Monica, California

Marie bought the last four daily newspapers off the newsstand rack. She hustled to a battered Saab station wagon, tossed the papers in the passenger seat and locked the car door. She proceeded south on foot, across a street congested with cars. The car horns sounded rapidly, not for the bumper-to-bumper traffic. Marie had inadvertently mesmerized the intersection. The twenty-five-year-old continued without a break of her stride, naively underestimating the power of her beauty. Of course men stopped and stared with their tongues wagging, but to Marie, that's what men did. It wasn't because her bronze skin glowed or her jet-black hair that hung down to her chin like black curtains for a stage of green eyes. It definitely wasn't the hourglass body she developed at thirteen and maintained with no exercise. Marie took these things for granted, everybody else didn't, especially other women, blue with envy. The sunburned asphalt heated the soles of her open-toe sandals. The legs to her blue denim jeans were rolled up on her calf muscles. A Prince "Purple Rain" t-shirt cut at the collar, exposed her bare shoulder with a colorful butterfly tattoo. The ventilation kicked out cold air in the tailor shop. The tailor greeted Marie and fetched her order from the previous day, two tuxedos tailored, cut and trimmed to the specific sizes she requested. The transaction occurred too quickly for Marie. A few more minutes under the booming air-condition is what she desired, but after paying the tailor, the sweaty scorching May day welcomed her back. She asked herself the same question for the thousandth time. "Why am I doing this?" Five years earlier, Marie arrived in the United States with a secretary job at a recording studio awaiting her in California. She dove into her new life with great enthusiasm. Marie's willingness to work hard elevated her to Lindsay Joy's personal assistant, pop music's brightest star. The three-time Grammy winner recorded at the studio where Marie worked. They became the best of friends. After a full year in her new position, Marie began enjoying the fruits of her labor. She leased a new apartment three blocks away from the beach in Santa Monica, finally got over her latest heartbreak and was contemplating buying a new car. A red convertible that would really piss off her ex. The future seemed bright until her past returned. How could she refuse the man who saved her life, financed her exodus to the U.S., and fulfilled the father role she desperately coveted? Marie was nineteen when the Guadalajara cartel sent hit men to her family's villa in Tijuana. She stayed the night at a friend's house, the decision saved her life. The next morning, Marie found her parents, grandmother, siblings, and pets dead. The murders were retaliation for acts her father committed against the Guadalajara cartel. When Enrique asked Maria for help, how could she refuse? She'd be risking everything but if it wasn't for Enrique, she'd have nothing.

Mickey leaned against the kitchen counter watching the portable TV next to the microwave. The locks clicked on the door, his arms crossed to retrieve two .38 caliber revolvers from separate shoulder holsters. Marie appeared in the doorway, juggling newspapers and suit covers. Mickey holstered the guns and rushed to help her.

"Thank you," she said, kicking the door closed with her sandal. They carried the items to the cluttered living room, where Matty slept.

"Hot enough for you?" Mickey's attempt to spark a conversation. He tried to make Marie feel as comfortable as possible with two notorious murderers camping out in her living room.

"Hot and humid," she said, turning to face Mickey. "I see your face has fully healed."

"Finally, I recognized this handsome fella in the mirror." Mickey said "Much better from the way you looked when I picked you guys up six months ago."

Marie unzipped a tuxedo out its cover.

"He got off a great sucker punch," Mickey shrugged.

"Yes, you told me. One great sucker punch caused all that damage." She laughed, which pleased Mickey even if it was at his expense.

"This should fit you perfect. I had it cut to your precise measurements.

Matty's I'm not so sure."

"Don't worry. Matty hasn't fit anything perfect since the third grade." Mickey put the white tuxedo jacket on.

"This is really nice Marie. Your taste is excellent." She gushed at the compliment. Mickey counted a money wad thick as a dictionary.

"This is for your troubles," he said. Marie refused the money like she always did.

"This is a favor for Enrique, I don't want anything. I just want to make him proud." Mickey admired her loyalty.

"Let's talk more about this award show," he said.

J. Edgar Hoover Building, Washington D.C.

Wayne Robinson kicked his feet up on a government-issued desk. His New York office could easily fit twice inside the one in Washington DC. The DC office came with a personal secretary and a view of the Department of Justice across the street. Wayne would catch himself spying on the Senators and Congressmen visiting the DOJ. He relocated a room's worth of personal property to a one-bedroom apartment near DuPont Circle. Wayne didn't have the time to enjoy his new dwellings, helping Sam Mitchell build the task force superseded everything. He opened an issue of Rolling Stone Magazine with diva Lindsay Joy on the front cover and flipped to a tribute for Continental Island Music Group chairman James Morrison. The American Music Awards (AMAs) were honoring Morrison with a lifetime achievement award this week. The article included two picture inserts. In one picture taken at an album release party in the 90s, Wayne recognized a cheerful Charles Freeman. Wayne placed himself in Mickey's shoes. If he was committing murderous acts of vengeance, who would be next up to bat? James Morrison? It made sense. Big Jim gained the most from Charles Freeman's conviction. C.I.M.G absorbed Dessie Stone Records, and many insiders believed Big Jim plotted Charlie Free's downfall.

"Would Mickey Tansy defend Charles Freeman's honor?" Wayne asked himself. He kicked off the desk so fast, he flipped out the chair.

Beverly Hills, California 8 hours later

"Pull over to the side of the road, now!" someone barked on a loudspeaker. Big Jim twisted around to see two sirens flashing on black Lincoln Navigators.

"What did you do Bernie?" Big Jim asked the chauffer. "Nothing, Jim."

"It's probably a routine traffic stop," said Josh.

"Who the hell has time for this bullshit?" A man tapped the tinted window.

"Can I be of some assistance, officer?" asked Big Jim.

"Mr. James Morrison, I need you to come with us." Josh spoke over Big Jim.

"What is this about? You haven't even identified yourself."

"I'm Special Agent Wayne Robertson with the FBI, and the gentleman on the other side of your limo is Special

Agent Sam Mitchell." Wayne took his FBI shield out a brown leather wallet.

"Where I go, Josh goes," Big Jim said. "What is this pertaining to?" Josh asked.

"You'll find out. Follow us." The two FBI agents drove ahead of Big Jim. The caravan rode to the Hilton hotel, where Big Jim stayed. Wayne showed them up to a suite, three floors below Big Jim's Presidential suite. "What the fuck are you doing?" Big Jim asked, studying the state of the art technology the Feds used to monitor their target, him.

"You're violating our constitutional rights. I'll have our lawyers on this first thing in the morning," Josh said.

"If you shut your mouth, you'll realize the FBI is not snooping on Mr. Morrison."

"So what are you doing?" Sam dismissed the seven agents he handpicked for the taskforce except Wayne.

"We're protecting Mr. Morrison," Sam said. Big Jim doubled over in laughter.

"Everybody loves Big Jim. I've made more people stars than Ed McMahon."

"There's reason to believe you're next on Mickey Tansy's hit list," Wayne said.

Josh shivered.

"Mickey who? The punk that's always on TV? Please, I've never met the man," Big Jim said.

"We know but can't prove you played a hand in Mickey's and Charles Freeman's money laundering case. If we can see through your masquerade, so can Mickey," Sam said.

Wayne butted in.

"We don't have to explain what Mickey does to people who crosses him. This man grew up with Mickey Tansy." Wayne unpinned a photo of Jackie's dead body off the bulletin board.

"Stabbed multiple times. You don't want this to be the last memory of James 'Big Jim' Morrison." Josh couldn't stomach the gruesome photo. Big Jim remained unfazed.

"I'm not worried. With my connections, he'll be another ant killed by a sledgehammer." Wayne underestimated Big Jim. They showed the photo of Jackie's corpse to intimidate him. Sam and Wayne didn't have any more tricks up their sleeves.

"Well then, gentlemen, if I'm not under arrest. I'll be continuing on with my day. Josh, let's go!" Big Jim said.

Los Angeles, California. The American Music Awards, One Day Later

Josh Stevenson made his usual rounds backstage at the Staples Center. The American Music Awards created an opportunity for major networking, same goes for the other annual music award shows. Josh met plenty of fallen stars desperate for comebacks at these award shows. If the star wasn't strung out on drugs or fame, you put them on a single with the newest chart topping artist and magic, they're relevant again. The best part, they owe their relevancy to you. That's the Big Jim power system in a nutshell. A favor now, for a favor later. Josh, dressed in a black tuxedo designed by Tom Ford campaigned like a young politician. He greeted the masses with a painted-on smile and warm handshakes. Josh met hundreds of people, but never forgot a name. When Big Jim's most trusted advisor knew you on a first name basis, you were somebody in showbiz. To the janitors at the Chrysler Building, it meant Josh was smart enough to remember the names of the people collecting the trash. Josh's protégé Lindsay Joy cradled three AMA trophies, while posing for photographs. A few falls ago, Lindsay sung lullabies to the children she babysat in her hometown of Grand Rapids, Michigan. A chance encounter with an A& R led to her singing for Josh Stevenson, which led to a multimillion-dollar recording contract. Josh decided not to interrupt her celebration. There would be plenty of time to congratulate Lindsay at Big Jim's after party.

The Blackberry in Josh's pocket vibrated with this text message. [RE: The Rafters, behind the spotlights, 3 minutes!!!!]

Wayne Robertson stood in the shadow of the Los Angeles Lakers 1972 Championship banner.

"What made you change your mind?" he asked.

"I made my decision after seeing the photo. If Big Jim finds out about this, I'm through. That's the deal, Big Jim doesn't catch wind of this," Josh said.

"However, you want to play this Josh. The balls in your court."

"Big Jim can't seem to get it through his brain that he's not untouchable. I'm not doing this to betray Jim, I'm trying to help him." Josh needed to hear himself say that more than he meant what he said.

"These are serious criminals. You're doing the right thing, Josh," Wayne said.

"Here is Jim's schedule for the remainder of the L.A. trip. If there's any confusion, text the Blackberry."

Marie's feet throbbed from running track and field in four-inch heels. Lindsay Joy swept every category she received a nomination in, bringing the total of AMA trophies to three on the night. Marie anchored the relay team of assistants. Paparazzi chased Lindsay's yellow stretch Hummer out the Staples Center VIP parking lot. In the backseats of the cozy limousine, Lindsay and her all female staff toasted champagne flutes overrunning with bubbly.

"To success," Marie toasted. The females yelped loudly. Marie swallowed the champagne in a single gulp and quickly refilled. The rest of the ride she sat silent. Nobody seemed to care. The girls were happy to be aboard the money train, heading straight to next year's Grammys. The Hummer hugged the curves of the winding roads climbing the Hollywood hills to Mullhound Drive. The mansion Josh rented was built into the hills, with four floors below ground level. The home belonged to a Colombian drug lord in the 1980s who contributed millions of dollars to its renovation. Two Russian men a half foot above six feet, wearing identical blue nylon shirts stood outside the massive wrought iron gate. Lindsay waved a sloppy "hello," out the sunroof. The international star was all the validation the bouncers needed. The stretch hummer entered the gates.

Big Jim tilted his head back and exhaled a cloud of cigar smoke. Three perfect smoked o's floated upwards. A black bowtie laid untied on a crisp white collar. A million-dollar diamond shined brilliantly on his ring finger with every flick of the hand rolled cigar. He was conversing about oil prices with a Saudi prince. The prince skipped the formal tuxedo for a white keffiyeh topped with a gold braid and a black robe trimmed in gold. The wealthiest man attending the party, the amount of power the prince wielded kept Big Jim babbling on about a boring subject. Lindsay Joy and entourage strutted into the party, saving Big Jim from another twenty minutes of barrels and spills.

The prince licked a thumb and index finger, then spread them over his thick eyebrows.

"Excuse me, Big Jim. Something urgent has come to my attention," he said. To Big Jim's left, the deputy director of the CIA entertained guests with tales of espionage. Loughlin flashed a skull head ring when his hand gestured to the rotunda. Big Jim snatched a champagne flute off a waiter's tray. The partygoers in attendance were decked out in their finest jewels. Their multimillion-dollar investment portfolios paid the price of admission. The best of the best, cream of the crop, for Big Jim to surround himself with anything less would be uncivilized. A crystal chandelier a couple hundred pounds in weight hung in the center of the rotunda. Big Jim approached it, puffing on the Cuban cigar, Loughlin coughed into a closed fist.

"You should get that checked out, Robert. It sounds worse each passing month." Loughlin gained control of his body spasms. "It's the weather. I'm allergic to the pollen," he said.

"When the seasons change, what'll be the next excuse, you're allergic to icicles?"

"Cut me some slack, Jim. I'm in the country for two minutes before I got your message, then I'm on another plane out west. Where do I find the time to schedule a doctor's appointment between the scions and the government? I got to take a crap with a stopwatch. "Loughlin said.

"The lodge comes before Uncle Sam and those third world countries you call home six months out the year." Big Jim dumped the Havana in the champagne flute.

"I'm upset I had to fly to California because you're scared of two hoods," Loughlin said.

"I've got the F.B.I spying on my hotel suite. I'm supposed to be next on a hit list. These punks are going state to state, leaving bodies. I think that's enough reason to be worried." Loughlin pulled Big Jim closer.

"The F.B.I is an incompetent agency who couldn't find a human head in a haystack. Those two junkies are making a mockery of them. They're desperate, Jim. You think you're the only celebrity they tried the good cop, bad cop routine on this week?" "What about the whole fiasco of setting Mickey up to take the fall with Charles. He has a valid reason for putting me on the chopping block," Big Jim said.

"I'm with the C.I.A. The elite," Loughlin paused for emphasis.

"We found Osama Bin Laden two years ago. We're waiting on the right time to kill the coward, so the President can build more momentum for the next Presidential election. I won't let them fuckers come within a hundred miles of you, Jim. Mickey Tansy and Matthew Hart will be dead in the next forty-eight hours."

CHAPTER 21

Mickey killed the lights to the Hummer in an underground garage large enough to fit a hundred vehicles. The garage was near its maximum capacity, which meant not many more people would be rolling in to crash Big Jim's after party. Matty fed a Kalashnikov AK 47 a banana clip and shoved a 10-round magazine inside a Colt .45 caliber handgun. Mickey dragged heavily on a cigarette, then plucked it under a Bentley. He double checked the cylinders to the twin.38 caliber snub noses and pulled the slide back on a Hecklar & Koch MP5 submachine gun, chambering the first round.

"This tux is hugging me the wrong way. I can barely breathe in this shit." Matty popped the top button on his dress shirt, revealing a patch of the bulletproof vest he wore underneath.

"You remind me of a three-year-old at a dinner party, fidgeting with buttons, It's bad enough you're so fucking fat, everybody can see the imprint of the bulletproof vest through your tuxedo,"

"This tux is two sizes too small," said Matty.

"We can't have you upstairs looking like the Hunchback of Notre Dame. Stay in the Hummer."

"You're not leaving me down here, we're two floors above hell. I'm going upstairs and I'm bringing Diana." Matty caressed the AK-47.

"I can move around without attracting attention. When I get Big Jim in my sights, bam!" Mickey shot an imaginary gun.

"I'll chirp you on the Nextel if shit gets thick. You remember how to work the walkie talkie?" Mickey asked.

"It's not rocket science. I hold this button and talk," Matty demonstrated.

"The code word is Ray, when I say Ray, you come upstairs and let dirty Diana do the talking."

"Why Ray?" Matty asked.

"I watched the movie last night on Showtime."

Wayne circled O-R-N-A-M-E-N-T-I-O-N diagonally across the crossword puzzle. "A thirteen letter word right in my face," he said excited. "I don't see the point in searching for words you'll never use," said Sam browsing through one of Wayne's crossword books.

"It's not about using words. It's about killing time on a stakeout. You expect us to sit and stare at two men and an iron gate for six hours?"

"I've done it that way for almost forty years. It's about maintaining focus, while you're crossing out 'ornamentation' you're missing clues everywhere."

Wayne rolled up the paperback puzzle book and accepted the challenge.

"Ok, what valuable clues are we missing?" he asked. Their two subordinates remained quite in the backseats of the Lincoln Navigator.

"That license plate on that yellow Hummer." Sam scribbled the plate numbers across a puzzle book.

"That's Lindsay Joy. She won record of the year at tonight's award show," Wayne said, watching the star scream out the sunroof.

"You're right Sam. That's real valuable information. She might kill someone with those awful vocals." That gave the other agents a good laugh. Sam balled up the sheet of paper he wrote the plate number on and chucked it across the road at the second Navigator.

"These are cold blooded killers hunting James Morrison. It's our job to keep him alive," he said.

"The security inside the party is tighter than the Whitehouse. Big Jim's having the time of his life. We're the ones with hemorrhoids and crossword puzzles," Wayne said.

"My men must be up and ready at all times!" screamed Sam. "I'm the squad commander. We flew to L.A. with an agreement, I lead the taskforce and you play the sidelines. You've questioned every decision I've made thus far," Wayne said.

"Ok, I won't question any more of your decisions. Matter of fact, I won't even stakeout in the same car." Sam reached for a pack of cashew nuts and a loaded .50 caliber Israeli Desert Eagle on the dashboard.

"I'll be in the other squad car, doing real police work," he said, leaving the SUV.

Mickey winked at the Russian manning the elevator. "Working hard or hardly working?" he asked.

"A bit of both," the Russian replied.

"I used to be an elevator operator before I made my fortune in the music business. The secret to this job is you got to break between floors and get your rest," Mickey said.

"I see why you were more successful at music." The Russian separated the vertical doors with a lift of an arm and push of a heel. He wasn't armed. Mickey scoped a scenery out of Lifestyle's of the Rich and Famous. The tuxedo Marie picked out blended in perfectly. The white jacket was cut wide to conceal the holstered revolvers. A live instrument band played a jazz rendition, composed by Duke Ellington. A waitress with raven hair and a face made up heavily in rouge and mascara offered Mickey a variety of smokes. He chose a cigar and instantly she held a flickering flame. "I see you're very good at what you do," Mickey said.

"I'm great at what I do." The flirtation delivered with the statement, gave Mickey the impression she wasn't referring to striking matches.

"I 'ma see how great you truly are. I'm looking for a friend, who happens to be the host of this party. Do you know him?"

"Big Jim Morrison," the waitress answered, quicker than a contestant on Jeopardy.

"Where can I find Big Jim?"

"He's one floor up, in the rotunda."

Mickey whipped out a hundred faster than her burning flame. "I'm great at what I do as well," he said.

"Are you from the L.A. area? You look so familiar," she asked, depositing the cash in her cleavage.

"No, I'm from Hell's Kitchen. You might've seen my last prison photo on the news." The waitress giggled and went back to earning her tips. On the next floor up, a country singer strung the strings to an acoustic guitar and serenaded guests with love ballads. Mickey casually walked the dance floor, enjoying the fine cigar, scanning every passing face. Big Jim's mug lived on billboards for weeks prior to the AMAs.

The house twisted like a maze but another waitress gave Mickey directions to the rotunda. In the rotunda, twenty people were scattered around indulged in conversations. Mickey looked up at the nude angels painted on the ceilings thirty feet high. Their private parts gracefully covered by bluish clouds as they winged around a priceless chandelier. Mickey put the burning cigar down on a linen tablecloth. He gripped the wooden handle to the revolver in his shoulder holster and followed behind an Arab. At a distance of four feet, Mickey aimed the .38 caliber at an oblivious Big Jim and screamed.

"James Morrison!"

The smile on Big Jim faded when he saw death down a small black hole. The headshot tumbled Big Jim over, brain matter oozed down the prince's keffiyeh.

The sounds of echoed screams brought Wayne out the trance of a crossword puzzle. The two Russian bodyguards standing outside talked tentatively in their earpieces and bolted into the party.

"Why would they leave the front gate unguarded?" Wayne pondered. He brandished the Mossberg shotgun and heard semiautomatic pistols being readied behind him.

"I want the entrance secured, nothing comes in or out unless I give the order," he instructed. Sam called Wayne to the other Navigator, waving the chrome Desert Eagle.

"Something is going on in there, Sam, and…"

Wayne broke off to open the text message from Josh Stevenson. [OMG! They're shooting inside the party. Hurry up, get in here!!]

Wayne read the text message aloud. The second Navigator emptied out and the eight members of the taskforce ran to the mansion's front gate. The first wave of frantic guests burst out the mansion, stampeding each other in their race for safety.

"You three watch the gate. Nobody leaves until the local police arrives. The shooters are still in the house," Wayne said. The three agents lined up in their shooting stances, forming a barricade between the guest and the gate. The confused mob halted at the gun line, a few braced themselves for a foray of bullets.

"FBI!"

The words reflected off their bulletproof vests in bright yellow lettering.

"I want everyone to lie flat on the ground and put your hands where I can see them!" The flock abided, sprawling on the dirt in their fancy attire.

"The rest of us are going inside. There's a security team in the house. Be aware of friendly fire. Any unknown armed assailants are to be put down"

Wayne turned and ran in a swift sprint. Sam willed the stiff sticks he called legs to keep up with the squad commander. The old titan wasn't too keen on taking orders, but he admired the way Wayne excelled under pressure. Sam fell in line and charged with the young herd.

Mickey was a hop, skip, and a jump away from the freight elevator when Loughlin's bullet struck the Kevlar vest harder than a heavyweight's fist. The force knocked Mickey forward and out the path of the next three bullets. The Oakwood walls splintered with every high caliber bullet piercing. Mickey sought refuge behind a twenty-foot ice sculpture of the Statue of Liberty. He spit two rounds out of each revolver, gripped firmly in both hands. Loughlin and the Russian guards countered by melting off Lady Liberty's torch arm, using Uzi submachine gunfire. The boulder of ice came close enough to fan Mickey a cool breeze before it broke to pieces on the floor. Loughlin communicated with the Russians in their native tongue and they spread out. Mickey counted three different sets of footsteps, the pair on the right tipped closer. He had three bodies to drop and only seven rounds of ammunition left. He chirped Matty on the Nextel, "Ray, Ray!" The room went silent for the longest minute. Mickey peaked out. The Russians and Loughlin's bullets chipped away at the thick base of the statue. The large chunks of ice rained over Mickey until the volley subsided. Loughlin & Co. disposed of the spent clips and reloaded. Mickey popped out and squeezed the trigger to the right-hand revolver in succession. The first slug punctured Loughlin's chest, mid-reload, his Uzi fell. The next slug ate through the deputy director's neck and a blood squirt erupted over six feet long. Mickey crouched down. In came the second volley of bullets. The top half of the sculpture crumbled into a million little pieces.

Matty heard the code word and left the Nextel in the cup holder. He strapped the MP5 on his back and held the AK-47. The underground garage buzzed with guests trying to break for it. The Hummer blocked the concrete ramp that winded up to the front gates. Horns blared, people shouted. A three hundred-pound gorilla armed for warfare made guests hover between cars. The freight elevator opened, another load of petrified millionaires hoping to cross the Underground Railroad.

"Everybody, get the fuck off!" Matty shouted, leveling the AK-47. The elevator operator tried to disguise himself in the crowd, but the blue nylon shirt gave him away. Matty smacked a palm and five fingers around the back of the operator's neck.

"Where's my friend?" he asked. The operator needed no explanation.

The dapper man in the white tuxedo jacket reeked of trouble.

"He's on the third floor. Don't kill me, I'm unarmed." Matty pushed the operator down to the ground and shot him. The freight moved at a turtle's pace. Matty kept looking through the spaces in the gated ceiling, holding the lever that mobilized the elevator. At last came the Roman numeral three. He aligned the freight elevator with the third floor, and removed the latch on the deadbolt. The upper half of the door lifted up and the lower went down. A statute of ice collapsed like a chopped tree in the forest. The Russian guards stood in a stupor after triggering empty guns. Matty chopped one down, immediately, using the AK-47. The other disregarded the useless Uzi and ran. The bullets that rattled the Russians back, left him sliding on his belly. Mickey rose and dusted off the ice debris.

"A second later, I'd be Swiss cheese," he said.

"That fucking elevator moves in slow motion." The ice crunched under their feet. Matty pulled the strap attached to the MP5 over his body. Mickey holstered the .38's and grabbed the machine gun.

"What's the best route out of here?" Mickey asked. Matty looked at the elevator, a vertical coffin. They'd be boxed in if someone cut off its mechanisms. He pictured the melee down in the garage and gazed at the ceiling.

"Up the stairs."

Sam Mitchell combed the east wing of the house with two G-men. Wayne hit the west, a man shorter than Mitchell, but what he lacked in manpower, he made up in firepower. The agents moved ahead of Sam, weaving through darkness on the main floor. The power inside the mansion cut off swift and suddenly. The flashlights propped under the handles of their handguns beamed spotlights, crawling up, down, and across antique furniture. The flashlights illuminated a pathway through the vast residency. The majority of the guests evacuated the East Wing for the underground garage beneath it or the West Wing's easy access to the front gates. A few guests missed out on the memo. The dull minded false alarms Sam & Co. found cowering underneath chairs or hidden in closets. Sam accidentally clattered a China dish under his heel. The younger agents shot him a quizzical look for the absentminded blunder. Sam's infatuation with a towering ice sculpture arrested his ability to discreetly pursue. The night owl carved out of ice in peculiar detail, marked the third sculpture he'd seen. A couple of rooms back, they past an iced eyeball atop a twenty-one-block pyramid, the symbol famously printed on the back of a one-dollar bill.

"These sculptures are symbolic. There's a deeper meaning within them, a message they're projecting," Sam said, investigating the watchful owl. The two special agents backtracked to observe a sculptor's tireless work and a preordained puddle of water. The pounding of feet upstairs diverted their attention. They zeroed in on the mahogany door, the gateway to the stairwell. Sam switched stances, legs spread apart, arms extended, holding the .50 caliber. The knob turned, a large body appeared in the doorway. The agents held their fire unsure whether the well- tailored intruder was a crook or a guest. Their flashlights momentarily blinded the intruder. Sam recognized the squinting face as Matthew Hart. In Sam's moments of recognition, a long object sprung up from under Matty like a kickstand under a bicycle, an assault rifle! Sam dove out of the line of fire, bullets ricocheting around him. The Desert Eagle gave a massive recoil, launching bullets at an empty doorway. Mickey and Matty changed directions back inside the staircase. The inflammation in Sam's knees resonated a red hot pain. The old titan managed to get up, a second agent sprung up next. The third remained down, clutching a gut wound in agony. The steel plate in his standard issued vest wasn't thick enough to shield off a high velocity, full-metal jacket round.

"Call for help," Sam said. "And don't leave until they get here." With cop-killer ammunition piercing armored vest, the special agent didn't object. Sam wobbled down a flight of stairs, every step irritating his knees. Sam blocked out the pain and leaned over the banister. Rapid gunfire from Matty's AK-47 jerked Sam back. An exit door slammed above Sam, but he could still hear Matty wheezing in the stairwell below him.

"They split up," he thought, calculating the odds of catching Tansy on bum knees as slim to none. Sam stayed with Matty. Down the next landing, Sam spotlighted the abandoned AK 47. The overweight thug wasn't the only thing running on empty.

The armored vest weighed Matty down. He dropped the empty AK- 47 and cocked back the Colt. The presence of the Feds on the premises caught them off-guard. Mickey instructed him to fetch the Hummer before dashing two flights above the main-floor. Matty preferred they stay together but there wasn't enough time to protest. There wasn't enough time to think, only time to kill. Then suddenly Matty slowed to a stop and kneeled on one knee.

An unbearable pain attacked him, feeling like a thousand pounds of pressure fell on his chest. Matty fell over and squirmed in the pitch black.

Sam shined the flashlight on Matty Hart in the midst of a heart attack. Sam himself knew the symptoms. He wanted Matty to recognize him, so Sam moved closer and Matty did recognize him. Sam could tell by Matty's expression.

"I've waited a very long time for this day."

Sam aimed the Desert Eagle at Matty. When the magazine emptied, a wisp of smoke curled out the Desert Eagle's barrel.

The discharge of a large caliber handgun stopped Mickey cold in his tracks. A part of him wanted to race back down the stairs but Matty could handle himself. Mickey pushed forward in the dark. The moonlight curled around expensive drapes, helping him distinguish a speaker from a five-layer cake, it took a couple minutes for his eyes to adjust. Mickey upped the pace, crossing over to the West wing. The West wing was larger than the East, with twice as many exits. Mickey planned to slip out the mansion disguised within the crowd. He moved the drapes aside on a floor to ceiling window. A quick glimpse outside deterred Mickey's plan from ever coming to fruition. There on the front lawn over one hundred guests laid stretched out.

The house has to be completely evacuated, he thought. Sirens blared loudly. The police sealed off the entrance to the underground garage. Matty and the Hummer were trapped inside. There was no way out. Cop cars flooded the front gates. Mickey head-butted the windowpane.

"Fuck! Fuck! Fuck!" he screamed with every collision.

"Tansy, drop your weapon!" a voice shouted behind him. An infrared beam dotted Mickey's tuxedo.

"Tansy drop your weapon or I 'ma shoot," Wayne repeated.

"Not if I shoot first." Mickey spun around, the MP5 sweeping the room, vibrating in his right hand, spitting out rounds. Wayne ducked behind a bar, liquor bottles and shot glasses shattered on the counter. Wayne sat up with his back against the counter. The broken bottles poured alcohol on his baldhead. The other FBI agent managed to get off a shot before leaping over a cluttered table. A bullet knocked Mickey down and the air clean out of him. Mickey felt his Kevlar vest. It curved the bullets full velocity.

"He's hit, I shot him!!" screamed the agent. The infrared beaming on his handgun.

"You ain't hit shit, cocksucker." Mickey stumbled back up.

"Tansy, it's over. The house is surrounded. It's only two ways out of here, handcuffed or a body bag. It's your choice," Wayne shouted.

"I choose the body bag." Mickey shot up the bar and staggered to the next window.

"Ok, you want the body bag. I'll be happy to accommodate you!" "Where's Matty?" Mickey asked, ignoring Wayne's growing frustration. "Matty did the smart thing. He surrendered," Wayne lied.

"Bullshit! You motherfucking liar, get down!!" Mickey screamed, firing his gun, sending Wayne's backup dodging for cover.

"I'm giving you a direct order to lay down your weapon, Tansy," Wayne said.

"No, I'm giving you a direct order to…"

A shotgun blast broke Mickey's sentence, sending him flying backwards, arms outstretched. Wayne cocked the Mossberg and shot it again. That shell carried an already flying Mickey out the glass window. His body plunged two floors, smashing a police cruiser's windshield. The cops on the ground scattered in sheer shock. Wayne stood in the window and sent Mickey down another shotgun shell.

Federal Prison, several hours later

Bobby rolled out a paper-thin checkered board on a limestone table. He unraveled the strings to a purple velour pouch, the kind jewelers used to store precious gems. Bobby appraised every chess piece he plucked out the pouch. He crafted the pieces out of rock mineral, he snuck from the yard. Bobby shaved, molded, and polished all thirty-two pieces. The stones glistened in the morning sun, Bobby assembled the chessboard and searched for a worthy opponent to invite to a game of chess. The refined chessboard was strictly for master players. Bobby kept a spare plastic chess set for mediocre chess players. The best chess players were elbowing for position near the yard's TV area. Bobby tried waiting them out, but eventually he packed up the chess set and joined the other inmates by the television.

"What's going on, Brethren?" Bobby asked Detroit.

"The pigs killed the white boys in California," Detroit said, upset, the criminal in him always rooting for the bad guys.

"What white boys?" Bobby asked.

"The Irish boys, your man Charlie Free's codefendant." Bobby's eyes grew wide.

"What! What!" he stuttered. "It's a tear-jerker, isn't it?"

"When the fuck did this happen?" Bobby realized he blurted the question out loud when Detroit answered.

"This morning or yesterday. I'm not sure the time's different on the left coast." Bobby muted Detroit. The yard started spinning, Detroit never seen Bobby so disorientated. He asked, "Are you alright?"

Bobby vomited.

A recent photo of Claire and Mia glued to the cell's mirror made Chuckie laugh. Their faces always put him in a good mood. The Polaroid captured them in a joyful fright on a rollercoaster ride. Chuckie laid the beige shirt he was folding on top of the three he already folded. The days seemed to pack on extra hours now that the parole board approved his release. In under two months, he'd be free as a bird. Chuckie pulled the Polaroid off the glob of toothpaste on the mirror and imagined his rollercoaster face.

"Charlie Free, top of the morning, bro. I've got something I want you to see," Dash said through the cell bars, interrupting Chuckie's moment of clarity.

"Good morning, Dash. What is it?"

"Get dressed and meet me in the yard by the TV area."

"Alright, cool."

Ten Minutes Later

Chuckie walked in the TV area, wearing a yellow Polo shirt, beige khaki pants, and white Chuck Taylor All-Stars. He sensed all eyes on him but remained calm. Dash descended down the bleachers.

"What did you want to talk about?" Chuckie asked.

"It's your co-defendant Mickey. He's dead." Dash's words took some time to sink in. Chuckie studied every crease on Dash's face to be sure this wasn't a hoax.

"Mickey and Matty died in a shootout with the FBI at a Hollywood Hills Mansion. The deputy director of the CIA died too. It's big news." Dash directed Chuckie to the television and continued the run down.

"A few bodyguards got killed, a federal agent wounded, but you're not going to believe this shit." The television screen showed an aerial view of the mansion on Mullhound drive, FBI agents roamed the grounds, some pushing black body bags to a black county coroner's van.

"They killed your former boss, Big Jim Morrison."

Chuckie didn't attempt to wipe the tears trickling down his face. This single act of valor, washed away years of resentment Chuckie held towards Mickey. Chuckie's childhood friends sacrificed their lives to revenge the person who ruined his. Josh Stevenson was on the TV screen speaking to news reporters, wrapped in a gray quilt.

"Let's walk. I don't want everybody to see me this way," Chuckie said. Chuckie and Dash circled the outskirts of the prison yard.

Bobby was jogging the outskirts, long dreads dangling out a tied- up bun. After the parole board granted Chuckie's release, Bobby ceased speaking to Chuckie altogether. So when the Rastafarian said, "Chuckie, I want to send my condolences. I'm sorry to hear about Mickey," Chuckie was surprised.

"Thanks, Bobby. I appreciate it," he replied.

Dash, aware of the tension amongst them, wanted to use Mickey's death to bring the former friends back together.

"Bobby, why don't you spin the yard with us?" Dash said.

"I can't, this is my workout hour, I'll see you guys later," Bobby said. Chuckie and Dash agreed, and continued their stroll, but Chuckie turned back around when he didn't hear any footsteps jogging away. Bobby was up on Chuckie in no time, holding a six-inch shank. The blade slid in Chuckie's belly like a car tire.

"I have to die in jail because of you, motherfucker," Bobby whispered in Chuckie's ear. Dash swung two wild hooks at Bobby, landing one. Bobby freed the knife from Chuckie's stomach and began chasing Dash. Chuckie lost his footing, his legs collapsed beneath him. The leaking blood stained the fabric of the knitted yellow shirt, turning it crimson. Chuckie felt his insides go cold.